Dragon Lover

by

Karilyn Bentley

Draconia Tales Series

This is a work of fiction. Names, characters, places, and incidents are either the product of the author's imagination or are used fictitiously, and any resemblance to actual persons living or dead, business establishments, events, or locales, is entirely coincidental.

Dragon Lover

Cover Art by *Tamra Westberry*

The Wild Rose Press, Inc.
PO Box 708
Adams Basin, NY 14410-0708
Visit us at www.thewildrosepress.com

Publishing History
First Faery Rose Edition, 2014
Print ISBN 978-1-62830-272-1
Digital ISBN 978-1-62830-273-8

Draconia Tales Series
Published in the United States of America

Fafnir felt one eye-ridge rise. Did she think to rummage around in his mind, to extract the memory of her presence? He'd like to see her try.

But he'd rather speak a promise.

What did I see?

A small brush against his mind, so slight as to be almost imperceptible. *Almost.* He slammed mental barriers in place, watching her brow furrow as she tried to remove his memory of her.

She probably could get away with reading others' minds, but not his.

"You saw me standing here." The High Priestess's voice jarred him back into the moment.

That's not all I saw.

"Yes, it is. Now, are you going to give me that ride back to the Temple or not?"

Having problems transporting?

"I'm still here, aren't I?"

Fafnir chuckled. *A ride then.* He knelt, offering her his back.

Her hand touched his shoulder as some of her bristle relaxed. "Thank you." She climbed to his back and sat, her weight a pleasant feeling against his scales.

He straightened, standing a bit taller, knowing she sat on his back, knowing she trusted him. Him. The Draconi liar, the male too afraid of his own guilt to admit his identity. But she didn't know that, did she? No, she felt pity toward him, pity for his years of captivity, his inability to change into human form, but no outright disgust. As annoying as pity might be, he could live with it. Her disgust, though, would shatter his heart into shards of shame.

Bloody effing sap.

Dedication

To my wonderful husband,
thank you for all your support and love.
And to Lill,
your hard work makes me a better writer. Thank you.

Chapter One

"You're late."

Aryana sucked in a breath and caught herself from tripping down the last few stairs. Falling into the secret underground chamber was not dignified High Priestess behavior. Serene movement befitted the position, not being startled out of an internal fantasy to land on her face.

She peered into the shadows until she spotted her friend and second-in-command, the Temple Healer Annaliese. "You almost broke my neck."

"Sorry. I thought you knew I was here."

"Didn't feel like taking part in the ritual?"

"I'm no longer young. I find it's become...well, it's too ritualistic."

Aryana snorted. *Her thought exactly.* All festivals of the Goddess ceased to enthrall as time slipped by. Perhaps that's why they were called rituals? "To be young again and not mind everything being timed. If only there was a male that you didn't have to time every stroke, every thrust." She shrugged, as if she didn't care. Better to feign ennui than to have Annaliese realize she'd been fantasizing of Fafnir, her newest problem...er, dragon.

For some unknown reason, thinking of the Harvest festival of the Goddess made her think of Fafnir. Made her fantasize about what he would look like in human

1

form instead of the dragon form he remained locked in. Made her imagine the feel of his hands on her body, stroking, bringing her pleasure. She shook her head. What was wrong with her?

Sexual fantasies were a thing of her past. Which was a clear indication of a deeper problem going back many years. Why else would she have embarked upon a relationship with a Watcher if not an attempt to regain lost feelings? While the sex was good, it was still, well, boring. Boring, boring, boring. She'd done it all before, and a forbidden partner didn't change things.

So she'd ended it. No use in handing her non-Draconi partner a death sentence for sleeping with the High Priestess.

Besides, it wasn't Enar she dreamed about. That privilege of late went to Fafnir.

Who was still in dragon form. Draconi do not have sex in dragon form. Reality didn't stop the fantasy from replaying. Maybe she should leave it alone and be glad she actually wanted a bed romp.

Aryana shook her head and walked into the chamber, using her magic to flick on glow lights as she went. She couldn't live in fantasyland when a ritual needed leading.

"I'm hoping that maybe this time…" The words hung in the air, a thick longing of Annaliese's desire.

"If the Goddess chooses." Chances were She didn't, but one never knew.

It looked as if Aryana was the only one who had experienced the other purpose this underground chamber served. For her, it became more than the space where the High Priestess controlled the sexual energies produced upstairs by the priestesses and their partners.

Despite Annaliese's presence beside her helping, or even controlling the ritual, nothing special happened for her friend. Only Aryana.

Why did the Goddess deem her worthy and not Annaliese?

"I can hope. What do you need me to do?"

Go upstairs. As if she'd tell Annaliese she preferred to enjoy her experience alone. She didn't mind the help. Really. She didn't.

"You can stand with me in the circle and help direct the energies. But first we need to cleanse the circle."

"As you wish." Annaliese walked toward the circle while Aryana grabbed candles, sage, salt, and water.

She turned to see her friend standing where requested, sweeping the circle clean and had to shake away a feeling of self-doubt, as if Annaliese should be the High Priestess, not her. *Odd.* Her magic had proven the stronger of the two. Otherwise, she'd be the assistant instead of the High Priestess. *So why the feeling?*

Must be one too many conversations with Alviss, Annaliese's father, over the last month. The male never did get over her becoming High Priestess instead of his daughter. Or maybe it had something to do with the old Seer claiming Aryana was his son's mate. A mated female could not serve as High Priestess.

But she wasn't mated, now was she? His son didn't believe the Seer, and had sought out his own fortune, disappearing from Draconia.

Her mate, according to the Seer. The only male for her, since only one mate existed for each Draconi. Provided the Draconi had a mate; not all did. Frankly, she thought Annaliese's brother had the right of it. The Seer's words had been cryptic, but more than her usual yes or no response to the question of a child's mate.

If she concentrated she could once again feel the smooth palm, knobby knuckles twisting the fingers as the old Seer placed her hand upon a five-year-old Ari's head.

Ah, this young's mate will come from the strongest family, a hatchling born to parents who thought never to have a son. Two days prior to her birth was he hatched and many years will it take to find her.

Never mind that many young hatched two days prior to her birth. Only one of those was from the strongest family, Alviss's line, born late in his parents' lives. The old Seer predicted similar words to Ragnor, casting their fates together.

Not that either believed the old female. No names were mentioned so perhaps she made a mistake. Besides, if they had been mates, wouldn't they have felt something for each other?

Had she even given him a chance? Being High Priestess had been her desire from a young age. A desire she'd made come true. Alviss had no business claiming she shouldn't be allowed to try out for the position, especially since her magic was stronger.

He still held a grudge after all these years.

If she could only avoid the council leader, her life would be perfect.

It never hurt to dream.

She placed the candles outside the circle and grabbed another broom to help Annaliese sweep out the energies, the first step in cleansing it. The first time she'd seen the circle, she couldn't believe the size of it.

Twenty steps across, ringed by silver runes, the size rendered her speechless. Her predecessor offered no plausible explanation for a circle that large.

But Ari knew why.

Which meant she couldn't be the only Draconi ever to discover its secrets. When they finished sweeping, Annaliese picked up the sage, lit it, and smudged the air, chanting softly under her breath. Aryana took the salt and water and sprinkled them over the smooth stone floor. She had to admit, things went faster with Annaliese's help.

Grabbing the yellow candle, she placed it on the east line. *Air.* A necessary element. With a flick of her finger, the wick ignited into flame. Annaliese took the red candle representing the fire element and headed to the south side of the circle, while Ari picked up the blue one and walked to the west line.

Setting the candle down, she waved her fingers and watched as a thin stream of fire lit the wick. *Water.* Without it they would die. She turned to see Annaliese place the green candle to the north and light it. *Earth.* Without earth they would have no food.

Air. Fire. Water. Earth.

Together with her assistant, Ari walked to the middle of the circle. She lifted her hands over her head and sent a small burst of magic upward, through the high ceiling into the joining room, letting the participants know all was ready for the ritual.

Spirit.

She felt the pulse of power, of magic, the ancient beat that drove life. Sexual energy poured down, covering her and Annaliese with its power, its life. Its need. She felt hands, thousands of hands, stroke over her skin, into her body as the priestesses and their partners moved in a set rhythm, a timed calculation of life.

The pulse moved inside, throbbing through her veins, filling her with desire. Faster and faster it surged, until she exploded in a wave of bliss, she and all her priestesses. The magic from the joining of dozens of couples rained down upon her, ready to be used, ready to help her transform into something else.

The purpose of the ritual was to take the energies and transmit them to the fields for abundance of grain and renewal of the fields for the following year's crops. She directed that energy now, sent it into the earth, deep underground where it would affect the soil and the crops.

But the energy had another effect on her. A transformation females did not experience. *Ever.* Only in myths and bedtime tales told to the young. Or in her secret chamber while standing in the middle of an enormous circle.

Ari had no sooner discharged the magic into the earth than she felt the pulsing begin. Internal organs shifted, bones lengthened, her back grew wings. Annaliese leapt in front of Aryana, moving out of the way of her growing body. A growing dragon's body.

She blinked and looked down her snout at Annaliese. Throwing back her head, she let loose with a roar that shook dust from the high ceiling. A dragon. A female dragon.

Who would've thought?

Clearly someone many years ago had. Hence, the overlarge circle.

She flapped her wings, then used magic to stop the

eddies from blowing out the candles. Annaliese needed to end the ritual and discharge the energies, not an errant wing-flap.

After wrapping the candles in an eddy-stopping spell, Ari put her wings through another up and down motion. Or two. What she would give to fly. To soar above the clouds. To fly to where the males locked in dragon form stayed. To see Fafnir again.

She should be researching how to turn the poor male back into human form, not thinking of using him as a stud. Must be all the sexual energy coupled with her previous fantasy.

Which was now running through her mind on a constant replay.

She saw Fafnir in her mind's eye. Saw him as she did the first time they met. Felt the tingle of energy, of banked desire when they touched. Her many-years-long lack of desire vanished as she thought about him, thought about his hands running over her skin, stroking her, making her scream her pleasure.

She wanted him. *Now.*

The thought no sooner raced through her mind than her body shattered into a million pieces, soaring through the stone walls into the air.

With a loud pop, Ari appeared in midair, hovering above the ground. As a dragon. *Uh-oh. This was not good.* Her first time as a dragon away from the confines of the circle and she appeared in the sky like a wayward meteor streaking toward earth.

She didn't even know how to fly.

Ari pushed against the air, wings flapping an erratic beat. So much for things coming naturally. Apparently one had to be taught to fly. She flapped her wings again, trying to stay in the air.

Falling was not an option. Landing and being seen as a dragon was unthinkable. She needed to stay airborne long enough to calm down and transport back to the circle.

Flapping her wings got her nowhere. Every muscle in her body trembled. She thought about the circle, tried to transport there, but her body wouldn't obey. Goddess's teeth, she was going to die. The only High Priestess in memory to transform into a dragon and instead of soaring, she drops out of the sky like a hailstone.

Aryana screamed as she plummeted to the earth on a wave of pure terror.

****

Fafnir stared at the tree-covered hill and sighed. Not tall enough. Too covered in trees. Even the cave was too small to enter as a dragon. No place nearby to accidentally slip and fall to his death. The land given to the males locked in dragon form was flat, comprised of waving grasses and berry bushes, punctuated by the occasional tree-covered hill. No place to put an end to his misery.

He had hoped to kill the one who kept him locked for more than two decades in a titanium-lined cell, unable to use his magic, unable to free himself. However, that man was dead, his son killed by the Watcher, Enar. Fafnir shivered. *Watchers.* Curse them all. Although he didn't mind Enar so much. Maybe he would have even liked the tall, blond warrior if they had met prior to his captivity. *Maybe.*

Now though…He sighed. Now, he hid behind names, behind lies. Hid. Like a coward. A coward unworthy to call himself Draconi. A coward who would rather plunge from a tall height to a bone-shattering death than admit his failings.

He looked down at the drinking pond, his reflection blurry in the dark water. *A dragon*. Not a broad-shouldered, curly-haired human, but a huge scaly dragon. Red scales instead of black hair. Thick stout legs instead of firm muscular ones. Not the form he wanted to remain in. Yet another reason to find a tall cliff.

He looked up at the sky, at the deepening twilight. Maybe he should have gone to the Temple with the other males to celebrate the Harvest festival instead of moping. Maybe he should accept living as a dragon instead of hoping to return to human form. Maybe he should get a new goal, a new hope.

Did his Watcher still live?

His lip curled. Now that was a worthy goal. Killing the male for telling humans how to capture him, for telling them titanium was the bane of Draconi. Yes, he could do that. He could live for that goal.

And then what?

A loud pop ripped the stillness of the air and Fafnir started at the unexpected sound. What now? He looked up at the darkening sky and saw a dragon fluttering around, clearly not used to its wings. Silly hatchling, trying to fly before being taught. He remembered trying to fly before being ready, remembered plummeting out of the sky, gliding to a rough landing.

This hatchling, though, didn't have the sense the Goddess gave him. Dumb goat had pulled his wings in instead of pushing them out.

He shook his head. He'd asked for a goal, hadn't

he? And the Goddess saw fit to give him this hapless hatchling to teach how to land. Perhaps She wanted him living a bit longer.

Put your wings out and glide, hatchling! He projected his thoughts to the struggling young one.

And surprise, surprise, the hatchling heard him. Shaky wings shot out, slowing his free fall. But not slowing it enough.

He felt the ground rumble as the dragon crashed into a clump of bushes not far from where he stood. What were hatchlings being fed nowadays to be so large as to cause tremors when they landed?

Gems?

Sighing, he strode to the downed hatchling, arriving in time to hear a moan. A rather feminine moan. Had the hatchling been carrying a female? No, he hadn't seen one. Didn't mean there wasn't one, though.

Are you all right? sat on his tongue, held there by some invisible force. Asking was the kindly thing to do, and yet, something made the words freeze in his mind. As he watched, the clump of bushes rustled, separating to reveal a tall form dressed in torn, dark robes. *A female.* Where was the hatchling?

He peered into the darkness of the bushes, but saw nothing except leaves. Come to think of it, there wasn't enough room in that clump of berry bushes to hold a hatchling. How did the female get there?

Fafnir cleared his throat, eyes narrowed as the female jumped, one hand darting to her chest as if to hold in her heart. He saw her face then, smelled her scent and felt a jolt through his veins unbecoming of a cloistered male.

Which is why he never wanted to be cloistered.

He liked bedding females, thank you very much.

He'd really like to bed this one. As if that was going to happen in his current form.

The High Priestess Aryana stood in torn robes, her long, black hair in disarray. The same female he'd spent his younger years trying to avoid and his later ones wishing he hadn't been so successful.

She had no idea who he was. With any luck, it would stay that way.

High Priestess? What are you doing?

Her eyes narrowed, her hand still clasped against her chest. "Fafnir? Is that you? What are you doing here?"

I live here. The more important question is why are you here?

"I, um, I...had an accident during the Harvest ritual. Why are you here instead of on the Temple grounds?"

Where's the hatchling you flew in on?

"Oh, um..."

A thought popped into his head. A thought so foreign, so improbable it was laughable. Females did not turn into dragons. And yet, there was no hatchling.

"I have to go. I need to finish the ritual."

Wait. Are you hurt? I can... What exactly? Offer to heal her scratches and bruises? As if that wouldn't be a dead giveaway as to his true identity. While males could be Healers, the ability was so rare as to be confined to only a few families. She would know his family lineage in less time than it took a dragon to spit a fireball. Which was a discovery he hoped to avoid. After what he did, the atrocity he never thought to commit and yet had, his family wouldn't want to admit he shared their blood. No, it was better to keep his talents and his identity hidden.

"You can what?"

I can fly you back to the Temple. You look a bit hurt. Injuries make it hard to transport sometimes. At least for the average Draconi. The High Priestess could probably transport semi-conscious and leaking blood. Truth of the matter was he wanted her to touch him.

Bloody sappy desires.

She pushed a shaky hand through her hair and breathed out a puff of air. "You may take me back. Only if you promise not to speak of what you saw. I can...make it so you don't tell. But I'd rather take your promise."

Fafnir felt one eye-ridge rise. Did she think to rummage around in his mind, to extract the memory of her presence? He'd like to see her try.

But he'd rather speak a promise.

What did I see?

A small brush against his mind, so slight as to be almost imperceptible. *Almost.* He slammed mental barriers in place, watching her brow furrow as she tried to remove his memory of her standing in the berry bushes.

She probably could get away with reading others' minds, but not his. Twenty-four years of captivity prohibited his use of magic, but not of mind-speaking. His feeble curse at the time of his capture coupled with his mind-speaking abilities wrecked havoc on his captors. The lord of River's Run wasn't the only one to become insane; he just happened to have the misfortune of standing directly in the way of Fafnir's curse. The others, well, they heard voices for a long time.

He curled his lip at the memory.

"You saw me standing here." The High Priestess's voice jarred him back into the moment.

That's not all I saw.

"Yes, it is. Now, are you going to give me that ride back to the Temple or not?"

Having problems transporting?

"I'm still here, aren't I?"

Fafnir chuckled. *A ride then.* He knelt, offering her his back.

Her hand touched his shoulder as some of her bristle relaxed. "Thank you." She climbed to his back and sat, her weight a pleasant feeling against his scales. Her touch was well worth the aborted attempt to end his misery.

He straightened, standing a bit taller, knowing she sat on his back, knowing she trusted him. Him. The Draconi liar, the male too afraid of his own guilt to admit his identity. But she didn't know that, did she? No, she felt pity toward him, pity for his years of captivity, his inability to change into human form, but no outright disgust. As annoying as pity might be, he could live with it. Her disgust, though, would shatter his heart into shards of shame.

Bloody effing sap.

Taking a hop, his wings expanded, lifting them into the air. Unlike the hatchling—or should he say Aryana, as odd as it might sound—he glided across air currents, the wind pressing against the membranes of his wings. He loved flying. Loved the feel of water droplets as he rushed through clouds. Loved the wind catching his wings, pushing him higher.

Loved having Aryana sitting on his back, letting

him care for her.

Where was the nearest rock to bang his head against when he needed one?

When one flies, it's important to expand the wings, to let the air currents push you higher. If you flap too quickly, or pull the wings in, you'll fall out of the sky.

She stiffened, her hands tightening their grip on his scales. *I will keep that in mind, if I ever teach hatchlings flight techniques.*

Ah. It makes for an interesting conversation, don't you think? How to remain in the air? How to fly?

How had a female managed to change? Maybe he imagined it. The thought no sooner came to him than he dismissed it. He did not imagine seeing a dragon flying. Or attempting to fly in her case. His fault had been to assume it was a hatchling flying since no grown male would flap his wings in that unknowing way. All males underwent training on how to fly once they hit puberty and after that, none flapped their wings like a green hatchling.

A female would, though. They never underwent training since females did not change.

Yet, he knew what he saw. He also knew getting her to admit it would be like getting a male to admit he fathered a child on a human and then abandoned it.

He needed a goal to make his life worthwhile and what do you know? One appeared. How did a female change into a dragon?

I wouldn't know. I'm female. Females don't fly.

Ah. Well. Males find the topic interesting.

Look! There's the Temple. Why don't you put me down here, so I can transport back. I feel much calmer now.

Sure she did. Tension traveled from her legs through his skin, transmitting her fear of discovery as surely as if she spoke. He wanted to know how she changed. Why she changed.

It wouldn't be a goal if he had an immediate answer, now would it?

As you wish, Priestess.

Banking to the left, he circled around the perimeter of the Temple, noting the crowd in the Temple Courtyard, as he landed behind the large, stone behemoth. His feet touched down on the path leading from the Temple to the Council's Chamber and his wings folded against his scales. He started to kneel, when he felt Aryana transport off him. She regained form a few feet away, the tears in her previously torn gown repaired, her hair, though, still mussed from the flight. Or the earlier landing in the bushes.

"Thank you for the ride." She inclined her head toward him. "I will—"

The rest of her sentence froze in the air as high-pitched screams sounded from the Courtyard.

Chapter Two

Aryana pivoted toward the screams, toward the explosion of a cacophony of voices, each vying to be heard. What happened? Ignoring Fafnir and the questions in his eyes, she transported into the noise consuming the Courtyard. Fafnir appeared in the Courtyard a few seconds later and the disheveled crowd buzzed around him.

Disheveled? With their torn clothes and faces covered in blood and dirt, the crowd looked like they had been on the losing side of a battle. How could that be? Fighting was not what the Harvest ritual inspired.

"High Priestess!" Someone spotted her and as one the crowd swarmed her way. She sucked in a breath and tried to swallow, her throat as dry as a desert, her palms clammy. What a ridiculous reaction to her people, the race she served. She should not be afraid of harm. Or of them discovering her earlier wing-flapping disaster. So why did watching them rush toward her make her heart double its rhythm?

Fafnir vanished only to reappear beside her, his tail forming a scaled barrier between her and the crowd as it curled around her legs. She released the fear snaking through her veins on a trembling breath, oddly calm in the sea of terrorized eyes.

"What is wrong? What has happened?"

A sea of voices answered in a discordant melody

and Aryana raised her hands for quiet.

"Not all at once. You there—"she pointed to an elderly male standing up front, blood pouring from a slash across his forehead—"what happened?"

"We have been attacked! The village of Tyne has been attacked!"

"Attacked?" How? Wards stationed at their borders protected Draconia from outsiders and in general Draconi did not attack each other. A brawl might occur now and then but nothing of this level.

"They were Watchers! None I recognized, but I saw their blond hair under their masks."

"Masks? Watchers wore masks?" She really needed to find a larger vocabulary, but after her surprising transport into flight, followed by finding the only Draconi whose mind she could not control and then hearing a village had been attacked, she was surprised her mind conjured up any words at all.

"They hid! We need help. We transported here for assistance, but we were unable to drive them off. There were too many of them."

Aryana felt her eyes widen. So much for her serene High Priestess look. Watchers raiding a village? Harming Draconi? Why? From the corner of her eye, she saw the priestesses running out of the Temple, a river of white in the blood-splattered crowd. She sent them a mental image of what happened and watched as they ran to the survivors.

"Please, go with the priestesses and let them tend your injuries. I will call warriors to go to your village."

Not waiting to see if they obeyed her, she closed her eyes and sent a mental call to her nephew Thoren. He served on the Council, the group of male Draconi and Watchers tasked with the protection of the Draconi. Some protection. They hadn't even seen the attack coming.

Thoren!

What? I'm a little busy now.

Tyne has been attacked. They think it was Watchers. You need to contact Alviss and send a group there now. I'm transporting there to see if I can help.

Wait! Ari!

She blocked whatever else he was about to say. The less she said, the faster he'd act. A subtle tensing of Fafnir's tail against her legs caused her to put one hand on the hard scales. When she opened her eyes, Annaliese stood in front of her, Fafnir facing away from her friend. *Wonder why that was.* She put the thought aside, focusing on her second-in-command.

"Did you hear what happened?" At Annaliese's nod, she continued. "I'm going to see about the village. See if I can help. I've contacted Thoren and he'll contact Alviss."

"Are you sure that's a good idea?"

"Having Thoren contact Alviss?"

"No. You going to Tyne by yourself."

She's not going by herself. I'm going with her.

Aryana blinked and schooled her face into a calm mask. Where did he get off thinking he could just up and follow her around like a lost puppy? Somehow she doubted Fafnir would take no for an answer. But did she really want him to? She liked the way his tail curled protectively around her, liked the way he had offered to take her back to the Temple, liked his willingness to go into danger.

Someone clearly needed to slap some sense into

her.

"Who are you?" Annaliese asked, her brows reflecting the curiosity in her eyes.

"This is Fafnir. Fafnir, this is Annaliese, the Temple Healer and my second-in-command. See, I won't be by myself. You don't have to worry."

"I'm assuming you want me to oversee all this." Annaliese swept her arm out, the gesture encompassing the survivors.

"Of course. You are in charge until I return."

Annaliese inclined her head, but kept half her gaze on Fafnir. *He is the one Thoren freed from Keara's village?*

He is. Why?

She shrugged. *He looks familiar.* "Safe journey." Raising one hand, she nodded and then turned to the huddle of survivors.

Ari took a deep breath, readying herself to transport when she felt her body disintegrate into a loose dance of particles. Not again. But this time, when she reappeared, she remained in human form. Thank the Goddess. Fafnir's tail remained wrapped around her legs and it took her mind a second to process he was the one who had transported them here. To Tyne.

Shadows cast from flames flickered across Fafnir's scales, which gleamed like rubies in the light. His tail uncurled, removing his protection, leaving her alone. Although how she could be alone with him still standing beside her, she didn't know. Didn't care.

He looks familiar. Ari heard Annaliese's words again, heard the longing, the surprise, as if the Healer stood by her side. While Fafnir didn't look familiar to her, he felt familiar, his touch drawing out memories she thought she'd forgotten. Memories of when she longed for love, for a family, memories from a time so long ago she had a hard time remembering. Goddess, she had been all of what? Ten? Eleven? She'd become an acolyte at twelve, her dreams of a mate forgotten in the excitement of serving in the Temple.

But one touch of Fafnir's tail against her legs and those buried, forgotten dreams rushed out of hiding like they wanted to see the light of day.

What was wrong with her today?

Getting out of her own mind, she focused on the scene before her.

Tyne.

Or what was left of it.

The remains of a bonfire, a typical occurrence for the Harvest ritual, jumped into the air, casting elongated shadows like clawing fingers across the houses surrounding it. The stench of burned flesh and death mixed with sulphur and charcoaled wood. Did she know a spell to keep breathing but not inhale the scent? It wouldn't do for the High Priestess to arrive with one hand firmly planted over her mouth and nose.

Since nothing came to mind, she continued breathing the stench with the hope her nose would become accustomed to it and stop wrinkling in protest.

Tyne was nothing more than a farmer's village, a group of homes surrounding an open area where gatherings and rituals took place. No walls surrounded the town, just as no walls surrounded any place in Draconia with the exception of the Temple. The wards set around their land kept out attackers, visitors, and other unsavory guests.

Except the one time several weeks ago when a

band of humans simply walked through the wards. But, they had been led by a rogue Draconi, who escaped. Despite the Council's efforts, the Draconi hadn't been found. Maybe he was behind the attack tonight?

While the thought of blaming all the destruction on the nameless Draconi gave her warm fuzzy feelings, the reality was, he couldn't have committed this atrocity alone.

Which brought her back to the report of Watchers being behind the attacks.

Why? Why would Watchers attack a Draconi village?

"It's the High Priestess!" a shout snapped her attention to the right, to a female hiding in the doorway of a building.

As if her appearing was the all-clear signal, villagers began streaming from buildings, some looking at the destruction, others clustering around her. Aryana turned to Fafnir, only to blink into an empty space beside her.

Where had the dragon gone?

****

Fafnir removed his tail from around Aryana's legs and disappeared. Invisible, he walked around the outside of the houses, looking for…something? Someone to pop up and say, *I caused this destruction, come and get me?*

He'd do better sticking by Aryana's side.

Where he wanted to stay.

Now was not the time to search his inner feelings. He needed to concentrate, to find evidence of the perpetrators.

Shadows flickered across the houses, fingers of

pain digging into the darkness. He heard a female shout, "It's the High Priestess!" and then confusion reigned, as a cacophony of voices rushed the last place he saw Aryana.

He almost missed the whimper in all the noise.

Behind one of the houses sat a small shed, obviously a storage building of some kind as he didn't catch a whiff of privy-scented air. As nothing moved in the shadows, he assumed the whimper came from the shed and headed in that direction.

Only to come to a stop.

Lying in front of the shed were two Watchers, both dead from the smell of things.

Fafnir's nose wrinkled. He hated the stench of death. Of decay. Which was why he never became a reconnaissance specialist.

He'd rather teach hatchlings how to fly.

Or High Priestesses.

He shook his head. *Stay in the present, not in your imagination.*

Having never worked for the Council or overseen investigations of the type lying in front of him, he couldn't be certain, but it seemed as if one of the Watchers tried to defend the shed. Something about the angle of the bodies, the way one looked to be slumped protectively in front of the door.

A half-sob escaped the shed, smothered as if by a hand. Fafnir dropped his invisibility spell and used mind-speak to project his thoughts.

Who's in there?

Who are you? A young one. Female. Scared.

Fafnir's teeth ground together, his nostrils flaring. *I am Fafnir. Close your eyes and open the door.*

The door creaked open, a small figure highlighted in the flickering shadows, her face screwed up as she squeezed her eyes shut. One hand rested on the door, as if to slam it closed at any moment. Her chest rose and fell, rose and fell, as if she had run a distance.

Between one breath and the next, he transported her to him, avoiding the Watcher's bodies her young eyes did not need to see.

A tear-streaked face stared at him a second before thin arms wrapped around his leg. Trusting him. A small piece of his heart broke. So this is what it would feel like to have his daughter touch him. To trust him. To look up to him as her savior.

But he wasn't her savior, now was he? If he ever saw his daughter, his only offspring, she would have nothing to do with him. How could she after the great loss he caused her?

This little one didn't know his failings, she only knew he saved her.

Come. Let's try to find... He almost said her parents, but thought the better of it in case her parents were among the dead. *Let's try to find someone you know.*

She nodded, still holding his leg with a death grip. Taking a deep breath, he transported them to where he last saw Aryana, in front of the village.

Keep your eyes closed. Last thing he wanted was for the young one to see the destruction, the death. The stench of it was bad enough.

Aryana stood in the middle of the town, next to the bonfire, surrounded by the villagers. What would his life be like now if he hadn't avoided her as a hatchling? One thing was for certain, he wouldn't be trapped inside a dragon's body, living life with the cloistered males.

A series of small pops sounded as a group of warriors, both Watcher and Draconi, appeared beside him. None of the males looked too happy to be there, especially the Draconi.

"Do you know what happened?" one of the males asked.

Tyne was attacked.

"So you don't know why either."

Would I be standing here if I did?

The male snorted. "Let's go." He gestured to the crowd surrounding Aryana. Eyes narrowed, the warriors marched into the center of the confusion.

Another pop to his right had him turning in that direction. Thoren and Enar. He made an effort to keep the snarl off his face.

"Hey, Fafnir. What are you doing here?" Enar walked toward him.

"Who do you have there?" Thoren asked, following the blond Watcher.

"I'm Elspeth. Do you know where my mommy is?" Elspeth poked her head out, disobeying his keep-your-eyes-closed order. Young ones.

"I do not. Why don't you stay here and we'll find out for you?"

"All right."

Thoren patted the girl on the head and walked into the crowd, leaving Fafnir with Enar.

"Where did you find her?"

Fafnir pulled his gaze from Thoren's retreating back and focused on Enar. *In a storage shed.*

"When the bad people came in, Mommy told me to run and hide. So I did. Lief followed me to keep me safe, but a bad person attacked him before I could hide. Do you know where Lief is?"

Enar looked at him. Fafnir shook his head.

"I don't know. I'll go help Thoren look for your mommy, all right?"

"Thank you."

Enar grinned and turned to follow Thoren.

How's Lily?

Enar glanced over his shoulder at Fafnir. *Good. She's really good. Stop by sometime.*

Only if you aren't around.

Enar made a gesture Fafnir hoped Elspeth didn't see. A chuckle escaped his lips. He might actually be learning to like that Watcher.

Stranger things had happened.

Like discovering he had a daughter.

He shook the thought off. Too much going on to get caught up in his own thoughts.

"Elspeth!" a female cried, her shout cutting through the cacophony of voices.

Small arms loosened their grip around his leg. "Mommy?"

The female took two steps forward, disappeared, and with a *pop* reappeared in front of them. "Elspeth!"

"Mommy!"

Fafnir backed away, giving the reunion space. He wished for the same thing Elspeth had, for his family to embrace him into their fold. For their forgiveness. For their acceptance.

For a life that didn't involve a youthful arrogant attitude.

Good thing Elspeth and her mother didn't know what a sorrowful excuse for a male he was.

A touch on his flank knocked him out of his morose thoughts. Elspeth's mother stood beside him, clutching her daughter to her chest, tears streaming down her cheeks.

"Thank you, thank you, thank you. I don't know what I would have done..." Her words faded into sniffles.

You are most welcome.

As if she felt his sadness, she offered another stroke on his flank before walking to where the bonfire leapt into the air, disappearing into the crowd. His scales felt lighter from her touch, as if all his troubles vanished with the removal of her hand, a feeling that rippled across his hide, burrowing deep inside his heart.

His prior actions might have branded him a failure, a coward, a poor excuse for a male, but he'd found Elspeth and reunited the young one with her mother.

Maybe there was hope for him after all.

Chapter Three

Aryana stared at the tents erected in the Temple Courtyard. Temporary housing for the displaced villagers. Once the Council warriors arrived at Tyne, she had taken the females and children and returned to the Temple. Helped erect tents. Swallowed steam every time she thought about the ruined village.

"Did you find out who did it?" Aryana jumped as Annaliese touched her arm. "Sorry. I thought you heard me behind you."

"It's all right." She loved the feeling of her heart jumping out of her chest. "No, I didn't find anything out. You?"

"I looked into their minds and only the elderly male saw blond hair. Everyone else saw males in black masks, no discerning features. Which isn't to say it wasn't the Watchers."

"But why would the Watchers attack? And attack a farming village at that. Why not attack a town if looting was the goal?"

"Maybe looting wasn't the goal. Remember how Enar said there was a plot to overthrow us?"

Aryana took a deep breath on the off chance it possessed some calming qualities. "The plot was to overthrow the Draconi, not the priestesses, and establish Watchers as rulers. The Council is supposed to be working on the threat."

"Clearly they need to step up the program."

"Maybe it wasn't Watchers. Most of Tyne's Watchers were killed defending the village. Would you attack your own race?"

"If my goal was to overthrow what I considered a dictatorship and you got in my way, then yes, I would kill a member of my race."

Aryana shivered. *Note to self: Do not upset Annaliese.*

"I suppose you're right. This fighting is all new to me."

"I know." Annaliese looked around the Courtyard at the city of tents. "Where is the male dragon who took you to Tyne?"

"He and the other cloistered males are guarding the perimeter of the Temple." Because nothing says love like a dragon brigade breathing fireballs on intruders.

"You never did say how you met him."

Aryana felt her cheeks warm. As the possibility existed someone could overhear their conversation, she projected her thoughts directly to Annaliese. Her complete failure at flying, her plummet into a berry bush, Fafnir's discovery.

Annaliese's eyes flared wide. "Oh my. Did you wipe his memories?"

"I tried. Trust me, I tried hard, but he prevented me. Never had that happen before."

A shadow flickered behind Annaliese and Ari focused on the movement. One shadow split into three.

"Help! Someone please help us!"

A female and two young glanced around the Courtyard, their faces wide-eyed with fear, even as Annaliese and Aryana ran to meet them. Aryana touched the female's arm, willing away her fear. The female took a deep breath, her tension releasing into the air on a puff of steam, while the youngsters darted behind her, clinging to her skirts.

Not again. What enemy existed who coordinated attacks on her people? "What happened?"

"We were attacked! Our village was attacked!" She shook free of Aryana's touch, and reached for her children.

"Goleb?" Annaliese asked, her head cocked to one side. It might not be polite to read minds without permission, but sometimes it helped.

"Yes, yes, Goleb. Please, you've got to help us!"

"I'll go." Aryana took a breath and swallowed the steam rising in her throat. Who was attacking Draconi villages and why? Was it the Watchers? If not, then who managed to get past the wards?

"Don't be ridiculous," Annaliese snapped. "Call the Council. You aren't trained to fight. It might be a trap."

"You think they want me?"

Her friend narrowed her brows. "It's possible."

"I was planning on calling the Council"—she wasn't completely brainless—"but I'm still going. They are my people and I am sworn to protect them."

"You're sworn to protect them religiously. Nothing in the vows mentions protection against an attack."

"I'm going and that's final."

Annaliese's jaw tensed, but she bit back her words and offered a nod. How could she consider not going? Not trying to help? She was the High Priestess, a repository of magic. And she knew a little something about Goleb no one else did.

Aryana closed her eyes and focused on calling Thoren.

What is it, Ari?

Another village has been attacked.

What! When? Where?

Goleb. A female and her young just arrived. I'm going to see—

You will do no such thing!

Aryana cut him off. Past experience proved he'd come faster if she ended the conversation before he started ranting. She opened her eyes, looking at Annaliese. "Take care of them. I'll be back."

Disappearing before her friend once again gave voice to going-is-a-bad-idea, she reappeared in Goleb. Another small farming village located miles away from the Temple, Goleb smelled of burned wood and freshly tilled soil. Magic thrummed beneath her feet, a music playing for only her ears. Unlike Tyne, the buildings had not been burned.

At least not from the side she stood on. Her transport landed her behind a row of homes, between the village and the fields, not in the middle of the square. All the better to hide on the off chance Annaliese was correct and the attackers wanted her.

Screams slammed through the open air, followed by the sounds of metal on metal. If any of those screams belonged to her people, so help her Goddess, she was going to charcoal every last one of the attackers.

And she might get the chance. With a cry of "She came!" a group of black-garbed males waving swords ran straight toward her. Aryana sucked a breath through dry lips. She was the High Priestess. She could incinerate them all.

She hoped.

Aryana stood still as the intruders surrounded her, circling, entrapping. Maybe Annaliese was right, maybe she was the target.

Aryana turned her lips in what she hoped looked like a you're-about-to-die snarl as she drew power from deep inside the earth. Goleb sat in the middle of a magical hotspot, a well of power bubbling to the surface like an underground stream. A well few felt and even fewer knew how to use. Lucky for her, she belonged in that small group.

"You want me? Come get me."

They moved nearer and she lobbed energy balls, *bam, bam, bam,* hitting the closest three in the chest, driving them to the ground. Here in Goleb with the magic coursing beneath her feet, powering her with the force of a gale wind, she was unstoppable.

A pain ripped through her skull, clouding her vision, driving her to her knees. Virtually unstoppable unless hit on the head. Maybe she should have noticed those behind her instead of focusing only on those in front.

Her vision wobbled, fading to gray with dancing black spots around the edges. She heard laughter, low and malevolent, and felt the air ripple as a weapon slashed toward her. Anger danced through her veins, mixing with the earth's magic, changing her, invigorating her.

She felt her bones lengthen, her skin ripple into scales, her head tilt back as her lips opened into a roar. The dragon filled her, exploding from its hiding place, scattering her attackers. If she hadn't been so scared, she might have enjoyed their gasps of surprise and fear.

What would she do if one of the villagers saw her change? Furthermore, how did she manage to change outside of the circle?

A sharp pain pierced her front leg and she roared with agony. One of the intruders had clearly overcome his fright and was busy trying to poke his sword through her leg.

Just because she had no idea how to use her wings, didn't mean she had no idea how to use her new set of sharp, pointed teeth. At a snap of her jaws, the sword clattered to the ground and the male screamed as his arm joined his sword.

The loss of his arm didn't stop the others from attacking. No longer caring if any villagers saw her, Aryana said a quick prayer for survival and threw herself into the fight.

****

Fafnir glared straight ahead into the darkness and saw nothing but the dark outlines of trees and grasses. Or was that grasses and trees? A glance to the right and left showed the other cloistered males who, like him, stood guarding the Temple, spread out around the perimeter of the walls. Although he doubted whoever attacked Tyne would dare to venture onto Temple grounds, he agreed with the guardian action.

After all, Aryana stood inside those walls.

He shook his head. One touch from her and a rush of emotions he didn't want surfaced. As if she'd ever return his feelings. The days of caring and sharing rested in a past best left buried. If she discovered his crime, the best he could hope for would be banishment from Draconia. No I-care-about-you-too feelings directed at him. He didn't deserve such niceties.

Guilt swallowed him, soaking through until his bones ached with the onslaught. His mind slipped into the past, reviving memories best forgotten, spinning them like strands of yarn. He should have fought harder, tried to escape, insisted his lover obey his orders.

They told him she'd died, their child along with her.

He'd grieved. Released his sorrow over the years spent behind titanium bars. Until he'd been freed, he'd believed his captors when they said his child died.

They lied.

And the guilt had surrounded him ever since.

A low-powered jolt twisted through him, as if an energy ball tore into his muscles, slinging him back into the present. What was that? Pushing his mantle of grief aside, he focused on the tingling stabs shooting across his legs, stabs that indicated an impending transport. Perhaps he would transport right out of his life and into someone else's.

No one could accuse him of not having an imagination.

Since he remained in his same body, his same life, and transporting was the last thing on his mind, why did it seem—

Before he could complete that thought, his body shattered into tiny, invisible pieces, pulling his essence across the land, transporting him a stone's throw away from a fight.

A small dragon, scales dark against the night, bit, clawed, and threw fire on five humans attempting to attack. Where was he? Why had he been brought here?

More importantly, how?

With a sweep of its tail, the dragon knocked the legs out from under one of its attackers, a roar of triumph bellowing from its mouth.

Yes! The roar of glee slammed into Fafnir's mind and with a shudder he realized who the dragon was.

And why he transported against his will.

He cursed.

He still didn't know where he was, but he knew he needed to get Aryana out of that fight and fast. Before a villager saw her in dragon form and did something dumb. Or, more likely, one of her attackers got a strike in. Casting a spell, he cloaked himself in invisibility.

Aryana!

She stopped moving and looked in his direction. A sword screeched against her scales and she screamed in obvious pain. He winced as steam began rising in his throat. They hurt her and they would die.

Become invisible and transport to me.

I'm not giving up.

I know. I'm replacing you.

Do you think I can't fight? She swept her tail to the side, knocking down two of the attackers.

As saying yes would get him nowhere, he stomped the word out of his thoughts. *I think the High Priestess is injured and needs her wounds tended. Come to me and I will dispense with the attackers.*

With a final sweep of her tail, she vanished. He felt a stirring of air as she transported to his side. Breathing a sigh of relief, he transported into the circle, taking her place. He dropped his invisibility spell and roared. The attackers jumped back, but he didn't give them time to escape.

Taking a deep breath in, he put the steam in his throat to good use, letting it power a rush of flame and fire. Two charcoaled humans down, three to go.

He clawed the nearest one, blood coating his talons. But when he looked for the last two, they had vanished. No, not vanished, ran off.

Fafnir gave a hop, stretching his wings, readying to fly, when the two running-away humans dropped to the ground, courtesy of Aryana's spell.

Turning his head, he stared at her. No longer a dragon, Aryana stood in her torn gown, her features marred in the darkness.

Are you all right?

I've been better. You?

Fine. Those two?

Asleep. For awhile. We need captives to interrogate.

Made sense, but he wanted to rip their intestines out and burn their bodies for the harm they caused Aryana.

How did you know to come?

Oh, right. As if he was going to play the share game and tell her the old Seer was correct all those years ago. She was his mate. He passed the mating test, which proved without a doubt she belonged to him.

Not all Draconi knew who their mates were. Most Draconi had to seek them out. To help in their quest, a test had been devised, a test that took a potential mating pair and put one of them in jeopardy. If the other one transported against their will to the one in jeopardy, then they were mates. No automatic transfer meant it was not a true mating.

A rather odd way to find a mate, in his opinion. It

seemed to work with others, but he had always wondered if it would work with him.

Now he knew.

Not that it mattered. Aryana could never know she belonged to him.

An ache took up residence in his heart and he shook it off.

He shrugged and hoped she'd leave it at that. *What about the villagers?*

By the Goddess, I got so caught up in the fight, I forgot about the villagers. She turned and ran toward the houses surrounding the middle of the village.

He glanced at the sleeping humans, decided they were going nowhere, and followed Aryana. She came to an abrupt stop, staring at a circle of dragons in the middle of the village. Inside the circle stood a group of black-masked humans, swords in a defensive posture.

Pop! Pop! To his right, a group of Council warriors appeared, and he breathed a sigh of relief. Their appearance meant he could convince Aryana to return to the Temple and check on her wounds. He smelled blood on her, and it wasn't the human variety.

One of the warriors turned to Aryana, his open-wide eyes a comical accompaniment to his slack jaw. "High Priestess. What are you doing here?"

"I heard of the attack and came to check on the villagers."

"Are you injured?"

The warrior took a step toward Aryana, but she held up a hand in defense. "I am fine."

"You should not be here."

I'll take her to the Temple. There are two unconscious attackers behind the houses. He nodded to where the attackers were. Before Aryana could protest, Fafnir wrapped his tail around her legs and transported them to the Temple Courtyard.

As soon as they reappeared, Aryana shoved away from him, her left arm held against her chest, her eyes flashing sparks under the light of the glow lamps. "How dare you? I needed to be there, to comfort—"

You are injured. You need to be here.

"What right do you have to transport me against my will?"

If she only knew. He froze the words wanting to escape his tongue, wanting to proclaim to all she belonged to him, locked them up tight. He wanted her to know and yet he didn't. Conflicted was not a state of mind he enjoyed.

He opted for a silent stare.

Narrowed eyes focused on him. The air around her shimmered and he flicked his tail around her legs before she could transport back to the village.

No.

"No? No? How can you stop me?"

By expending a lot more effort than he planned. Goddess's teeth, she was powerful. Only with extreme effort did he manage to hold onto her and stop her from transporting. By the time she swayed, putting out her uninjured hand to collapse upon his tail, he panted with the effort exerted.

Stubborn female.

Who had clearly lost a lot of blood and needed tended to sooner rather than later.

Running the layout of the Temple through his mind, he tried to remember where the healing room for the cloistered males was located. Never having been there in his current form, he tried pulling the memory from when he was a hatchling, running the Temple corridors with his mother.

The memory came to him, the location of the room at the end of the infirmary wing. One room only, one extra-large room, since dragons rarely got sick. Or injured for that matter.

Scales protected against a lot.

At least the scales on male dragons. Judging from Aryana's wounds, female dragons possessed flimsy scales more for show than protection.

Who knew?

It wasn't like he'd ever heard of a female dragon. Those sightings had been relegated to long, long ago in a time far, far away. Fables. Tales told to children at bedtime.

How did Aryana manage to change into a dragon when no other female could?

His goal loomed before him, joined with the more pressing matter of taking Aryana to the healing room before she fainted from blood loss.

Closing his eyes, he focused on the healing room for cloistered males and transported them there. Aryana collapsed onto his tail, her fingers clinging to the spiked ridges of his scales as if they were a lifeline in raging waters. Her touch simultaneously soothed him and aroused him. What a combination.

Did all mated males feel this way toward their mates? How would he attain his goal of discovering how she changed into a dragon with these bloody emotions pinging around his veins?

He was in dragon form. Even if she felt the same way toward him, and that was a huge if, he couldn't carry those feelings to their obvious conclusion. Dragons didn't mate. They couldn't. For a dragon to mate with a female was abhorrent, repellant, taboo.

And that did nothing to stop his feelings.

Bloody feelings.

Where did they get him? Nowhere fast.

Instead of over-thinking matters, he should be calling for a priestess to come tend to Aryana.

As if he'd called, the door banged against the stone wall, one infuriated priestess storming through the opening. Green eyes flashed worry that bled into anger, and she glared at Aryana as if holding back a physical strike. He remembered that look from when he was a hatchling and shuddered involuntarily. No reason to shrink against the wall, no reason at all. The anger wasn't directed toward him.

For the moment anyway.

She stood, lips pursed white, her anger wrapping around her like a cloak too heavy to wear. Annaliese, the head Temple Healer, was the best choice to heal Aryana.

And the last person he wanted to see.

Chapter Four

Aryana sat on Fafnir's tail and prayed she wouldn't faint. When was the last time her energy had ebbed this low? During her testing for High Priestess? No, not even then. This tiredness went far beyond the exhaustion that drained her after the testing of her powers.

At the sensation of liquid dripping down her skin, she looked at the tear in her gown, at the blood draining from a gash the length of her forearm.

No wonder she felt weak. And fighting against Fafnir hadn't helped any.

None of which explained how he managed to transport her against her will. She was the High Priestess, for Goddess' sake. A tremendous amount of power resided in the position, not to mention her own innate magical abilities.

Very few Draconi possessed powers stronger than hers and most of them were confined to one family, those members who carried the blood of Alviss and his long dead mate Eir. Perhaps Eir had distant relatives, of whom Fafnir was one, since to her knowledge, only Annaliese and Keara remained of Alviss's line.

So who was Fafnir to possess magic enough to overpower her will?

A mystery to answer once she could sit upright without the room spinning like a ball rolling down a slope.

"What happened?" Annaliese stormed into the room, her anger visible in tendrils wrapped around her head, her mouth flattened into a thin line.

Aryana shivered as a wave of exhaustion attempted to shove her over. Remaining upright took more energy than she expected, energy she needed to heal. But with Annaliese exhibiting uncharacteristic anger, and anger directed her way, blood loss was the least of her problems.

Her friend's eyes snapped worry, relief, and anger in varying amounts, and Aryana felt like a child scolded for inappropriate behavior.

Not that she had behaved inappropriately.

Maybe she should have stayed at the Temple.

And miss out on the fighting? No, I'd do it again.

Did she just answer herself? Yes, yes, she did. Clearly she needed healing and fast.

She's lost a lot of blood.

Aryana glanced at Fafnir and attempted to turn it into a glare. If only to prove that as a grown female, she could answer questions herself. Not that she seemed to be answering questions, but still. She could.

She hoped.

Maybe she needed his overprotective arrogance as the ability to open her mouth and speak seemed beyond her capabilities. Why was he being so protective? Because she was hurt? No, he had been protective of her all night, even before her injury. He acted like a mated male. Acted like she belonged to him, like she was his mate.

The thought was preposterous. He couldn't be her mate. First off, she spent her life rejecting the prediction she possessed a mate. And even if she was wrong, only one mate existed per Draconi and hers died years ago.

Didn't he?

"What!" Annaliese stared at Aryana, her anger morphing into worry.

Aryana shrugged the shoulder of her injured arm. "It's bleeding." Did that small voice really belong to her?

Annaliese's brows raised, then dipped as she hurried over, her anger forgotten in her obvious concern. "Let me see."

She grasped Aryana's wrist, her other hand held above the skin ran along the length of the gash, absorbing the pain. Her lips moved as she turned her hand palm up. A roll of bandages appeared in her palm, which she used to bind the gash. Aryana watched as blood continued to seep through the pristine white cloth, soiling it.

Still holding Aryana's wrist in her hand, Annaliese turned to Fafnir. "She needs to be moved to a bed in one of the healing rooms."

This is one of the healing rooms.

"This is one of the healing rooms for the cloistered males. As you can see there is no bed. She needs a bed. Now release her so I can transport her."

No. Transport a bed here so I can remain by her side.

Annaliese snarled at the dragon, steam seeping from her ears, circling her face.

Aryana placed a hand on her friend's arm. "S'all right. He can stay with me."

Annaliese's eyes narrowed, the steam still drifting

from her ears. "Fine." With a wave of her hand, a bed appeared on the other side of the room. "Release her, so I can transport—"

Before she made it to the end of the sentence, Aryana felt her body split apart, its particles coalescing on the bed. Annaliese still stood by Fafnir's tail, her mouth open in an expression of surprise.

Aryana stifled a smile. "He's good about that. Transporting."

"I see." Annaliese hurried to a cabinet in the room where she removed a bowl and bandages along with a jar of ointment. She turned toward the bed, muttered a curse, and with another wave of her hand transported a nightstand beside the bed.

Aryana alternated between watching her friend gather supplies and staring at the fresco on the ceiling. This room featured clouds and mountains floating across the ceiling in broad strokes. No frolicking dragons in here. Which stood to reason seeing as cloistered males no longer frolicked. At least not with female dragons. She glanced at Fafnir as the thought went through her mind.

I do not frolic with males.

Good. I find I don't like that thought.

He chuckled. *So, you'd rather I frolic with females?*

I'd rather you frolic with me. Oh great, did she just say that? Judging by how his eye-ridges popped halfway up his forehead, the answer was yes. Clearly Annaliese needed to work her healing magic and fast before she spewed any other best-left-unsaid thoughts.

Would you now? The words whispered across her mind, low and seductive. If she hadn't been suffering

43

from blood loss, she would have appreciated its timbre.

Well, not right now.

Obviously not.

Don't go anywhere.

Don't worry.

"Here we go." Annaliese hurried to the bed carrying the bowl filled with water, which she placed on the nightstand along with the other supplies. "I'm going to remove your sleeve, clean your wound, then repair it. All right?"

"Thank you."

As Annaliese cut off the now-soaked-through bandage along with her sleeve and cleaned her wound, Aryana watched Fafnir lay down, curling his tail around his body, his gaze never leaving her face.

Why is he here? Her friend's mind-spoken words cut across her thoughts, jarring her back to reality.

Long story.

I think we have time.

I'm sorry. You were right. I should have stayed here.

That doesn't answer the question.

No, it doesn't.

Why did you leave?

They are my people. I couldn't see them hurt.

Were they hurt?

I don't know. I was attacked as soon as I arrived.

You were what!

Ouch! Aryana jumped as the cloth used to clean her wound pressed hard against the gash.

Sorry. What happened?

Masked humans with swords spotted me and attacked.

Annaliese raised a brow. *You must have fought well to only have this one gash.*

You could say that. I turned into a dragon.

You what?

Turned. That's why there is only one gash. Then Fafnir arrived. I'm not sure how he knew to come there, but he took my place and together we incapacitated the invaders. Then the Council showed up, Fafnir grabbed me, and you know the rest of the story.

Annaliese glanced over her shoulder at Fafnir for a moment before focusing again on her work. *Will he tell what he saw?*

I don't think so. He seems rather protective of me. But I'd like to keep him close in case. Feel out the situation.

As you wish. Just promise me you won't go running off to attacked villages in the middle of the night again.

Worried about me?

The corner of Annaliese's mouth stretched into a grin. "I think it's clean so I'll say a spell to heal the skin and to replenish your blood supply. After which you will sleep, understand?"

Aryana nodded. Sleep sounded like a wonderful idea. Best idea ever. Tomorrow would be the day for discovering why Fafnir insisted upon protecting her. Why he followed her to Goleb. Why his magic was as powerful as hers. Then she could work on finding a spell to turn him human, to force him from his dragon state.

Although that might be more for her benefit than his. In his human state, she could bed him.

But first she needed Annaliese's healing spell to work its magic, to invigorate her body, to restore her drained energy.

The healing spell weaved its way through her veins, closing her wounded skin, restoring her lost blood. Despite the healing, exhaustion flooded her body, and it took her a moment to realize the healing spell also carried a spell for sleep. Annaliese's warm hands touched her forehead, stroking as one would a child. Or a beloved friend.

"Sleep, Ari. Sleep and heal. Peace to you."

Aryana's lids grew heavy as the spell coated them closed. Giving herself to the welcome sleep, she drifted away on a wave of peace.

****

Fafnir stretched, his claws raking against stone. Stone? He tensed as fear stabbed a hole in his gut. Was he back in his cell deep underground? His lids flipped open, heart racing a wild gallop, his breath uneven.

Not a cell. A healing room in the Temple.

The tension bled out of his muscles and a couple of deep breaths later, his heart rate calmed. He shook his head.

Would he ever stop having flashbacks to his time in captivity? At least he recovered quicker now than he had when first freed.

The soft sounds of snoring brought his head around. Aryana lay in a bed, covers pulled to her chest, her lashes dark against her cheeks. Morning light streamed from the windows, bathing the room in washes of pale pink and orange.

His mate.

What a fool he had been. Who was he kidding? It appeared his foolish behavior started as a hatchling and only worsened over the years. One would think as he aged he would grow out of such behavior, and yet here he sat, refusing to admit his true identity.

A fool and a coward. What a combination.

With the wisdom of ten-year-olds, he and Aryana had made a pact to ignore the prophecy of the old Seer. After all, the Seer's usual predictions consisted of telling the parents of a baby whether that baby possessed a mate, not who that mate was. To his knowledge, they were the only couple predicted to be mates. And the prediction was a bit loose, no names attached.

Not that it kept their parents from deciding their fates lay together.

As a young hatchling, the last thing on his mind was taking a mate. And Aryana had a strong desire to be a priestess. Who was he to get in the way of her dreams?

So he ran. Had affairs with non-Draconi females. Fell in love with one. Deeply in love. Which only strengthened his belief the Seer erred in her prediction. How could he be so in love with another if the fates decreed he and Aryana belonged together?

But the love he'd felt for Mabbina held a dull gleam to how he now felt about Aryana.

The door creaked open, startling him from his thoughts. Annaliese walked into the room and Fafnir dropped his head, closing his eyes to slits, pretending to be asleep. She glanced at him, but her attention focused on the High Priestess as she walked to the bed.

One more person he didn't want to see. What a yellow-bellied rabbit. He should pop his head up, refresh her memory as to his true name and allow her to wallow in excitement over seeing him again.

Who was he fooling? She probably would just as soon banish him as welcome him.

It had been a month since he'd returned to Draconia. Plenty of time to greet his family members. Instead, he hid.

He didn't deserve Aryana. How could he be the mate she deserved if he couldn't even work up the nerve to speak to his estranged family? Did they even think of themselves as estranged? Maybe they would greet him with pleasure. Maybe they would be overjoyed to see him. Maybe they would welcome him home.

Or maybe they would see what he did, how he left his daughter to rot in a village in Cautasia, to be raised by non-magical humans and think what an irresponsible muddle he made of his life.

Why would his family want him?

"You seem troubled." Annaliese's whisper caused him to jump, his lids snapping open, a snarl crossing his lip before he wiped it away.

Don't you know better than to disturb a sleeping dragon?

"My apologies. You seemed troubled."

You don't say? He kept the thought to himself. She couldn't help her curiosity.

Healers wanted to help others, felt driven to ferret out the cause of pain and unhappiness, even when they should leave well enough alone. As part of their nature, they could no more stop caring than they could stop breathing and expect to live.

Therein lay their problem. Especially for one such as he, who wanted to keep his secrets nice and tight inside. Bottled up, locked down and allowed to fester like dead flesh left in the sun.

No wonder Annaliese wanted him to play the sharing game. He probably smelled like rancid meat.

Bad dreams.

"Hmm. While I have a tonic for that, in your case it seems like something internal eating away at your heart."

Was he that obvious? After years spent in a cell, he forgot how to hide his emotions from others. What had his jailers cared about his thoughts, his emotions? Not one thing.

But Annaliese did.

Healers.

He would not transport away from her and admit to being guilty as charged. He would not. He was a grown dragon. Grown dragons did not run from their problems, they faced them head-on.

Fafnir swallowed, as if that would help loosen up his dry throat. No such luck.

Perhaps you are right.

She blinked at him, a silent entreaty to continue. The almost-unnoticeable spell caressed his scales, his head, whispered for him to find relief by sharing his problems.

His eyes closed. He wanted to tell her, to speak with her as he had all those years ago, to wallow in her comfort.

But what if she didn't offer comfort? What if, instead, she rebuked? What if she threw him out of the Temple?

He shook his head.

"You are the first Draconi I know of who was held captive for so long behind titanium bars. It is only natural you would feel like you didn't fit in here anymore."

It is more than that. Did those thoughts actually slip out?

Judging by the way her head cocked to the side and her eyes widened in encouragement, the answer was a yes. He shut his eyes, trying to work up the courage to say what he needed to, what he didn't want to admit.

She placed her hand on his side. "When you are ready, I am here. I am always here, Fafnir. You do realize that, right?"

He drew in a deep breath, overwhelmed by the emotions her words provoked, the way they transported him back to when he was a hatchling seeking comfort. Without thinking, he answered the way he always answered her question.

Yes, Leesie, I know.

Her eyes flew wide, her lips parting, her whole body freezing as she clearly contemplated his words.

Son of a goat. Was he an idiot or what? If you wanted to hide in a crowd, it helped not to say words that singled you out.

Stop putting it off and tell her who you are. Before he could act on his own words, Aryana moaned. Annaliese's gaze flitted to her patient before returning to his. "Ragnor?" she whispered. "Is that you?"

Ragnor no longer exists. Because his embarrassment and cravenness obliterated his ability to call himself by his given name. Better he choose another than admit his failures.

"Annaliese?"

Both he and Annaliese turned to look at Aryana, who had rolled on her side to face them.

"Ah. You are awake." Annaliese glanced at Fafnir as she placed a hand on his snout. *Please don't leave until you've talked to me.*

He closed his eyes, unable to look her in the eyes, unable to see either acceptance or rejection written in their depths. He gave a quick jerk of his head.

"How do you feel?" Apparently satisfied with his answer, Annaliese walked to Aryana, leaving Fafnir to his thoughts.

What had he done? *What you should have done a month ago, fool.* Was he really going to tell Annaliese who he was? *Yes, you blithering ninny.* Was it a sign of insanity if he answered himself? *Probably.* But what did he expect after all those years in a cell with no one to talk to? Perhaps Annaliese would understand. She did, after all, ask him not to leave until she had spoken to him.

That had to be a good sign. Her concern slid across his scales, burrowing deep into his soul, comforting him as it had so many times when he was young. He wanted to talk to her, needed to express his guilt, his shame. He wanted forgiveness from the one person who always gave it to him growing up.

His sister.

Chapter Five

Aryana watched Annaliese walk toward the bed, her face the pale shade of a light-colored sheet, her normal serene composure shattered. What had happened? Had someone died?

Slipping into her friend's mind took less effort than expected. Encountering a mental wall around jagged memories gave her pause. Clearly whatever upset Annaliese had nothing to do with the current attacks on Draconi villages and everything to do with the past. That much she could tell. But what made the past appear?

And why was Annaliese blocking the memory?

Too painful? Or did her friend know she'd try to read her mind?

Probably the latter.

Whatever bothered Annaliese would eventually be told. Neither kept secrets from the other for long. As much as she wanted to comfort her friend, Aryana decided to wait.

"I'm feeling much better. Thank you for the healing. How are you?"

"I'm fine." A lie on so many levels. Annaliese's hand shook as she touched Aryana's arm, her eyes staring at the fresh pink scar as if she'd never seen one like it.

"How are the refugees? Has the Council talked

with any of them yet?"

Annaliese drew in a deep breath, closed her eyes and gave her head a small shake. When her eyes opened, only lingering memories showed in their depths, proof she won the battle over her past. "They are doing as well as can be expected. I have not seen a Council member, but then, I have not spoken to the refugees this morning."

"Then how do you know they are well?"

"The other priestesses have interacted with them. Their injuries have been tended to. Mostly they were frightened."

"As well they should be. Any word on who attacked?"

"I have heard nothing."

The "as usual" went unspoken. Aryana sighed.

"I will need to go speak with the Council." She'd rather clean the latrines with her tongue.

"Only if you are healed."

"Oh, I'm healed all right. I feel fine." She tried to shove Annaliese's hand off so she could get up, but her friend grasped her arm like she was an anchor in a rocky sea. "Annaliese?" Aryana looked at her arm and up to her friend's eyes.

All right, then. Perhaps the battle within still raged. Annaliese's haunted gaze cut like shards into her soul.

"Are you all right?"

"I believe you are well enough to visit with the Council. Perhaps they can tell us who is attacking our villages." Annaliese released her grasp on Aryana's arm and began sorting through the vials sitting on the bedside table. One bottle went to the back of the table while another one came to the front. Over and over, the work of a distracted mind.

Aryana swung her legs out from under the covers and placed a hand on her friend's arm.

"I'll be all right. I just need some time to myself." At Annaliese's whispered words, Aryana squeezed her friend's arm.

"I'll be here when you need me."

"Thank you."

With a wave of her hand, Aryana dressed in the set of white robes she wore around the Temple. On rare occasions, she used magic to dress, preferring the way the material flowed through her fingers as she wrapped it around her body, the smoothness of the cloth as it brushed her skin. But her use of magic this morning was twofold.

She, the uninhibited priestess, felt shy undressing around Fafnir. Perhaps she should have Annaliese examine her head instead of her arm. Or not. Feelings were feelings after all, no matter how strange. Shyness aside, she needed to appear before the Council with due haste, and using a snap of the fingers instead of the physical act of dressing sped up the process.

The quicker she could persuade the Council to tell her who attacked, the quicker she could help her race set up defenses against the invaders. Provided they talked to her.

Thank you, Alviss. Her disagreement with the elderly Draconi affected her ability to address the Council, even with her sister's husband and now her nephew, Thoren, warming two chairs in the stone chamber.

But the attack on the villages would be top on their agenda this morning and she needed in on the discussion. The fear of standing in front of the group of males needed to disappear. She was the High Priestess, and fear was not an option.

Liar, liar.

"I will be back and give you a report. Fafnir, would you like to come with me?"

The dragon's eyes widened. *I do not wish to appear before the Council, but I will escort you to their chamber.*

"Have you appeared to them since you have returned home?"

He licked his lips and focused on a corner of the room. *I have not had that privilege.*

"I don't blame you. Are you ready?"

"Will you return, Fafnir?" Annaliese asked, a vial clutched in her palm.

Fafnir swallowed. *I will.*

What was that about? Why did her friend need to speak to Fafnir? Maybe he was injured too? He hadn't mentioned anything, but then so often males didn't talk about their injuries.

At least not while still injured.

"All right then. Let's get this over with." Aryana walked to Fafnir, touched his side and together they transported to the stone chamber of the Council.

Bright sun blazed into her eyes and she squinted in self-defense.

I will wait for you here.

She looked up at Fafnir, glad he stood away from the sun. "It might be awhile if you need to speak to Annaliese."

I will wait.

"Thank you. Wish me luck."

Luck to you. He brought his muzzle close to her cheek, his breath hot upon her skin. She felt what seemed to be lips, human lips, kiss her cheek. Warmth flooded her veins, dashing to her core, giving buoyancy to her limbs.

Fafnir belonged to her.

Now where did that thought come from? In no way did he belong to her. Obviously, her bored-with-males mood had spilled over into her current situation, forcing Fafnir into her mind's eye as a potential cure for her boredom with a bed-romp.

Not like she could have romp with a dragon. Not in her current form anyway.

She refused to think about changing into a dragon. Not now. Not when she was about to see Alviss. He might attempt to view her mind and the last thing she wanted on it was her attempt to fly and fight as a dragon.

The less the old male knew of her personal life, the better.

Which meant she needed to push Fafnir from her thoughts too. A little hard to do when his kiss lifted her feet from the ground.

She glanced at her feet firmly planted on the ground.

All right. So his kiss hadn't made them float, but it sure felt like air between her soles and the grass.

As soon as she finished talking with the Council, she would start researching turning Fafnir back to human form. Selfish? Yes. But no one had to know that little fact, did they?

Sometime during her parade of thoughts, Fafnir took a step back, watching her like a wolf would a rabbit. Leaving her trembling from his touch, a continuing rush of feelings coursing through her, giving a lightness to her step as a wave of empowerment swept over her. Face the Council? Not a problem. As long as she knew Fafnir waited for her, she could do anything.

Giving the dragon what she hoped wasn't a besotted smile, she opened the tall, wooden doors and entered the stone realm of the Council.

Only to come to a complete stop.

Where was everyone? Shouldn't someone be in the chamber?

"Hello?" Her voice echoed off the stones, bouncing around the room, encountering a whole lot of air and empty chairs.

Sunlight sliced through the open doors, shining sparks of light on dust motes floating through the air. Thirteen carved wooden chairs sat in a semi-circle opposite from the door. A table sat against one curved wall as if someone shoved it into place.

Nothing moved but the specks of dust in the air.

So much for talking to the Council.

She stepped back out, closing the doors behind her.

That was quick.

"No one was there. I've never seen the place empty." And it worried her. Where was everyone?

Shouldn't someone remain in the chamber?

"That's my thought, but I guess not. I'm not privy to the way they work." If only tension didn't exist between her and Alviss, she might know why the Council disappeared. Temperamental old male.

Where do you think they went?

"Your guess is as good as mine."

I'd guess back to one of the villages.

57

"All right. Which one first?"

Tyne. That's where it started. Although the Council could have split so half of them are at Goleb.

Her thoughts exactly. Nice to know her mate held the same thoughts she did.

Wait, wait, wait. Fafnir was not her mate. Her mate had died many years ago. So why did she feel like Fafnir belonged to her?

Clearly it had something to do with turning into a dragon. Memories she needed to banish from her mind prior to talking to Alviss.

Perhaps if she found the Council and forced them to tell her who attacked the villages, all these Fafnir-is-mine thoughts would leave her alone.

But did she really want them to?

Aryana gave herself a mental shake. *Focus, focus, focus.* "Let's try Tyne. Ready?"

****

Throughout his life, Fafnir had heard tales of a mated male following his female around like a half-witted fool, a behavior said to be pure instinct, unavoidable. A behavior he never thought to exhibit.

Accompanying Aryana to Tyne, however, placed him among the rank of besotted fools. The last thing he needed to do was run into a Council member. He'd managed to avoid appearing before any of them since his return, despite repeated requests to drop by for a chat. After a month of refusing their invites, it surprised him they hadn't tracked down his avoiding arse and hauled him in for questioning.

Although he supposed other things of greater importance occupied their attention. Like villages being attacked or a banished Draconi returning to terrorize and invade Draconia. All things much more important than one renegade, previously captured dragon with self-esteem issues.

Still, why press his luck and appear anywhere in their vicinity?

Being with Ari tended to make him forget things, forget he failed his daughter, forget he lied to everyone he met about his identity. He needed to remember his failures, remember why he could never admit he was her mate, remember he could not be who she needed him to be.

A loser. A failure. A craven male.

Or maybe he wasn't such a poor excuse for a male. Following his mate around and attempting to keep her from harm ranked under actions of a real male. Perhaps he needed to modify some of his thoughts.

What a novel idea.

One he'd consider once he successfully avoided Council members in Tyne.

Which happened to be a problem he shouldn't have wasted time worrying about. They arrived in Tyne in the same place they appeared the night before, right outside the village on the path leading into the circle of homes.

Sunlight warmed the ground, brightening the streaks of charcoal shadows that darkened so many of the houses. The charred remains of the Harvest festival bonfire smoldered in the middle of the square, the scent of death hanging in the still air.

Males and females scurried between houses, knocking down the damaged parts of their homes, dragging the remains of buildings to the center of the square where they stacked the wood into a pile. Using magic might make the process go faster, but hard work helped calm a grieving mind.

Opposite from where he and Aryana stood milled a group of Draconi Council soldiers, talking to a group of Watchers. A brief glimpse around the village showed no signs of the thirteen Council members.

Thank goodness.

"I'll go ask them where the Council members are. Did you want to walk over there with me?"

If you don't mind, I'd rather stay here.

"As you wish." Ari took a deep breath, squared her shoulders and started walking through the ruined village.

He watched her stop and talk to the villagers, offering little touches on their arms and backs, her smile visibly relaxing a few of the females. Did she enjoy being High Priestess, dispensing wisdom and peace to those hurt or ill? As a youngster, she wanted the position for power, for a way to strengthen her magical abilities, to gain knowledge of the arcane energies coursing through Draconia. Did she still feel the same or had her reasoning changed as she aged?

Maybe he'd ask. Right after she told him how she changed into a dragon.

"They aren't here." Fafnir started at Aryana's words. "Sorry, I thought you saw me walk up."

Daydreaming halfwit.

He offered her a half-smile. *Did you speak with the soldiers?*

"Didn't have to. The villagers said that the Council members who were here left a few soldiers to guard Tyne and disappeared to Goleb shortly after dawn."

That still doesn't explain why no one is at the

Council Chambers.

"I know. It's a bit odd. Maybe they'll tell us when we arrive at Goleb. Are you ready to go?"

As ready as he'd ever be. Perhaps no one would notice him. It could happen. Mated males were such fools.

As soon as she touched his flank, they transported to Goleb, arriving to a frantic buzz of noise. Voices raised in anger, coupled with females wailing, sent a shiver of unease through his scales. What had happened? When they left last night, it seemed as if the villagers had things under control and that was before the Council's soldiers arrived.

Clearly, some terrible event had occurred since then.

Aryana stiffened, her eyes seeking the source of the wailing, her head tilting to the side.

Can you tell what the problem is?

"Grief." She started walking toward the sound. "But I don't understand. I saw the villagers chasing down the ones who attacked. They were dragons, for Goddess' sake, not in human form."

You were hurt.

The glare turned on him could melt ice. Fafnir shivered and took a step back as Aryana's voice burst through his mind. *My scales aren't as thick as a male's. And it would do you good to keep that knowledge to yourself.*

Of course. Just because he was a besotted fool over his female didn't mean he was a complete and utter idiot.

Her skirts flared as she whirled an about-face and marched around the corner of the nearest house. A jolt of lust shot through him, a silent vibration across his scales. Since when were angry females attractive? No wonder mated males became besotted fools, nothing their females did upset them.

Instead of knocking some sense into his head by banging it on the nearest wall, he followed Aryana around the corner of the house, which gave him a glimpse of the commotion. A group of Draconi and Watchers surrounded several crying females. It looked like the Watchers belonged to the Council. He recognized a few from before his captivity, along with Enar who he heard now served on the Council. Tension filled his muscles, stiffening them, as he froze in place.

The one person he wanted to avoid, needed to avoid, stood on the opposite side of the distraught group, staring not at the wailing females, but straight at Fafnir.

That look burned through him, immobilizing his limbs, momentarily prohibiting him from subtly using illusion to change his appearance. Nothing he did would keep Alviss from recognizing him. He knew the risk of following Aryana, knew it like he knew the sun would rise in the morning, and yet he could no more stop trailing behind her than he could still the pounding of his heart.

Time for him to face reality, to admit his true identity and stop hiding behind a false name. He gulped.

"Moira?" Aryana stepped forward, her gait stiff and jerky. His thoughts crashed into the present as he focused on the female she addressed.

One of the crying females looked up, her eyes red and puffy, swollen like a bruise. "Ari?" The female shoved past those gathered around her and stumbled toward Aryana. "They took her! They took her!"

Aryana caught the female by the elbows as Balthor and Thoren hurried toward her. "Took who, sister?"

"They took my baby! They took Jaythena!"

Chapter Six

Her sister's words crashed through Aryana like a waterfall of ice, stealing her breath. Two tries later she managed to choke out, "What?" Surely she heard wrong. Jaythena was her youngest niece, seventeen years old, a pretty girl still in the unstable phase of having her magic unlocked, the phase where her powers fluctuated out of control.

It had only been two weeks since Jaythena came to the Temple for her unlocking ritual. Two weeks since Aryana spent the day repairing the destruction left after the ceremony. *Two weeks.*

And now she was gone?

Despite the stability issues of her newly released magic, Jaythena should still possess the ability to ward off a kidnapping attack. She should be able to channel some of the energy into harming her attacker.

Unless she possessed little to no magic.

Moira fell against her shoulder and Aryana wrapped her arms around her sobbing sister.

"Jaythena was in Goleb?" Her brain turned over as if walking through sludge, unable to accept the evidence as truth.

"She was visiting a friend," Balthor said, his lips pressed into a thin line, his eyes blinking a rapid staccato as if to ward off tears.

"How? How was she taken? Her powers had been

unlocked."

Thoren stepped closer, vibes of anger radiating off him like bursts of lightning. He glanced at his mother, then his father before focusing on Aryana. *Her magic seems to follow the same path as Mother's.*

Aryana tried to swallow her caught breath and got all of nowhere. Moira's magic, if it could truly be called magic, lay in her fertility, not in demonstrable powers. Unlike other Draconi, Moira could not snap her fingers and dress herself. If after their unlocking ceremony, her daughters blew up a table, she was unable to wave her hand and repair it. To the casual observer, Moira possessed no magic.

However, Draconi females had trouble getting pregnant. Even among mated couples, it could take centuries to have a child. Some families conceived two children and considered themselves blessed beyond measure. More than two was a rarity. So Moira's family of six living children and six unhatched eggs—eggs with the potential to hatch into male young—placed her in a category all by herself. Unheard of. A rare form of magic thought to be possessed by only one.

Aryana swallowed the stab of jealousy that always erupted when she thought of Moira's fertility and allowed her mind to trip down a jagged path to a conclusion she feared.

Jaythena is pregnant?

It's too early to tell, but her power fluctuations stopped. Mother said the same happened to her after her unlocking ceremony.

And Moira had lost the child even as she gained notoriety for being the only Draconi female to get pregnant from the unlocking ritual. Aryana swallowed.

"I'm going to kill them." Judging by Balthor's raised eyebrow, she spoke the words aloud. Just as well. Spoken words held strength.

I'll help. Fafnir's words might not be spoken aloud, but they held strength nonetheless. As they had when she prepared to enter the Council chamber. As they would forever.

Forever? *Stop behaving like a girl with her first crush and focus on what needs done.*

"You won't be alone." Steam snaked from Thoren's ears, his brows a black slash across his forehead as his fists curled and uncurled.

Enar stepped beside him and Aryana waited for a streak of unwanted longing mixed with remorse to jolt through her heart, like it did every time she saw the tall Watcher.

Nothing. Maybe enough time passed for her to stop missing their chats in bed after a night of passion.

Praise the Goddess. Dealing with unwanted feelings resulting from a dead-end relationship instead of focusing on finding her niece ranked lower on her to-do list than servicing males.

A puff of warm air struck her back and she turned her head to the source. Fafnir stood behind her, his lip on full snarl mode, his eyes glaring daggers at Enar.

Surely he didn't read her mind about her former lover. Thoren knowing was bad enough. Only through a mutual understanding between the two did she manage to avoid him telling others about her illicit relationship. Sure, she could slip into his mind and cause him to forget the entire conversation, but invading her own nephew in that way just didn't seem right. Erasing another's memories was tricky business. Potentially harmful business if she extracted the wrong memory. Something only to be used in extreme emergencies, like observing her dragon form crashing to the earth.

Now reading others' minds was a whole different matter. Most people didn't realize she slipped inside and took a look around. Most couldn't stop her even if they did realize her ability.

Most people did not include Fafnir. For whatever reason, she couldn't peer inside his thoughts, which left her reading his body language.

It didn't take a genius to deduce he had issues with Enar. The Watcher in question stepped around the grieving family, and she slanted her stance to see him bump a fist against Fafnir's flank.

"Fafnir, my dragon, how are you?"

Aryana bit her lip to ward off the smile threatening her mouth. Clearly Enar wasn't bothered by Fafnir's off-putting behavior.

Good thing. She needed all the help she could get to find Jaythena. First things first. *Head in the moment, Ari.*

"How did it happen?" Steam billowed out her ears as she pictured Jaythena in her memory. Thought about what the poor female must be going through.

Decided a simple death wasn't enough for the one who took her. A painful, long death sounded like a winning plan.

Moira took a step back, dashing a cloth under her eyes. "She came to visit a...a...friend." She darted a quick glance to her mate before squeezing shut her lids. "I cursed my daughter." The words, spoken in a whisper, floated to Aryana's ears, but they struck with the power of a hammer.

"Nonsense, Moira. It's not a curse. It's just...different. That doesn't make it bad." Envious, yes, bad, not so much.

"But if it wasn't for me, she wouldn't have come here. She would be h...h...home." And there went the tears.

Before Aryana could wrap her arms around her sister, Balthor grabbed his mate into a hug, whispering something in her ear. Moira relaxed against him, tears still running down her face, but her sobs seemed to subside.

Aryana raised a brow.

Calming spell, Balthor mouthed.

"All right. So she came here to meet her friend. The town was attacked. What happened then?"

"A group of Watchers dressed in black, as if that would help disguise them, appeared from nowhere and began attacking the villagers. Unlike Tyne, these villagers turned into dragons and cornered most of them, but some managed to grab Jaythena before her friend could stop them. He said he was knocked unconscious and when he awoke, she was gone." Thoren's jaw clenched, his hands knotting into fists.

"How did Watchers appear from nowhere? And in coordinated attacks?"

Balthor's eyes narrowed. "We suspect a Draconi helped them. We'd also like to know what you and a dragon were doing here when the village was first attacked."

Aryana swallowed. At least no one besides Fafnir saw her turn into a dragon. She hoped. "A mother and her child appeared in the Courtyard saying Goleb was under attack. I immediately transported here and saw a group of Watchers attacking. Before I could do anything, Fafnir"—she gestured to the looming dragon—"appeared, knocked a group of attackers unconscious, and returned me to the Temple. I came as soon as Annaliese released me."

"You were injured?"

"It was nothing."

"So, this is the mysterious Fafnir." Alviss shuffled his way across the packed dirt to stand in front of her, peering at Fafnir with a gaze sharpened by years of observation.

Muscles drew taut despite his squint aimed at Fafnir, and she forced her limbs to relax. From the corner of her eye, she saw Fafnir bristle as she stiffened, a sense of displeasure roiling in the movement. Was it possible he acted protectively toward her?

Despite the moment's situation, a wave of happiness crashed through her, and she swallowed a smile. No male ever cared about her like that. No one.

A subtle magic pulsed from Fafnir's direction, subtle enough that only her heightened senses noticed and she wondered if Alviss knew Fafnir cloaked himself in a disguise. A disguise? Why would he do that? Sure, Alviss intimidated everyone he met and she'd rather not deal with the elderly male, but disguise herself to avoid him?

Why?

Yet another mystery about Fafnir she needed to unlock. After she found Jaythena and killed the kidnappers.

Eyes narrowed, she glared at Alviss. "Yes, it is, but what's more important is what happened to my niece and how and why a group of Watchers attacked two Draconi villages. What are you doing about that?"

Was that a hint of red crossing the old male's cheeks? Maybe he overexerted himself shuffling to where they stood. "We are interviewing the captured Watchers and attempting to extract information."

"Any success?"

"These things take time."

Those things would go a lot faster if the Council let her talk to the attackers. "May I talk with them? We in the priestesshood have secret ways of getting tongues to loosen."

"You would allow us to watch?"

As it was impossible for Alviss to see her tunnel into the Watchers' minds, root around, and extract information, why not? "Of course. We should be willing to work together for the good of our people, should we not?"

Alviss snorted, his cane thumping against the packed dirt as he began his slow, shuffling walk to the other side of the square, forcing her to follow. Fafnir's breath raked hot on her back, his vague magical illusion brushing against her skin. No time to think on his magic-enhanced appearance, she needed to focus on the upcoming interrogation.

In order for Alviss and his Council not to realize she and other higher-ranking priestesses slipped into and out of minds at will, she needed to persuade the captured Watchers to verbalize their thoughts. A simple spell, one she'd used since the unlocking of her powers.

No problem.

Alviss led them across the square, past the houses lining the open area, and out into the fields beyond the village. A group of Draconi and Watchers, Council members and those who worked for them, stood in a circle surrounding those she assumed to be the previous night's attackers. Alviss waved at the closest males, a gesture for them to step aside and let the two of them through. They stepped back into place behind her, leaving her and Alviss to face the intruders.

Five males sat on the tilled dirt, their black cloaks thrown to the side in a heap of cloth, their blond hair streaked with blood. Aryana swallowed. Her entire life she believed the Draconi to be calm, peaceful, not prone to violence. Violence happened rarely and was punished quickly when it occurred.

The males' appearance dashed her beliefs.

Only her anger sustained her, kept her feet moving forward. They knew who took Jaythena. They helped. And they had no qualms about killing Draconi.

Why should she be repulsed by their black eyes, their bleeding noses and lips, the careful way they drew in a breath? In one act, make that two acts, they turned from allies to enemies. She should not feel compassion for their injuries.

She could not stop her emotions any more than she could stop her feet from continuing their slow Alviss-like shuffle to the closest Watcher. The scent of blood stained the air and she fought to swallow the bile rising into her throat. A couple of swallows later, she knelt by the male.

"Tell me where they took the female."

He turned to her, his features too swollen to show surprise, but she felt it radiate from him nonetheless. He spat on the ground, a bloody stream of saliva hanging from his torn lip. "No."

She heard growling from the circle and held up her hand. "Are you sure?"

"Not talking."

It took no effort to slip in to his mind, to rummage through his thoughts. Unlike a Draconi mind, she had no barrier to barge through, no wall surrounding his innermost thoughts. Even Enar put up a resistance, poor though it was, but this Watcher knew not how to protect his mind from assaults.

Stealing toys from a hatchling.

Now to get him to talk. Alviss did not need to know what she saw inside the male's mind, he needed to hear the Watcher talk. She sent a spell of persuasion, a wave of energy convincing the Watcher to confess his secrets aloud. He stared at her, his eyes blue slits in his now-slack face.

"Why don't you tell me who told you to attack?"

"The hooded Draconi." His speech slurred through swollen lips.

She ignored the gasps from his comrades in crime and continued her questions.

"Do you know his name?"

"No."

"Do you know where he took the girl?"

"That wasn't part of the plan."

"What was?"

"Attacking. Overthrowing the Draconi. Letting all know we are the strong ones. Why else would we be their guardians if they weren't useless?"

A shudder passed through her as she pulled out of his mind. He didn't know where they took Jaythena. He knew other things, things with the ability to terrorize her dreams and haunt her waking moments, but the twisted images couldn't stop her from questioning another Watcher. Surely out of all the captives, one would know where her niece had been taken.

She moved to the next Watcher, Alviss shuffling along to stand next to her. For once, his presence didn't bother her.

"Tell me what you know about the girl." This time she didn't bother with niceties, such as giving him a chance to answer. She slipped into his mind, sending a wave of persuasion to ride along her question.

"What girl?"

He didn't know. She moved to the next one, and the one after him. Maybe none of them knew. Her hands shook as she stopped in front of the last Watcher.

"What do you know of the girl?"

"He wanted her for his."

"Who?"

"The hooded Draconi."

"Why?"

"Said she belonged to the bitch priestess and he was going to take her. It wasn't planned. He saw her and decided right then to have her. So we got her for him."

"Where did he take her?"

"To our hideout."

"Can you take us there?" After seeing it in his mind, she could take herself there, but that wouldn't help Alviss and crew arrive.

"Yes."

"That's good. You've been very helpful. This male will take you to your hideout."

Alviss gestured a Draconi reconnaissance expert over along with the expert's Watcher and together the two younger males carried the injured attacker away. Aryana turned her back on the captives and prayed her legs held as she marched out of the circle. As before, anger lent strength to her body, despite her shaking hands and dry throat.

Fasolt took Jaythena. At least she assumed it was Fasolt. Over a month ago, when the hooded Draconi first broke through the Draconian ward line threatening her life, she assumed the Council would take care of the problem. Why should she fear a disgruntled Draconi she'd banished from Draconia?

But instead of coming after her, it appeared Fasolt decided to attack her family. Perhaps he thought to make her hurt with pain equal to what she forced on him. He wanted revenge for his banishment. He wanted her to die.

He had no idea what an infuriated High Priestess was capable of.

He'd learn.

Once they walked through the ring of Council cronies, she whirled on Alviss.

"Why did you not take care of the hooded Draconi, of Fasolt, before now?" If only the Council had done their job, Jaythena would be here with them, instead of captured by that female-hating bastard.

"We couldn't find him."

"With all the resources of the Council, you couldn't find one bloody goat-sucking Draconi?" She sucked in a breath. The High Priestess must not yell at the elderly leader of the Council. The High Priestess must exude serenity at all times.

Her predecessor's voice echoed in her head as she fought to get her breathing under control. One of

Alviss's bushy white eyebrows played a game of touch-the-hairline as he stared nonplussed at her.

"A goat-sucking Draconi, eh?" Was that a smile attempting a run on his lips?

"I apologize for my language." But not her outburst. He deserved that. The Council should have caught Fasolt, or whoever the hooded Draconi was, before now.

Her hands shook and she clasped them together before they did something stupid, like hit a Council member.

"I didn't think you had it in you. We have been looking for him, but he seems to have disappeared into thin air. We strengthened the ward lines and have posted guards around the area where he came into Draconia. Scouts have scoured the land, but have not found anything. It's as if he disappeared."

"Then how do you explain two villages being attacked in the same night?"

"That was due to the Watcher rebellion." Alviss sighed and shuffled in the direction of a log.

"It would seem the hooded Draconi is helping the Watchers."

"It would seem that way." He lowered himself onto the log, planting his cane between his legs. "Ahh. Old bones don't like to stand for long."

Aryana paced before him. Thoughts twirled through her mind, a jumble of questions, plans, ideas. How long until she could leave and find Jaythena? Why did the Watchers want to overthrow the Draconi? What did they think they were overthrowing? As far as she knew, they coexisted in Draconia. Although she had no idea why Watchers guarded Draconi.

"Now, Aryana." The use of her name instead of her title drew her feet to a halt as she turned to Alviss. "Why don't you tell me about the dragon you came here with? What was his name? Fafnir?"

She opened her mouth to tell him and then closed it. Something in his manner, the expression on his face, the tilt of his head, warned her that his question had a deeper agenda.

Why was she not surprised?

"He's been very helpful since Tyne was attacked last night. He and the other males in dragon form have been guarding the Temple from intruders. He agreed to accompany me here." She shrugged. "Will you be searching for Jaythena now?"

"Yes, yes. Of course. Don't worry. The one who took her will die."

Just not right away, went unsaid.

"Thank you. I will go see to my sister." Did Alviss realize her plans? *Calm, serene movements. Do not rush.*

She walked between two houses and saw Fafnir standing where she'd left him, beside her family and Enar, his illusion still in place. Did the others notice? It didn't so much change his facial appearance, as it changed the way his body moved, the way his scales lay. She recognized him, but if she hadn't seen him in years, she might not.

Why did he not want Alviss to recognize him?

"Moira, Balthor, one of the attackers knew where Jaythena was taken. The Council is going to get her."

"I'll go with them." Thoren patted his mother on the arm and headed toward where she left Alviss.

"Me too." Enar followed Thoren.

Balthor rubbed his hand across Moira's back. "Thank you for interrogating them."

Aryana gave him a nod as she drew her sister into a hug. "Do not worry, sissy, she will be returned."

"Thank you." Moira sniffed as she drew back into Balthor's embrace.

Aryana turned to Fafnir. *Ready?*

Where are we going?

To kill the bastard.

Chapter Seven

Killing the bastard sounded like a good idea to Fafnir. Harming a Draconi female was unthinkable; to kidnap one was punishable by death. And leaving meant he didn't have to face Alviss.

For years behind bars he imagined what he would say to his family when he saw them again, how happy they would be to see him. Until he Changed. Insecurity snuck in. Perhaps they would think him less than a male for being captured, for being unable to fight his way out of his cell. When Thoren freed him, he was hesitant to state his true name, wanting to wait and see how his family reacted to his imprisonment.

And then he saw Keara lying on the ground, her face immobile from drugs given to control her movements, and realized she was his daughter. His daughter.

Hard on the heels of that happy revelation came the thought that he'd abandoned her, left her alone to be raised by humans, caused harm to a female. Despicable.

How could his father want to speak to him? To do anything but cast him aside, banish him from Draconia? He'd harmed a female; he should be punished.

Guilt and shame might run thick in his veins, but he wanted to remain in his land, to live among his people. To see his mate.

What was he thinking? Even if he wasn't in dragon

form, their being mates created all sorts of problems. Namely that he'd have to admit his true name, a name better off hidden, thought of as dead.

A name he could never again think of as his.

And on that morose note, he focused his attention on Ari, on how her body vibrated with power. Or maybe that was anger. He'd like to see her hum with passion, passion directed at him as he thrust into her welcoming warmth...

Really, Fafnir? In case you haven't noticed your sizes don't match.

But they would if she was in dragon form.

And with that thought, his mind journeyed to the land of never-going-to-happen.

"Are you all right?" Bright green eyes penetrated his thoughts, jarring him out of his fantasy.

Good thing dragon scales hid embarrassment. *Yes. Where will the killing occur?*

Hold on.

A touch on his flank was all the warning he received before she transported them to a meadow surrounded by woods. Good thing they arrived in the meadow and not in the trees. Large dragons and close-spaced trees did not belong together.

Sucking in a deep breath of pine-scented air, Fafnir looked around the meadow. Wind whistled through branches, leaves moaning in protest. Aryana stood eyes closed, palms facing the ground, energy rippling along her arms as she drew magic from deep inside the earth.

When her eyes opened, they glittered with unholy rage. She pointed to the north. *They are in a cave by the bend in the river.*

Shouldn't we wait for the Council to appear?

And run the risk of him getting away? I think not.

In case you haven't noticed, I'm too big to follow you through those trees and I don't want you going alone.

Your concern is appreciated, but I've banished him once, I can do it again. She turned, walking toward the tree line.

Pride swelled in his chest, followed by a deep thud of fear. His mate was brave, but foolhardy. What if she died? Nonsense. He might not be able to trace her footsteps through the trees, but his wings and vision worked fine as did his ability to turn invisible.

Casting an invisibility spell, Fafnir spread his wings, pushing against the air. Gliding on the wind, he circled above the trees, keeping track of Ari as she wove between tree trunks, autumn's falling leaves allowing glimpses of her raven-black hair. On several occasions, she glanced upward, as if she knew he flew above her.

What did she expect? Him to stay put in the meadow while she walked into danger?

Maybe he was gallant after all.

Ahead in the distance, the river snaked to the left, falling across large granite rocks in a splash of white waves. A dark opening gaped in one of the rocks. The cave. The hideout of Jaythena's kidnapper.

With a flap of his wings, he sped toward the opening, looking for a place to land and wait for Aryana. The only place large enough for him meant landing on top of the cave itself. Touching down on the tips of his toes, he tried to land as quiet as possible to avoid giving himself away. As no one came running out of the cave, he assumed he succeeded.

Rushing water poured down the rocks, slamming into a froth of white foam as it hit the bottom of the streambed. If he had found this place only days ago, he would have tucked his wings against his flank and taken a dive, hoping to drown in the crash of water against rocks.

But now, those thoughts fled into the distance like a passing storm. He needed to keep Aryana alive. To discover how she changed into a dragon. To claim her for his mate.

Maybe he needed to take that dive into the rocks. It might knock some sense into him.

Aryana appeared at the tree line, staying in the shadows as she peered around a trunk to eye the cave. Her gaze flicked to the stones he perched upon and her eyes narrowed.

Couldn't stay put? Her voice cut through his thoughts.

He flashed his teeth, his lip pulling up as she shook her head. Fingers waggled at him as she vanished.

His heart thumped an erratic beat despite knowing she wrapped herself in an invisibility spell. Where was she? He stared at the path she should take from the tree line to the cave, hoping to track her. Nothing. His ears pricked forward as he strained to hear her steps above the roar of falling water.

Nothing.

Muscles tense, he held his breath, listening to the wail of the pines, the roar of the water. Where was she?

And then he heard the whisper of a shoe on rock and his breath rushed between his teeth on a whistle he hoped no one heard. A rock slipped, thumping its way down the slope, its splash soundless, lost in the roar of the falls.

She was in the cave. He perched on top of the opening, too big to fit inside and help his mate.

Bloody dragon's eggs.

****

Aryana took a breath and tried to still the erratic beat of her heart while she watched a stone fall over the ledge into the whirling waters below. Maybe looking down wasn't such a good idea. Neither was materializing on the edge of the cave and losing her footing, but it was a little too late for that now.

At least she cast an invisibility spell before appearing on the ledge. Weaved into the layers of the spell twisted magic gathered from the land, forming a cloak that rendered her invisible to sight and smell and masked her footsteps.

Unless she stepped on the lip of the cave's entrance and jarred loose a small stone.

A figure strode out of the darkness, a male in a cloak with the hood pulled over his head, sidling next to her as he peered over the ledge and then looked up to the sky. A heady aroma of herbs wafted from his robe, a scent triggering a memory she'd seen in Thoren's mind. A memory involving his mate Keara who had been captured and drugged by a hooded Draconi. Like the one standing in front of her.

Was Jaythena similarly drugged?

Aryana struggled to remember the name of the drug used on Keara and drew a blank. But she remembered what it did, how it inhibited the victim from acting out their will. How it made them a puppet to their captor, able only to act on the suggestions of the one who gave them the drink.

She shuddered.

If this bastard standing before her had harmed one hair on Jaythena's head, death would be a welcome relief for his slimy arse.

While the male continued to look outside, she slipped deeper into the dank darkness, heading toward the faint glow of candlelight flickering in the stone depths. Water dripped in an even rhythm, splashing against stone, each plunk causing a spike of anxiety.

What if Jaythena was dead?

The passage turned and she followed the path, walking into a circular room aglow with dozens of candles. In the middle of the room Jaythena sat on a slab of rock, hands and feet tied, a blank look on her tear-stained face. Purple blotches dotted her cheeks, while dried blood scabbed her lower lip. One shoulder of her dress hung halfway down her arm, the tear exposing the top of her breast.

Joy at seeing her niece alive morphed into rage. Aryana growled. Dead. The male was dead. Steam hissed from her ears, billowing out in a cloud to surround her head. Females were prized, protected despite all costs. The punishment for harming one was banishment or death, depending on the extent of the female's injuries.

The last time she'd seen a female injured this badly, she had banished the male, Fasolt. She wanted to kill him, to wring his life out in slow measure, to watch him suffer as he had caused another to suffer. Instead, she listened to the plea of the priestess, the one he harmed, listened to the female who would rather have her attacker live than be the cause of his death.

Silly female. But Aryana did as requested,

banishing the male, changing the wards so he couldn't return to Draconia.

She should have turned him over to the Council to be killed.

Jaythena continued to stare straight ahead, only the rise and fall of her chest giving evidence to her living. Still as stone, except for her even, steady breath. Ari clenched her fists, ignoring the bite of her nails into her palms, and tried to convince her feet not to march back to the main area of the cave and kill the male. Her niece's safety came first.

Then she could kill the bloody bastard.

Jaythena, can you hear me?

Aunt Ari? Where are you? He's here. He's coming back! You've got to help me! Don't let him touch me again!

Her panic rocked through Aryana like a blow.

Can you move?

No. He drugged me. Forced me to drink it. I couldn't stop him. Help me!

Footsteps echoed off the stone walls as the hooded male approached. "Ah, don't you look the sight." An herb-laden breeze rustled the hem of Aryana's robes as he walked toward Jaythena. Aryana's breath caught. A churning ball of ice took up residence in her stomach as she glimpsed his face within the shadows of his cowl. A face she hoped never to see again.

His hand cupped Jaythena's cheek in a parody of a lover's touch. "You have helped me destroy that bitch priestess you call aunt. Destroy her from the inside out, just like she did me."

He knelt in front of Jaythena, hands on the edges of his cowl. "Did I ever tell you what she did to me? No?

Let me show you."

His hands shoved back his cowl, showing short black hair to Aryana, but exposing his face to Jaythena. Aryana heard her niece's mental scream, the sound slamming through her mind, firing her rage.

Fasolt.

Even with his back to her, she knew him. Knew him the moment he passed her, the moment she glimpsed beneath his cowl and saw a face covered with jagged white scars.

Scars she gave him. Scars she shouldn't have wasted her time giving.

She should have stabbed him in his vile heart instead of banishing him. Good thing she learned from her mistakes.

Time enough to remedy that error once she transported Jaythena to safety.

With a wave of her hand, she thought about Jaythena transporting to where Fafnir sat on top of the cave. Any second now her niece would disappear from this bastard's vile clutches. Any second.

Why did her magic not work? She tried firing an energy ball at Fasolt—the scum's hand currently fondled her niece's breast—and nothing happened. Aryana screamed her frustration, the noise echoing off the stone walls, only for her ears. Fasolt didn't move.

How did her invisibility spell remain, but not her ability to work magic? Only titanium inhibited a Draconi's magic and very little of that was in Draconia. What were the chances of a deposit being in this cave?

Just her luck.

Perhaps it wasn't titanium. After all, her invisibility spell remained in place. The spell used magic from the land, magic that co-existed with whatever metal deposits were in the cave. Perhaps the land's magic masked the titanium's effects. Provided a vein of the metal ran through this cave.

Whatever the reason, she needed to move around the cave, to try working her magic from another spot. Titanium's effects only extended so far and if she got beyond that, her magic would function.

Keeping her eyes on Fasolt, she backed out the way she came until she stood where the path crooked into the main part of the cave. Taking a breath, and willing the magic to work, she again attempted to transport Jaythena out of the cave.

Nothing.

Her heart pounded and she fought to gather her thoughts. Why did it not work? Was she not far enough away?

Aryana stared at her palm, willing an energy ball to form. The blue-tinged ball flickered in her palm as she sucked in a breath. All right. If that worked, then why couldn't she transport Jaythena out of the cave?

After several more transporting attempts, her breath came in shallow gasps, her heart echoing a fast tempo in her ears. Her magic refused to penetrate the small chamber where her niece sat tied. Why was that?

Who cared? Magic did not work where Jaythena was held. End of discussion. The why didn't matter. How to free her did.

At least her invisibility spell worked. Which made little sense, but she had no time for figuring out why. She needed to get Jaythena out of Fasolt's clutches.

Now.

But how?

She needed a distraction. Like a rock thrown against the wall, drawing Fasolt out of the small chamber into the larger one. And lucky for her, loose rocks abounded in the cave.

Picking up one, she threw it hard against the opposite wall. The rock hit with a thud, dislodging smaller rocks, which cascaded down the wall in a dust-spewing mini-avalanche. Fasolt hurried out of the chamber, clearly looking for the source of the noise.

Not waiting to see his next move, Aryana darted into the small chamber, running to Jaythena.

Hold on, Jaythena, I'm going to get you out of here.

Just transport me.

I can't. My magic won't work in this chamber. She fingered the knot on the rope holding her niece's feet, struggling to untie her before Fasolt returned.

Hurry!

I'm trying. The knot gave—thank the Goddess—and Aryana started on the rough rope binding her wrists together. *Are you sure you can't move?*

Yes! He drugged me. Get me out before he returns!

One more yank and the ropes loosened, falling to the floor. *All right, you're untied. I'm going to have to drag you out.*

I don't care! Just get me away from here before I act on his orders.

His orders?

Hurry!

No time for questioning what she meant. Aryana pulled her niece off the stone slab, holding her under her arms, and dragged her out of the small chamber. Fasolt stood staring at the wall of collapsed rocks, head tilted to the side as if asking the wall what happened.

When she laid Jaythena on the ground, Fasolt turned around, clearly attracted by the noise.

"Noooo!" Fasolt screamed, his yell slamming against the stone walls of the cave, shaking pebbles loose to bounce against the ground.

Oh, holy Goddess help me! Aryana waved her hand praying the transportation spell worked. With a tinny pop, Jaythena disappeared from view and Aryana released the breath she didn't realize she held.

Fasolt ran toward her, anger morphing his scarred features into a vision of avenging evil.

Aryana fired an energy ball at him, watching as it threw him into the rough stone wall, his breath released in a hiss of steam. Dropping the cloaking spell, she readied another energy blast.

"You shouldn't have returned."

His eyes widened then narrowed as his lip curved in a snarl. "Bloody bitch. You shouldn't have banished me." He turned his hands palms up, his eyes narrowing as he formed two small, flickering energy balls.

How could a male stripped of his magic form energy balls?

Before he threw his weak excuses for energy balls, she lobbed hers at him, but he ducked to the side, missing the blast, which struck the cave wall. Rumbling shook the stone beneath her feet, jarring loose more stones. Aryana took a step back as several pebbles rained upon her head.

Ouch.

She shook off the pain, focusing on the only thing that mattered. Fasolt.

He crouched beside a stalagmite, eyes glittering

with anger or terror. Probably anger, judging by the way steam circled his scarred face.

"Look at me!" His voice struck her like a blow, snapping her gaze to his. "Look at what you did to me!"

"I should have killed you. Scarring your face was a kindness."

"A kindness? All I did was express my disappointment in not seeing the Goddess."

"By beating my priestess."

"It was an accident!"

"What? Your fists accidentally slipped into her face?"

"The bitch smarted off to me! What did you expect?"

"I don't know. Restraint. A conversation. Asking for return of your offering."

"I needed to talk to the Goddess! And all I got was silence!"

"She doesn't always appear."

He jumped to his feet. "I needed Her!"

"Why?"

"To tell me why my mate had to die!" Fists balled at his sides, he stepped forward.

Aryana sucked in a breath as she stared into eyes crazed with trembling rage. The loss of a mate wrecked havoc on the surviving Draconi, even more so if they had bonded their life-forces. But she had never heard of a surviving male turning to abuse of females.

"I'm sorry for your loss, but that doesn't excuse your behavior. Or kidnapping my niece." She readied another ball of energy, balancing it on her palm. "You know death is the penalty."

"Of course. The precious Draconi female. You

know what?" He took another step forward. "You females aren't any better than us males, you just think you are. And you get by with all sorts of evil behavior because no one bothers to stop you. You should all die. And you will. Even if you kill me, I've planned your extinction. And you can't stop it." His laugh shot shivers across her skin, raising chill-bumps across her flesh.

Drawing her arm back, she took aim at his chest, wondering as he mirrored her movements empty handed. Aryana lobed her energy ball, only to feel something heavy strike her shoulder, spinning her sideways. Her blast of energy went wide, slamming into the cave's wall as her back hit stone. Numbness encased her arm, while her lungs struggled to suck in air.

Breathe, Aryana, breathe!

With a gasp, her lungs remembered their expansion duty and drew in air like a dragon about to expel a fireball. Good thing too as Fasolt leapt in front of her, hands reaching for her throat.

She ducked, trying to dart to the side. Pain shot through her injured shoulder, the throb radiating outward. Hands grabbed her arms, twisting her around, throwing her backward. Her head struck the ground, sending black dots dancing around the periphery of her vision.

An energy ball flew her way, the air sizzling in its wake. Without thinking, she batted it to the side. She needed to do...something. Needed to defend herself...somehow.

Why couldn't she think straight?

How hard had she hit her head?

Another energy ball flew, slamming into the stone wall as she countered it. The ground pitched and she tried to sit up. Or maybe the ground pitched because she tried to sit up. Nausea roiled in her gut as she slapped at another energy ball.

"Not so hot now, are you?" Fasolt stood over her, the white scars streaking his face shining in the dim light coming through the cave's opening.

She needed to protect herself. Needed to form...a spell.

"Die, bitch!" Magic poured out of his hands, slamming into the shield she managed to throw over her prone body.

A shield spell hastily thrown together.

A shield not made to withstand the amount of magic thrown against it.

An ache settled in her chest, a tremor running through her limbs as she fought to hold the shield, fought to save her life. Why couldn't she remember a stronger shield spell? Didn't she know a spell that could repel Fasolt's magic? She was the High Priestess, the reservoir of power, a conduit for the Goddess.

And she couldn't think of a stronger spell?

How hard had she hit her head?

A roar shattered the air, dropping rocks from the ceiling as it reverberated in waves against the stone. Good thing she had her shield, feeble though it was. As stones dropped onto his scalp and shoulders, Fasolt stopped throwing magic and covered his head with both arms. Aryana kept her shield in place and breathed a sigh of relief.

Fafnir.

His appearance ignited a burst of warmth that

penetrated the thought-stopping fog smothering her mind. He cared enough to come to her rescue. And didn't that knowledge give her a warm, floating feeling.

Or maybe that feeling had to do with the hit-the-head-on-a-rock routine she just experienced.

Air dragged through the cave, speeding toward the opening as if sucked out by a wind funnel. Or an enraged dragon.

A plume of fire shot over her head, blistering the air into crackles of sound as it sped toward Fasolt. In the time it took her to blink, the bastard disappeared and the fireball sank into the stone with a blast that shattered shards across the chamber.

The ground shook, continuing to rumble long after the stone shards dropped to the ground. She might have been knocked hard enough on the head to forget spells, but she knew enough to get out of the cave before falling rocks obliterated its existence. Taking a breath, Aryana dropped her shield and transported out of the cave, landing flat on her back in the same place she had sent Jaythena.

Wind battered her body and she turned her head to stare at the spectacle in the sky. Two dragons screamed their rage, wings batting air as teeth and talons scraped and clawed against scales, the sound sending shivers spiraling through her veins. Sunlight glittered against their scales like red rubies on fire, little bursts of light blinding to behold.

A wave of nausea swept over her and she rolled onto her side, trying not to gag. Spiked daggers of pain shot across nerve endings as she tried to use her injured arm. Small prisms of light danced across the ground, and she closed her eyes to avoid the whirl of color fighting in the sky.

Why did a concussion pick now to hold her in its clutches? Laying around nauseous and half-witted when Fafnir fought for his life was not in her plans. What if Fasolt hurt him while she lay curled on the ground?

She hadn't known Fafnir for long, but it didn't take long to realize how much he meant to her. Or to know she needed him with her. What would she do if he died?

Aunt Ari, move! Jaythena's voice slammed into her mind, jarring her from her thoughts, her lids flying open at its strength.

Jaythena stood over her, arms upraised, a large rock balanced in her palms. The lack of expression on her niece's face, coupled with the screams of fighting dragons, sent chills racing through Aryana's limbs.

And then Jaythena dropped the rock.

So this is what was meant by an unmitigated disaster.

Aryana muttered a curse as she waved her hand, the spell tossing the rock aside. See, she did know a spell. They didn't call her the High Priestess for nothing.

Aunt Ari, I'm so sorry, I can't help it. Jaythena took a step toward the fallen rock. *He told me to kill you. I can't stop!*

A slug moves faster than I can think. Aryana bit her lip, trying to come up with a spell to stop Jaythena's drug-induced murderous tendencies. Batting aside rocks until the drug wore off was unacceptable.

Aunt Ari! Help me!

Jaythena held the rock again, her frantic mental voice a contrast to her expressionless face.

Without thinking, Aryana whispered a sleep spell,

the magic reaching deep into Jaythena's mind, turning off her higher functions. Jaythena crumpled to the ground, the rock falling from her fingers.

Sleep sounded like a good idea. The pull of unconsciousness beckoned, the cool touch of a calming friend, filled with peacefulness. Glancing one last time at the sky, Aryana watched Fafnir battle Fasolt.

Splashes of red, mixed with the whoosh of wings, caused another bout of nausea, and she closed her eyes against the myriad of colors.

Sounds drifted away as unconsciousness pulled her into the comfort of oblivion.

Chapter Eight

Fafnir roared in pain as Jaythena's kidnapper bit into his wing, damaging the tender membrane. In retaliation, he clawed a gash down the other dragon's neck, blood dripping off scales to fall to the ground. Pain shot into his shoulder, each flap of his wings sending explosions of white agony across the limb.

He risked a glimpse at Aryana huddled upon the ground like a broken toy as the other dragon circled around for another pass. He needed to pay attention to the fight. Watching her collapse led to the bite on his wing. A distraction when he needed to remain focused.

But seeing his mate lying still as a corpse sent a stab of pain twisting through his chest, a sharp panic spreading outward. Nothing eliminated the knowledge she received her injuries from the dragon flapping around in front of him.

Flapping a little bit lopsided due to a torn wing membrane.

Breath sawing in and out of his lungs, Fafnir countered an attack of talons and leapt onto the other dragon's back, teeth aiming for the thick muscles of the neck. Rage clouded his vision. This male hurt his mate. This male must die.

One shake of his head was all he needed to kill the bastard, to avenge his mate.

His mouth opened, jaws snapping closed...on

empty air. *What just happened?* Fafnir stared at the space of air that used to contain the male's body. A quick scan of the area proved he flapped alone in the sky.

How did Jaythena's kidnapper disappear? And where for that matter?

Right as he started to fly toward Aryana, the air thundered with dragon wings, an explosion of sound as a dozen dragons appeared in the sky. Council warriors. He hated to tell them they arrived too late.

One minute he hovered in the air and the next, his body flew backward, hurtling toward the ground. Fafnir shot his wings out, trying to break his fall, screaming as the wind caught his injured wing. He felt a spell wrap around him, cushioning his body as it lowered him to the ground.

No! You targeted the wrong dragon. That's Fafnir, not Fasolt. Thoren's words slammed into his mind, followed by a rush of apologies from another voice.

Mistaken identity. *What irony.*

A downburst of air rushed past him as the dragon warriors hovered above the ground. One landed, shifting into Thoren. Fafnir's lip twisted and he swallowed the snarl. No reason to snarl at the one who freed him from his titanium prison and stopped him from landing like a fallen boulder upon the ground. Really. No reason at all.

"Where's Fasolt?"

He disappeared. He hurt Ar—the High Priestess so I attacked him.

"And my sister?"

She lives. They are up there. He gestured with his snout toward the cliff. When would Thoren leave so he could check on his mate?

Thoren's jaw tensed, eyes closing as he drew in a deep breath. As he released it, he opened his eyes and locked gazes with Fafnir. "Thank you. We'll take care of things."

With a brief glance at one of the dragons, Thoren disappeared, the flock of warriors vanishing with him. Fafnir took a deep breath, preparing to transport to Aryana, when he saw the warriors appear on top of the cliff.

No! Bloody Council and their sense of propriety. He deserved to take Aryana to the Temple. Aryana was not their mate. She was his. His.

But a glance to the currently empty cliff told him he wouldn't get the chance to comfort Aryana. The Council warriors transported themselves, Jaythena and the High Priestess away, presumably to the Temple.

He roared.

"It's not your place to take them for healing."

Fafnir started, the rest of his roar dying in his throat as he turned in the direction of the voice. A voice he'd recognize anywhere. His breath froze in his lungs as the inside of his mouth turned into what felt like a desert, dry and sandy. Good thing he didn't need his mouth to talk. He doubted his lips could form words.

The moment he'd anticipated and longed for during his years of captivity and yet avoided once free, blindsided him. What should he do? Admit who he was? Run?

After fighting the battle to avenge his mate, he no longer felt like a coward. At least not a complete coward.

But faced with his father he stood like a fool on the

battlefield, eyes wide and limbs shaking.

Of course he could always write off the shaking limbs as a result of the fight. Whatever made him feel better.

Alviss shuffled over to Fafnir, his cane thumping in the grass with each step.

"We would have caught him if you hadn't engaged him in a fight." Alviss rolled right over Fafnir's beginnings of a snarl. "And yet I appreciate your defense of the females."

What did he say to that? Apparently nothing, his head bob taking care of words.

He really needed to speak up. This hiding-his-identity game had continued for too long.

"Go find the healing priestesses in the Temple. They'll fix you right up."

And the High Priestess?

Alviss's bushy brows slammed down, carving a vee between the white hairs. "She is safe. As is Jaythena. They are being cared for by the Temple Healer. Get along with you."

Fafnir took a breath. He could do this. He could tell his father who he was. *Right?* But before he formed the words, Alviss waved his hand and Fafnir felt his body disintegrate, only to reappear in the dragon healing room of the Temple.

His breath released in a rush of air. Was it relief or regret flowing through him? Or maybe that lightheaded feeling had to do with his wing shooting bright-white agony into his shoulder.

At any other time, avoiding his reveal to Alviss would be relief. But he wanted it over with. Wanted to admit his true identity to his father, even if Alviss shunned him. Once he admitted it to Alviss, then he could admit it to Aryana.

Maybe she would claim him as mate.

Maybe the earth would open up and swallow him.

"Are you injured?"

Fafnir turned to the voice, only to suck in a breath of air. Keara, his Halfling daughter, stood in the doorway, dressed in a white gown, her long red hair pulled back into a braid.

She looked like a cross between her mother and Annaliese.

Yet another person to whom he needed to admit his true identity.

Greetings, Keara.

"Fafnir!" Her face broke into a smile. "I didn't recognize you."

I'm sure recognition is a little hard when you are covered in blood as I am.

She walked inside the room, closing the door behind her. "Let me get a look at your injuries." A gentle touch against his wing, a probing touch against a gash across his scales. He flinched.

How is Aryana?

Keara raised an eyebrow. A pause and then she answered. "She hit her head pretty hard, but don't worry, Annaliese is tending to her. They sent me to care for you."

Fafnir let loose a sigh of relief. Praise the Goddess Aryana would be all right. *I'm happy you came. Thank you for letting me know. When may I see her?*

"I will have to check with Annaliese since the High Priestess is her patient."

And Jaythena?

Steam snaked out of Keara's ears as she snarled. "That bastard gave her the same drug he did me. But she'll be all right once it wears off. Physically anyway."

At least she was alive. When Aryana sent her to me, I could not get her to speak. She just stared into space. He knew the stare as the drug's effect, but still, Jaythena's whole affect gave him chills to see.

"That's the effect of the drug. That herb should be banned!" Her fists clenched, and she sucked in a few breaths until the steam stopped its circling dance around her head. "Changing the topic. It's been awhile since I've seen you. Where have you been hiding?" After clenching and releasing her fists and another deep inhale, she walked to a wall shelf containing bottles and jars of herbs. Running her finger along the label, she selected a half-full jar and put it on a long wooden table set against one wall of the room.

Here and there. How do you like working in the Temple?

"I hate these white gowns. They get dirty all the time, and the laundress is forever having to use spells to get them clean. Other than that I enjoy it."

Is Thoren treating you well? Because if not, he'd be glad to char his hide off.

"Oh yes! I love being his mate. He's a lot of fun. Except when he belches. Do you know he set the curtains on fire the other day? What's wrong with him? Is that common male behavior?"

Fafnir choked. *Maybe you shouldn't feed him spicy food?*

"Maybe he should learn not to belch fire. Now, let's start with the tear in your wing. That looks like it hurts the worst."

Her hand rested against the slash, and he couldn't help the indrawn breath. Healing magic poured from her hand, cascading over the torn wing, suffusing him with warmth. It reminded him of his mother's magic, of the way the older Draconi healed, the feel of her touch. A magic not experienced since before his capture, since his mother died.

From the corner of his eye, he saw the yellow and blue ball of healing magic surrounding his wing, knitting together the torn membrane. The white-hot agony ceased its relentless crawl, and he breathed a sigh of relief.

Thank you. That feels much better.

She dropped her hand, pulling away the warmth of her touch. "You are welcome. I'm learning to heal without draining myself. I can almost do it without thinking now. So much easier than when I used to live in River's Run." A small frown creased her brow, unwanted memories taking a run across the smooth skin of her face.

I'm sorry you had to grow up there. I'm sorry you were not taken to Draconia when you were born.

She shrugged. "It's not your fault." Ah, but it was. "Anyway, if I had been raised here, then I wouldn't have known my grandmother. We had our differences, but I loved her." Keara walked over to the table and picked up the jar of ointment. "She fostered in me a love for healing."

That is a family trait. You were born that way.

"Well, there is that. So it wasn't all bad." Dipping her fingers in the ointment, she began spreading the cool substance across the former tear in his wing.

Do you blame your father for leaving you there?

"Did he leave me there? According to Alviss he disappeared. I'm assuming before I was born. So if I wasn't born, and he didn't know I existed, then how can I blame him?"

It's a male's duty to ensure his Halfling offspring are returned to Draconia.

"Truly? Because before he mated me, that was Thoren's job, to find abandoned Halflings and return them to Draconia. The Council spends a lot of time on that activity. Apparently there are a lot of males who don't realize they have children."

So much has changed since I've been gone.

"I guess so. But at any rate, I don't blame my father. I really wish he hadn't died so I could know him. I never knew my mother."

I have many stories about your mother. The words slipped out before he could stop them and Keara's hand stilled against his wing.

"How did you know my mother?"

What did he say? *Keara, you are my daughter?* No, too overly dramatic. *Your mother was my lover?* Then she would have to deduce things herself. *The loss of blood is causing me to hallucinate?* No, he was done with hiding and lying. Telling her while she healed his wounds was not how he imagined it happening. While in his cell, as a captive, he assumed his lover, Mabbina, had taken their child to Draconia as he instructed her to do. Then his captors told him she and the babe died in childbirth. So when he saw a drugged Keara after Thoren rescued her, looked at her features and realized she was his daughter, his joy turned to horror.

He'd failed his child.

And yet, he wanted her to know him, wanted to

know her. Wanted a friendship with his daughter, his only offspring.

The stillness in Keara expanded until the very room itself seemed to be waiting on his answer.

I used to know your mother very well. I came to River's Run often and we became friends.

"You knew her well?"

I did.

"I hear you have not presented yourself to the Council for questioning."

What did that have to do with Mabbina? *True.*

"Why?"

I believe that gash under the scales is bleeding. On my flank.

"Sorry." Shaky hands probed, lifted a scale. He failed to stop the involuntary flinch and foot stomp. A faint chink indicated Keara placed the ointment jar on the stone floor. Another round of healing magic poured into his injury, and he leaned into it, allowing the energy to penetrate into the gash.

Ah. You are very good at what you do.

"Thank you. Why haven't you shown up to talk to the Council? They want to know who imprisoned you so they can stop it from happening again."

They know who imprisoned me. Simon's father. They know I cast a spell to render my captors insane. What more do they want? Would they go after his Watcher? Or was the male protected by the Watchers on the Council?

"What Watcher?"

Maybe he transmitted those last two sentences. *My Watcher and I did not get along.* A bit of an understatement. *He was there when they captured me and told them about titanium's effects on Draconi. I'm not sure if my spell touched him as I never saw him again.*

"That's horrible! Thoren and Enar are best friends so I guess I thought all Draconi-Watcher relationships were the same."

They are unique in their friendship.

"Well, I still think you should go to the Council. It makes you look like you are hiding something."

Pride laced his heart, followed by a good dose of fear-of-discovery. His intuitive daughter saw past his barriers into his soul, peeling away the layers of shame to stare at the root of the issue.

He still needed to tell her their relationship.

Perhaps I am.

"Really?" Her voice dropped to a whisper. "Why?"

He was a grown male, a defender of his mate, a dragon in his prime. He could tell her who he was. Really. He could.

If I tell you, will you tell?

"I swear on the bones of my ancestors that I will not tell anyone."

Well, then. You are correct. I am hiding. I do not want the Council, or others, to know who I am.

"But why?"

He swallowed. *It's embarrassing.* At her puzzled stare, he stumbled along, gaining confidence as he spoke. *I come from a powerful family, I carry great magic. And yet humans locked me away in a cell for twenty-four years, three months and two days? How can I tell my family who I am?*

"But we don't hold that against you. Even Alviss and the High Priestess would be stopped by titanium.

No one would blame you for it. You need to talk to the Council. It will be all right." She bent to pick up the jar, coating her fingers in the chalky white substance before applying it to his wound.

And I harmed a female.

Her hands stopped smoothing the herbal ointment over the former gash in his flank. "What did you do?"

My captivity meant my daughter was harmed. It was not intentional, but it was the result. They will not forgive me.

Her hands started moving, rubbing a bit more forcefully this time. "Well, I think you've been moping around wherever you've been hiding for too long. Do you really think someone is going to blame you for whatever happened to your daughter when you were captured? Did you plan to be captured? No? Then how can you think that?"

You have not lived in Draconia long enough if you think my indirect harm of a female will not be punished.

"You have been away too long if you think it will."

Hmph. He snorted and stamped his foot.

"Where's your daughter now?"

Beside me. Not the smoothest reveal, but from the quick intake of breath and loss of blood to her face, it seemed to accomplish its goal.

Crash! The jar of ointment fell from Keara's fingers, shattering against the stone floor. Fafnir twitched a talon at the mess, reforming the jar, never taking his gaze from Keara's face.

"Me?" she squeaked. "I'm your daughter?"

Does that...offend you?

"Offend me? Why would you think...oh. No. I'm just surprised is all. Are you sure?"

He raised an eye-ridge. Did she think he wouldn't recognize his own daughter?

"Dumb question. Sorry. I'm just, well, just surprised. And happy. Oh, does this mean no one else knows?"

Yes. And I would appreciate it if you'd keep it that way.

"Even from Thoren?"

He sits on the Council.

"For how long? You can't go around not telling people and expecting me to keep the secret forever."

He sighed. *I know. I haven't figured out how to tell them yet.*

"You know, I've been working on a spell with the High Priestess to turn you back into a human. If you'd like, I can turn you and then you can tell them. In your human form."

What spell? There was hope for him?

"It's buried in one of the old Temple scrolls. The writing is different than what we use now, but we've been able to decipher it. It seems to say that when a Draconi goes through his Change with no female and is stuck in dragon form, it's because he has too much power, like a switch stuck in the open position. A person who absorbs energy, like me, can absorb the excess energy and cause the Draconi to resume human form."

What are the consequences?

"It seems you might never be able to change back into dragon form. You'd be stuck a human. We think."

Not a problem. He'd had enough of being stuck as a dragon. Nothing wrong with being in human form, provided he kept his magic.

106

So the Draconi's magic is not damaged?

"It doesn't appear to be."

Pop! Aryana transported into the room, stumbling forward. *Pop!* Annaliese appeared behind her, grabbing Aryana's good arm, holding her steady.

Aryana! What are you doing here?

"I told you to stay in bed!" Annaliese spoke simultaneously, giving Aryana's arm a little shake.

"I told you I had to see him."

The two females played a game of stare-and-glare, before Aryana shook her arm free of Annaliese's grasp and took a step in Fafnir's direction. Fafnir stepped away from Keara and met her halfway.

What are you doing out of bed?

Checking on you.

"All right, you saw him. Now let's put you back to bed." Three strides later, Annaliese stood by them, hand reaching for Aryana's arm.

Everything in him protested at his mate being removed from his side. *There is a bed in this room. She can stay here.*

"Again?"

"Again?" Keara parroted.

"Great idea." Aryana took a step toward the bed. After a glare and a huff, Annaliese helped her get situated under the covers and then disappeared, a trace of steam circling where she stood.

Where did Annaliese go?

"To get the correct herbs. This room isn't as well stocked."

Perhaps she should be in different room, but he rather liked having her here with him. Where she belonged.

How do you feel? He took a step closer, drawing in a deep breath, trying to smell the extent of her injuries. Nothing but the pungent scent of herbs.

"My head hurts. But my arm feels better."

Pop! Annaliese appeared by Aryana's bedside, holding a basket that she set on the table by the bed. One by one, she picked bottles and jars out of the basket, setting them on the table until they filled the small space.

"Are you comfortable?" Anger laced her words as she glared at Aryana.

A growl crossed Fafnir's lips before he could stop it. Annaliese whirled to face him, eyes narrowed. He tried to stop the steam building in his throat and draw in a breath. Annaliese worried about his mate, nothing more. No need to throw a growling fit. Really. No need at all. He swallowed the remaining burst of steam and attempted to turn his lips into a grin.

Sorry.

"I don't want to hear from you right now. I need to complete this healing." She turned back to Aryana, pointing a finger at his mate. "You keep interrupting me."

"I—"

"Hush. Talk later."

Holding her hands over Aryana's head, Annaliese began muttering words of a healing spell. Keara touched Fafnir's flank, drawing his attention to her.

"Step back and let her work. We don't want to interfere with her spell."

While his body raged for him to get as close as possible to his mate, his mind knew Keara spoke the truth. Getting between a Healer and her patient never ended well.

Especially for the interferer.

As Keara smoothed more of the soothing salve over the gash in his flank, Fafnir watched as Annaliese placed Aryana into a deep sleep. The words of her spell coupled with Keara's healing magic, wrapped him in a wave of relaxation.

Which ended the moment Annaliese stopped casting her spell and turned to him. She pointed a finger in his direction.

"I'm getting tired of casting that spell."

Do you think I have control over her?

Never taking her narrowed gaze from him, she spoke to his daughter in what Fafnir called the big-sister voice. "Keara, thank you for your help. You may go tend to your duties now."

Keara ventured a glance at him before speaking. "I'm not finished."

"Yes. You are. I need to talk to...Fafnir. Alone."

"But—"

It will be all right, Keara. Let me speak to her alone. We have things to discuss. Starting with his hiding-and-lying state and moving on to his potential banishment. No problem. Nothing to worry about.

"I'll return later."

I'd like that.

She nodded and disappeared, leaving the jar of salve sitting on the floor next to his foot.

Annaliese continued to glare at him, her gaze moving across his face, down his chest, over his talons, her anger encircling him like a blanket. Nothing he didn't deserve. "You did not wait like you said."

Things came up.

"Things more important than talking to your family after years of being thought dead?"

Good thing dragon hide hid heated cheeks. *Do you still claim to be my sister?*

"Ragnor! How can you think that? You are my brother! My kin. How can you think I'd no longer call myself your sister?"

I've changed. If she only knew how much.

One hand gestured at him. "Yes, of course. You're stuck in dragon form. That doesn't explain why you didn't say anything to us when you returned."

Words boiled out, a stream of self-directed vitriol, releasing emotions trapped inside. *If I said something to you, you'd banish me. I'm a failure! I failed my daughter! I caused a female to be harmed. How can you allow me to live in Draconia, knowing who I am?*

"How can I not?"

His mouth opened, closed. Did she mean what he thought? Was it possible she accepted him, despite his failures?

Is it no longer customary to banish a male who harms a female?

She crossed her arms, head tilted off-center. "Did you mean to harm her? Did you physically abuse her?"

Of course not! But I did not ensure Keara returned to Draconia. She suffered. Because of me.

"And Keara is the reason you have not come to see me since you've been home?" One eyebrow rose and despite the ire in her tone, he knew her anger, born of grief and disappointment, began to subside.

Her words resonated inside, making what he thought of as clear-minded reasoning sound...illogical. *Father would not be pleased I caused her harm.*

"Father would not be pleased if you returned home with a fortune's worth of jewels. Do not base your beliefs on him."

Interesting. Wonder what happened between the two? *What is your issue with Father?*

"Besides the way he treats Aryana?"

Fafnir failed to stop his growl. *What do you mean?*

"He doesn't like to share things with the priestesses. Which is why we don't know what is going on with the village attacks. But that is another story. I can't believe you didn't come to see me when you returned home."

I didn't think you'd accept me. I thought you'd banish me.

"You said that. I can't speak for Father, but I do not consider you to be at fault for anything Keara went through. Yes, she was left in Cautasia, but you did not mean for her to be, and you cannot help that you were captured and held as a prisoner. If you deserved punishment, you have already received it."

A small flame ignited in his chest, spread through his limbs. Hope. *Truly?*

"Truly. Besides, the female has to press the charges, and Keara doesn't believe you were responsible for her injuries."

Lowering his head, he tapped her shoulder with his snout. *I apologize, Leesie. I should have come to see you.*

She rubbed his snout, pulling his head down to rest her forehead against his. "Ah, brother mine. You always worried overmuch. I am glad to see you again."

And I you.

Bang! Bang! Bang! Both Fafnir and Annaliese

jumped as knocking vibrated the door. "Annaliese!" *Bang! Bang! Bang!*

"That doesn't sound good." Annaliese gave Fafnir a pat on the side, dashed fingers under her eyes and walked to the door.

"Enter!" The door flew open with a wave of her hand and a young priestess stumbled through the opening.

"My apologies, Healer, but we have a situation."

"What is wrong?"

The priestess glanced at Fafnir and back to Annaliese. One black eyebrow raised.

"It's all right. You can speak freely in front of..." Annaliese's voice trailed off as she looked over her shoulder at him.

I'm Fafnir. He gave a nod to the priestess, whose eyes widened upon hearing his name.

"Fafnir? You are the one who rescued our High Priestess and fought Fasolt?"

That would be me.

"Oh!" Her hands clapped together, fingers pointing to the ceiling. "It's an honor to meet you!"

Honor? She thought meeting him an honor?

"He is not why you came. What—"

"Oh, apologies, Healer. One of the refugees has gone into labor, the baby is not coming quickly, and the mate is fighting off all attempts to assist. We hoped you could calm him."

"Of course." Annaliese turned to Fafnir, mouth open as if caught in the middle of a sentence, an apology written across her face.

She had nothing to apologize for. *Go. We can catch up later.*

I'm sorry. This might take awhile. Would you watch Aryana?

Of course.

Her arm will be healed when she wakes. I'm not sure about the head injury, so don't let her leave until I see her.

All right.

The priestess darted glances between the two of them, clearly in a hurry and wishing Annaliese would join the urgency party.

Words are not enough to tell you how good it is to see you. Even from across the room he saw the gleam of tears in her eyes. He blinked in understanding.

Same here, Leesie.

She looked as if she wanted to say something and regret tinged the smile shot his direction. Waving the priestess in front of her, Annaliese walked out the door, shutting it behind her.

Fafnir blinked at the door until it no longer wavered before his blinking eyes. Then he continued to stare at it, part of him unable to believe Annaliese refused to banish him. Another part wanted to run after her, to crawl in her lap, to let her touch on his head bring him comfort.

Right. As if a full grown dragon could fit in a female's lap.

When the shock of acceptance wore off, about the same time he grew tired of staring at the still-closed door, his attention snapped to Aryana. His mate. Would she accept him like Keara and Annaliese did? Or would she reject him?

Now that he finally admitted she belonged to him, the thought of her rejection stung. And it was only a thought. If in reality she rejected him...he refused to go there.

For the first time since his return to Draconia, the sense of failure plaguing him lessened. He felt...light, weightless, like he flew without spreading his wings. No, he could not tell Aryana who he was. Not while he remained a dragon.

Perhaps Keara did find a spell in the Temple archives that would turn him human. Perhaps. But he refused to put too much hope in the spell's accuracy. Too much hope and he would be disappointed when nothing changed. As far as he knew, no dragon had ever returned to human form once stuck in dragon form. *Not a one*. The chances of him being the first were rather slim.

He had a better chance of finding a cliff to jump from.

A thought left untouched since a certain female dragon fell from the sky.

Soft snoring focused his gaze on Aryana. The reason for the lack of cliff-jumping thoughts. *His mate.*

He'd love to fight Fasolt again. This time to the end.

Aryana made a snuffling noise, a little huff like a small dragon. He wondered what she dreamed. Maybe flying? Maybe her dreams were about him.

The idea, when it struck, came like a spark of sunlight on a diamond, bright and brilliant. Simple. Yet daring. And probably against several laws.

But it would tell him what she dreamed. Whether or not she held affections for him. If he stood a chance. The only variable being could he pull it off without her knowing.

Chapter Nine

Aryana ran through the familiar dreamscape, searching for an elusive person, or was it something hidden? Whatever it was, she hunted in vain. Trees, bushes and brightly colored objects joined to hinder her search. She couldn't let them. She needed to find…to find…what, exactly? Or should that be, who?

Her breath came in short gasps as she circled in place, always looking, never finding. Where was it? What was it? Why could she not find it? Didn't it know how much she needed, make that wanted, to find—

A glimpse of the object floated in and out of her thoughts. A brief touch, leaving her knowing and yet forgetting in the same second. Ari clenched her teeth, fists tightening until her forearms ached.

Right when she considered blasting the nearest object into oblivion, she heard a rustle to her left.

"Aryana!" A male voice stroked against her skin, firing streaks of heat straight to her core.

The object of her search.

She knew now what she'd been running toward. The object she wanted to find. The one she kept buried deep inside her heart, locked away, hidden from discovery.

Her mate.

After all these years searching various dreamscapes, she found him. The one the Seer had predicted. The one she refused to acknowledge. The one long believed dead.

But as this dream was all she had of her mate, she'd go with it.

Even if it meant ignoring the annoying little voice whispering she'd never caught Ragnor before. *Stupid little voice*. Dreams could change.

Aryana focused on the direction of his voice and walked toward him.

"Ragnor?"

Silence echoed through the woods. Even the trees dripped with tension as if they knew she said the wrong thing. But what was so wrong about calling his name?

"Ragnor? Where are you?"

This time the response boomed through the trees as if he stood beside her. "Here. Over here."

She turned and sucked down a breath. Where trees stood only seconds ago now lay a meadow, complete with blue sky, multi-hued wildflowers, and her mate.

Ragnor stood two stone's throws from her, his black curly hair brushing his shoulders. She'd forgotten his hair curled every bit as much as his sister's. Black lashes framed green eyes, his olive-hued skin burnished in the sunlight. A loose white shirt, the laces untied at the neck, tucked into gray trousers. He stood behind a red-checkered blanket, one hand outstretched toward her, a silent beseeching plea.

Tension flowed around his body; his throat tightened as he swallowed. Why was he nervous? Did he really think she'd refuse him?

She did have a past history in refusing him, a mutual decision, although technically still a refusal. But past history lived in the real world, not the land of dreaming. The male standing before her was a product of her imagination, a figure only alive in her dreams. And her dream mate should not look nervous.

Striding forward, she smoothed her hand down the front of her gown. Why was she wearing a gown? A sexy male stood in front of her and for the first time in a long time, she wanted to stretch him out and have her way with his body.

Why not? It was only a dream.

With a snap of her fingers, the gown disappeared. His eyes widened, the muscles of his throat tensed as he swallowed. Without saying a word, she grabbed his hand, placed it on her waist and pressed her lips against his.

Pleasure shot through her veins like a bolt of lightning. He paused only for an instant, as if shocked by her boldness, and then his arms tightened around her, pulling her against him. The rough linen of his shirt scratched against her bare skin, a thin barrier between their flesh.

Grabbing handfuls of the fabric, she broke the kiss and yanked it over his head. Her hands traced the thick pads of his pecs, brushing against the curly hair dusting his chest. Under her fingertips, his skin felt alive, as if Ragnor stood beside her clothed in flesh instead of the ethereal vapor of a dream.

The oddities of dreaming. Not that she offered complaint. Not at all. Already this dream was better than any she'd had in...well, ever.

"Eager, are we?" His chuckle sent sparks of pleasure straight to her core.

"Hush." She covered his lips with hers. No use ruining a perfectly good dream with talking.

His hands stroked her sides from her waist, up to her breasts, grazing the undersides with his thumbs before stroking back to her waist. Over and over, driving streaks of pleasure straight to her core.

She needed him in her. Now.

Her hands stroked down his chest, across the flat planes of his stomach, reaching for the laces on his trousers. Untying them took seconds. Helping him push them down meant breaking contact with his lips.

"I did not expect to find you this eager."

Didn't the male have better things to do with his lips than form words? "It's my dream. And it's been awhile." And even then, this craving, this urge to crawl inside him, to bond their life-forces for eternity never existed.

Was the intensity stronger with mates?

Or just in dreams?

Didn't she have better things to do than determine the complexities of a dream?

Yes, yes, she did. One naked male coming up.

Once Ragnor's trousers dropped to the ground, Ari hooked her foot around his ankle and tumbled backward onto the blanket, pulling him on top of her.

His smile and chuckle lit a small part inside she thought dead. "Like that, did you?"

"A male can't complain about an eager female."

"A male can do something about that eager female." She raked her nails down his back and squeezed the firm muscle of his arse.

His eyes flared, then darkened with lust. "So he should."

When his lips covered hers, she sighed her pleasure. Holy altars, but the male could kiss. She played with his hair, running her fingers through the curly strands, as his lips trailed a path to one breast. Drawing her nipple into his mouth, he flicked his tongue across the sensitive bud in a rapid rhythm.

"Mmm, Ragnor, that feels good."

She felt his lips turn into a smile against her flesh before he released her nipple with a pop. He blew across the nub, flicking a finger over it as his lips drew her other nipple into his mouth.

The melody of pleasure he wrote into her skin drove her toward a peak of ecstasy. And then his talented lips left her breasts, skimming across the skin of her stomach, kissing down, down, until he reached the tender flesh of her mound.

His hooded eyes glanced to hers, as if asking silent permission. She answered with a smile from deep inside, hoping he noticed her soul's expression of joy radiating from her face. The corners of his lips turned before his tongue swept across her folds, lapping at her core.

Ari closed her eyes, body arching under his touch. Streaks of bliss consumed her, so real, so intense, her mind trembled on the edge of believing it reality.

His tongue continued to lick over her folds, circling her bud, over and over until he latched onto the sensitive skin, lightly scraping with his teeth. Pleasure slammed through her veins as he continued to tease her nub. When he inserted a finger inside her channel and stroked, rubbing her inner pleasure spot, she swore she shattered into splinters of gold.

As she drifted back to consciousness, he thrust into her, filling her, searing her to her soul. Her eyes opened, watching his face as he rode her, as he branded her his. *His.*

Not so scary now.

She should never have let him go.

If wishes were jewels, she'd be wealthy.

Her hands stroked down his back, her ankles clasping around his hips, pulling him closer.

"You feel so good, Ari." Ragnor's breath teased her ear, his hair brushing her cheek.

"Mmm. So do you."

In and a slow glide out, again and again, her hips rising to meet his, countering each of his thrusts. Tension circled inside, spinning her in eddies of pleasure, her breathing joining his in a symphony of small gasps and moans. His hips slammed into hers, harder, faster, over and over, until she didn't know where she ended and he began.

She screamed his name as her body shattered, his cries joining hers as together they rode a wave of bliss. She felt his shaft thickening, widening, locking him inside and knew he fought the urge to mark her as his. To bite her shoulder, showing all a visual reminder she belonged to him.

Her gaze met his. "Do you want to join our life-forces?"

His eyes widened. "You would let me?"

"It's a dream. Why not?" It was a dream after all. She could do whatever she wanted. What were the consequences?

He closed his eyes, rested his forehead against hers. His muscles tensed, then he shook his head, pulling back so he could meet her gaze. "I cannot."

He rejected her. Her dream Ragnor rejected her. And why not? Her subconscious clearly went along with what would happen in real life. The knowledge failed to stop the sting of rejection from hurting.

"Of course not. You're only a dream. A good dream, but a dream all the same."

"Maybe I'll join you again here. If you do not mind?" One eyebrow cocked a question.

Since when did dream lovers beg to return? "You are welcome in my dreams any time."

His lips turned, teeth flashing white. "I'd like that."

Rolling them onto their sides, his shaft still imbedded deep inside, he wrapped his arms around her. Aryana snuggled into Ragnor's arms, closing her eyes, content to lie in the circle of his embrace, the bright sun warm on her skin. Amazing how her subconscious mind remembered details about his body, the feel of his skin under the pads of her fingers, the brush of his hair against her flesh, when her conscious one possessed no memory of what her fingers felt when they touched his skin.

Probably because she'd never touched Ragnor the way she had in this dream. What a shame it was only a dream. If she could see him again she'd tell him what a fool her younger self had been. How she needed him by her side.

Or would she? Being a priestess was the only thing she'd ever wanted. The childhood fantasies of love and mates lay long buried, resurfacing only recently, when she grew tired of males wishing to bed her.

Although that wasn't completely true. She wanted Fafnir to bed her. Little chance of that happening, even if the ancient spell reversed his entrapment in dragon form. Of course, the spell might be for reversing some other change, it was so cryptically written.

And why was she even thinking such thoughts in her dream? Shouldn't she encourage Ragnor in another round of bed-play before someone woke her?

But when she opened her eyes, Ragnor was gone, along with the blanket, the cloudless sky and bright sun. In their place dark storm clouds blew in, chilling the air, pelting her with little stabs of anxiety. Where had he gone? Why had he left her alone?

She needed to find him.

Right when she got to her feet, someone shook her shoulder.

"Aryana! Shh, shh, it's all right!"

Aryana's eyes snapped open. Annaliese stood over her, one hand on her shoulder. Reality greeted her in the form of the healing room. Remnants of her last moments in the dream gripped her like shackles, the squeeze of anxiety dissipating under Annaliese's soothing touch.

"You had a bad dream."

"Not entirely." Aryana stretched and drew in a deep breath. Heat rushed to her cheeks as she smelled the musk of her arousal. Despite wanting to keep the dream to herself, sensitive Draconi noses meant all in the room shared in her personal dreamland activities. Talk about embarrassing.

Especially since Fafnir lay across the room, nostrils flaring, lip turning with apparent understanding.

Yes, that would explain the embarrassment. Wanting him but dreaming of another.

How hard had she hit her head yesterday?

"How are you feeling?" Annaliese's lips turned at the corner as if she fought a grin.

"Better, thank you. How are Jaythena and Moira?"

Her grin flattened as her voice dropped to a whisper. "Moira is fine. Physically Jaythena will be fine. Emotionally? I cannot heal emotional damage. At least not as fast as the physical." She took a deep breath. "In retrospect, we should have turned Fasolt over to the Council instead of banishing him."

"Banishment seemed a good idea at the time." Aryana swallowed the steam boiling in her throat. "How were we supposed to know what he'd do?" Although she should have realized a male that disturbed would plan some sort of revenge.

"Next time we will not be fooled. But we cannot focus on him now. You're more important. How are you feeling?"

Aryana tilted her head to the side. "When can I see my sister and niece?"

"When you finish telling me how you're doing, I'll send them in here." Arms crossed, Annaliese appeared an unmovable statue.

Healers. "My arm feels fine. My head hurts a bit."

"Let's check it out." Annaliese ran her hand over Ari's arm, little pulses of magic testing the injury, determining if it needed another round of healing. "You're right, your arm is fine. Let's see about the head."

Another round of healing magic poured across her scalp, sank beneath her skin, probing, soothing. Annaliese hummed in the back of her throat, one side of her lip raised into a wry grin, as she shook her head.

"You need to take it easy for the next couple of days. You have a nasty concussion."

Ari raised a brow, leveled a look at her friend. "I've never known you not to be able to heal one in a day."

"Most Draconi don't find themselves in a collapsing cave. You almost died. You need to rest."

Who was she to disagree? Especially if Fafnir stayed in the room with her.

What was it about the dragon that quickened her heart? Burned passion through her veins? Made her desire a male after all these years? What was wrong with her? Dreaming of her dead mate while lusting over a male caught in dragon form? She should be worried about her niece and Fasolt's impending capture.

Maybe Annaliese was right. Her head needed to heal.

In more ways than one.

She risked a glance at the dragon in question. Fafnir's lip kicked up, one eye closing in a wink. Heat splashed into her cheeks and she glanced away.

She had no reason to be embarrassed, and yet the feeling persisted. What if he saw inside her mind? Realized it wasn't him she dreamed about?

What is wrong? Annaliese touched Ari's arm, a gentle comfort.

I...nothing. Not going there. *Just thinking.*

Annaliese raised a brow, shot a sideways glance to Fafnir. Returned her gaze to Ari. One brow cocked a question.

I can't help how I feel even though I don't understand why I feel that way.

Her friend's lips twitched as she tried to smother a smile. *I see. You find yourself attracted to the dragon.*

And I'd appreciate it if you'd keep that to yourself.

Annaliese's lips twitched, but sadness permeated her gaze. *It is not my secret to tell.*

Well, that was an odd way of swearing silence. And why was her friend sad? Perhaps she sympathized with Aryana falling for a male locked in dragon form. Or perhaps Annaliese thought her crazy for the unattainable feelings. As if she could help how her heart felt.

But all was not lost. An ancient spell needed deciphering, one that would—hopefully—return Fafnir to human form. Now that Annaliese told her to rest, it seemed plenty of time existed for her to work on uncovering the spell's secrets.

Who knew being bedridden could have a pleasurable ending?

Chapter Ten

When Fafnir winked, his mate's cheeks turned as red as a dragon's scales, her throat moving as she swallowed and avoided his gaze. He wanted to do more than wink, more than stay on his side of the room. Joining her in another dream topped his current fantasy. Just to see if she would repeat those words she said, words he knew she'd never say in real life. She'd asked him to bond with her. Of course she thought him a dream, but still.

She asked.

She didn't realize he and Ragnor were one and the same. No matter.

She asked.

His mate wanted to bond with him. And didn't that make a male stand a little taller.

It might make him stand a little taller, but it created another problem. What would Aryana do when she realized the overlarge dragon in her healing room was really her mate?

Jump for joy? Cast him out? Wish she'd never met him?

Why couldn't he foresee this problem when a hatchling? Maybe then the two of them would not have thought themselves above the prediction of the old Seer.

What would he do if Keara managed to reverse his

current locked-in-dragon-form predicament? How would he face Aryana as a human?

The door to the healing room flew open, ushering in a red-faced, ear-steaming Thoren. So much for worrying about future conversations with Ari.

"Aunt Ari." Thoren gave Fafnir a nonplussed glance before heading toward Aryana.

"Thoren!" Aryana sat straighter in bed as she faced her nephew. "Shouldn't you go see Jaythena and your mother?"

"I already have and was told you were also in a healing room. Why didn't you wait for the Council instead of going after Fasolt on your own? Now you're injured and he escaped." Thoren glowered next to Ari's bed, his face a mask of righteous anger.

"What?" Aryana's eyes narrowed. "You expected me to sit around wringing my hands while he kidnapped my niece when I could do something about it? In case you forgot"—one finger pointed at Thoren— "I got her out."

"And you got injured. And he escaped."

A snarl twisted Fafnir's lip. No one spoke to his mate in angry tones. *You might be her nephew, but you will not speak to the High Priestess that way.*

Thoren turned to him. "You should not be encouraging her to put herself in danger."

Steam puffed out Fafnir's mouth. *You think I wanted her to face Fasolt on her own? In case you forget, she is the High Priestess and can do as she wants.*

"Now, now." Annaliese stepped forward, palms facing the two males. "Your discussion is disturbing my patient. Take it outside."

"Oh, they can stay right here," Aryana slapped a hand against the bed, "and get it out of their systems."

"Their argument is disturbing your peace."

"Thoren's going to disturb it a lot worse if you don't let him have his say."

Fafnir stood a little taller. She said Thoren, not Fafnir. Not that her words stopped him from growling at his daughter's mate. Hot-tempered youngster. What Keara saw in him...Fafnir choked on the thought. Did he even have a right to critique his son-by-mating?

Thoren threw his hands out. "It's not my intention to inhibit your healing."

"Of course it isn't." A grin tinged Aryana's lips. "We all know you're worried and have to yell out your emotions. Get on with it."

Thoren crossed his arms as his ears stopped billowing steam and turned red. "I am not yelling."

Ari waved her hand back and forth, her eyes twinkling.

A sigh escaped Thoren's lips and he ran a hand through his hair. "Jaythena's a mess. Mother's not much better. Fasolt escaped and we've been unable to track him. And there are no further leads on the Watcher rebellion. At least another village wasn't attacked in the night."

"Well, that's a start."

What are you doing about the attacks? Fafnir took a deep breath, releasing it slowly. Peaceful and calm voices made for a pleasant conversation. Even if the topic was less than soothing.

Thoren made another pass through his hair with his hand. "The Council Watchers are talking to the Watchers in their village. Seeing if anyone will come forward."

Good idea. Because they all want to volunteer to be charcoaled by the Draconi.

Annaliese bit back a laugh while Aryana fought a losing battle to keep a grin from twisting her lips.

Thoren shook his head. "You know as well as I do they'll be a bit more discreet about it than I made it sound."

Just jesting with you. Fafnir offered a toothy grin. *Did the attackers mention anything?*

"Nothing other than what we knew. That they are throwing off the yoke of Draconi rule by overthrowing us. And we have no magic. Not sure where they got that one."

"And," Ari said, "they've undoubtedly been aided by Fasolt."

"Who wants revenge on you," Annaliese added.

"It appears so." Thoren ran a hand through his hair. Fafnir drew in a deep breath. Perhaps jealousy over his current lack of hair follicles rode his scales, but that hand-through-hair nervous tic of Thoren's made him want to growl. "If you stripped Fasolt of his powers, how can he disappear and use his magic?"

Why did you strip him of his powers?

Aryana pulled her attention from Thoren to him. Steam hissed out her ears as a snarl pulled her lip. "He beat one of my priestesses."

What? Fafnir forced his raised eye-ridges to drop and his mouth to close. Males beat females? Until now, he'd never heard of a Draconi male hurting a female. Females were cherished, loved. They held the power of the Goddess within their bodies and were treated as Her vessels. To hit one was a punishable crime. Worse than him abandoning Keara to be raised by humans.

"Claimed he failed to see the Goddess during their session, but that was no reason to hit her."

And that's why you banished him?

"Yes. I thought stripping him of his powers and banishing him would solve the problem."

Why didn't you kill him?

"I didn't want to bring the matter before the Council."

He opened his mouth to ask why not, then shut it when he realized the reason. Her feud with his father. What a mess. All the way around.

"As I was saying"—Thoren crossed his arms—"if you stripped Fasolt of his powers, how can he disappear and use his magic?"

"We don't know if stripping a Draconi of his powers always permanently works." Aryana glanced at the ceiling and back to her nephew, a tint of red peppering her cheeks. "And I was in a rage when I did it. Never work magic in a rage, my mentor always said. Guess I didn't listen."

"I helped you," Annaliese interjected. "And even if his magic wasn't stripped from him, he was still banished. He should not have been able to get through the wards. Ever. So how did he? That's what you need to figure out."

"The wards were weakened."

The wards don't weaken unless someone makes them weak.

"That is true." Annaliese glanced to Aryana before focusing on Thoren. "Did he have help getting back into Draconia?"

"He had a regiment of soldiers and the lord of

Keara's village with him. Clearly something went wrong with the wards. Even if they let Fasolt back in, they should have repelled the humans."

Lily came through them.

"She was with you."

The soldiers were with Fasolt.

"But he should not have been allowed in."

"Clearly you have more problems than you thought." Aryana drummed her fingers once against the sheet where it covered her legs. "Did you not assess this issue when it occurred?"

"Of course we did." Thoren crossed his arms and gave Aryana a glare. "We strengthened the wards. It was unclear how they became weak. There was no magical signature around them. No red flag stating who tampered with them. Perhaps they grow weak over the years."

"If I recall, it was only in that one spot where they were weak. Are you saying it was a coincidence that Fasolt found the only weakened spot in the ward-line and exploited it? That's too coincidental for reality."

Sounds like he had help.

"Who'd help an outcast?" Thoren raised a brow at Fafnir.

His friends? Was the male dense?

A headshake negated Fafnir's answer. "No self-respecting male would continue a friendship with one who abused a female and was banished for it."

"Maybe his friends have no self-respect?" Annaliese cocked a brow.

"Did you even ask?" Aryana matched her expression to Annaliese.

"It was not brought up. At least I didn't hear about

it."

Find out who's helping him and you'll find Fasolt.

"He needs to be destroyed." Thoren smacked a fist against his palm. "What kind of a male does what he has?"

"He claims to have lost his mate."

"That might lead to some crazy behavior and grief, but not violence. Alviss did not blow up villages when he lost his mate."

He almost destroyed the house. Fafnir caught himself before projecting that thought. A quick glance at his sister showed she remembered the same event. A grieving Alviss, sparks flying from his fingers as furniture burst into a thousand splinters. Somehow Annaliese managed to spell him into an uneasy sleep, while Fafnir repaired the destroyed furniture.

No one ever needed to know the depths of his father's grief. How the older male almost died with his mate. According to his father, appearances meant everything.

Good thing the old male thought him dead.

"Father is Council Leader. Fasolt does not have that much magic."

A rap banged against the door, stopping the conversation as all turned toward the sound. Before anyone spoke, Keara darted into the room like a rabid dragon chased her. She kicked the door shut behind her as she rushed toward Aryana.

"Keara." Annaliese's eyes narrowed. "What brings you here?"

"Little One!" Thoren stepped into her path, drawing her into his arms. He brushed a kiss across her lips before releasing her.

Fafnir might wonder why Keara mated Thoren, but after that kiss and the glow in Thoren's eyes, he had no doubt his daughter was well loved. Which was more than he could say for how he treated her the past twenty-four years.

Keeping a hold of Thoren's hand, Keara ignored Annaliese and spoke to Ari.

"I know I can perform the spell for reversing Fafnir's dragon form and I want to try it soon."

Hope glowed in Aryana's eyes as she glanced toward him, but she banked the look before facing Keara. "How do you know? Last I looked the old scrolls were in the Older Language and the spell needed deciphering."

"The Archivist read it to me. I know what to do. Will you let me?"

"Ask Fafnir."

Of course I'll let her. He couldn't hide forever. And he was getting tired of being in dragon form. Celibacy was not a state of being he enjoyed.

Especially when his mate asked him to bond.

In a dream. It still counted.

But would she accept him for her mate?

Maybe remaining a dragon wasn't so bad after all.

Who was he kidding? He hated being in dragon form constantly. He never realized how much easier life was as a human. How useful it was to have a thumb. Or a hand. Or a bed-romp for that matter.

Maybe that was why he was so depressed. Lack of bed-romping. Luckily the cure for that stood before him, offering to turn him back into a human.

No more hiding when in human form. Too many people would recognize him, even after twenty-four years. And no guarantees Ari would want to be around him, let alone bond with him. Or tell him how she became a dragon.

Fafnir took a deep breath. Trading scales and four legs for skin and feet was well worth revealing his true identity.

When can you work the spell?

****

Aryana sat on the bed with Keara beside her, trying to read the passage from the old scroll. Deciphering spells, rummaging through old scrolls, the parchment brittle beneath her fingers, ranked high on her enjoyment list. Perhaps she would have studied under the Archivist if she hadn't been so eager for the position of High Priestess.

Written on a new scrap of parchment, the spell held none of the flavors of old age as fresh ink glittered on the page. The Archivist copied the passage for them since she refused to let the brittle scroll out of the archive room. During the time it took the older priestess to make the copy, Aryana visited with Moira, Thoren left for a Council meeting, and Fafnir disappeared to talk with Annaliese.

She wondered what that talk was about. Annaliese acted like she knew Fafnir, but if that were the case, wouldn't her friend and closest advisor tell her who the dragon was? Especially since she knew Aryana's feelings for him?

"Aunt Aryana." Keara touched her hand. "Are you all right? You looked distant for a minute there."

"Just thinking." And since she didn't want Keara to know who invaded her thoughts, she added, "About everything that's been going on. We need to find out who's behind the attacks, and I'm stuck in the healing room."

"I'm sure the Council will discover the perpetrator and bring him to justice."

Undoubtedly, but not in the time frame she wanted. After all, a month had passed since Fasolt entered Draconia. A month. And the Council had yet to find him. Compared to that, discovering the cryptically written spell seemed easy.

Aryana made a noncommittal noise. "Now, are you sure you can work this? It requires much more energy absorption than you are used to."

"Of course. It's the same principle as when I helped Thoren through the Change."

"Yes, and that left you near death. How do you know this won't?" Thoren would blame her if something happened to Keara.

He'd be right.

Aryana possessed magic in abundance, her own, the land's, and the occasional touch of the Goddess's. Even with all that power, she could no more work this ancient spell than she could return the dead to the living.

But Keara could. Return the dead to the living, that was. But could she work the spell?

Aryana swallowed. What if Keara couldn't? What if she got halfway through the spell and, Goddess forbid, died? What would happen to Fafnir if the spell remained half-complete?

"I've been practicing since then. I've learned what to do with the energy, how to convert it so it doesn't damage me. Don't worry, no near death experiences for me again."

"I know you believe that, but there are too many unknown variables. Perhaps Fafnir should stay as is." At least he was alive in dragon form. Which was more than she could say for her mate.

Aargh. Why did she have to think of her dream? She had enough on her mind without adding to the mix.

"No!" The force behind the word startled Aryana and she gave a little jump. "I'm sorry, but no. Fafnir has to be changed back into human form. If I have the ability to help him, then shouldn't I? Besides, I thought you wanted him changed. I see the way you look at him."

Heat splashed against her cheeks. Was it that obvious? "Leave me the spell, let me review it and pray for guidance. I'll get back with you." Keara sat still, staring at her like she grew a pair of wings. "Go on now. Leave me alone."

Keara looked at the parchment while placing it beside Aryana on the bed. Her green gaze flashed upwards, eyes narrowed. "I can do this. Trust me. I know what I'm doing."

With those words, she strode out of the room, the skirt of her white gown swirling around her ankles as she pulled the door shut.

Ari let out a breath. Of course Keara thought she could perform the spell. She was young, powerful, with a thin slice of pride that had grown since she arrived in Draconia. Pride could do a lot of things. Raise a person up or cause them to fall.

What would the outcome be in this case?

Her fingertips traced the words, the spell warm under her skin. Even copied, the words gave a physical warning to those who would dare read them aloud. She wanted Keara to be right. Oh, how she wanted. To see Fafnir in the flesh. To feel the touch of his skin against hers. To care for a male.

But dare she risk Keara's life?

Perhaps it wouldn't be a risk. Perhaps Keara would speak the spell with the power of the Goddess behind her and work magic like no one living had ever seen.

After all, Aryana had turned into a dragon during the Harvest festival. What was one more act of rarely seen magic?

Ari picked up the piece of parchment with the copied spell and read through it again, translating the Old Language into the modern one. She pushed back against the pillows until she sat straight, then crossed her legs, placing the parchment on her lap. Resting her palms on her knees, she closed her eyes and began her prayer.

Maybe the Goddess would deign to show her what to do.

But all she saw behind her lids was Ragnor's face. Her dream lover. Her dead mate.

So much for asking for the Goddess's wisdom. It appeared she was on her own.

On one hand, she wanted to see Fafnir in the flesh instead of scaled. She wanted to see if the attraction between them could turn into something more.

On the other, the thought of Keara harmed sent an arrow of fire burning into her stomach.

She couldn't conscientiously choose her selfish desire over the wellbeing of one of her people. As the High Priestess, she was charged with the safekeeping of the Draconi. How could she knowingly send one into danger to soothe her own desires?

"Shouldn't the decision be Fafnir and Keara's?"

Aryana jumped, eyes snapping open, her heart pounding an uneven rhythm behind her ribs. Annaliese stood at the foot of the bed, hands folded in front of her waist, her face a false mask of innocence.

"Shouldn't you stay out of my mind?"

"You spoke it aloud."

"Oh." Well, that was embarrassing. What else did she accidentally say?

"You should let them decide."

"I hold ultimate responsibility for all Draconi. Part of my duties include keeping Draconi as safe as possible. I can't knowingly send Keara off to work a spell that might kill her. What kind of High Priestess would I be if I didn't watch over my people?"

"Ensuring safety does not mean refusing others that which they want to do. You cannot prohibit everything in hopes of saving one from harm. What kind of High Priestess would you be if you did that?"

"So you think I should allow it."

"Yes. I think both Fafnir and Keara deserve a chance to prove themselves."

Both? What did Fafnir have to prove? "I suppose."

"And you know as well as I that once Keara sets her mind to something, nothing will stop her. At least if you approve it, you can supervise it."

"She couldn't do it without approval. The spell requires the Harvest circle." The same overlarge, silver rune-lined circle that turned her into a dragon at the Harvest festival.

Annaliese's brows rose then crashed. "Are you sure?"

"You know another silver circle where females

138

fly?"

"There are more uses for that circle than we thought. Maybe research should be put into reading and translating the old scrolls. Wonder what else we'd find in there we've lost over the years?"

"Plenty of things, I'm sure. None of which will help me make a decision."

"What would you decide if it was you performing the ritual? If Keara weren't involved?"

No hesitation. "I'd do it. But that's not the problem."

"You are included in the keeping Draconi safe and sound vow. How can you not give yourself the same rules as you force on Keara?"

As usual, her second in command had a point. The logic failed to help her feel better about sending Keara to a possible early death.

"What if she dies?"

"We mourn her death."

"I take it you are for her working the spell."

"I think she can do it with no harm to herself. She should be allowed to make the decision. She knows the risks."

Aryana closed her eyes and pressed the pads of her index fingers against the bridge of her nose. A deep breath in, a slow release of air. "She is overconfident in her abilities."

"No, she's not. She has a lot of magic for a Halfling. She'd been practicing on absorbing magic without doing harm to herself. Allow her to prove her abilities. You'll be surprised at the result."

"Surprised in a good way or a bad one?"

"That remains to be seen. But I'm confident Keara

will survive intact with little consequence."

Was Keara living the surprise? What else could Annaliese mean? The Healer worked closely with Keara, which meant she had a better grasp than did Aryana on the Halfling's ability to perform the spell without causing herself harm.

Perhaps she feared unnecessarily for Keara's safety. Perhaps her nephew's mate had stronger powers than she thought. After all, Keara was a death raiser, a talent reserved for fables, tales told to the young, but not believed. She probably could return Fafnir to human form with little to no harm to herself.

Annaliese was right. As usual.

So why did she still feel so nervous?

Chapter Eleven

Fafnir sat in the dragon-sized purification pool outside of the Temple, watching the water lap against his scales as weak light from the late morning sun washed him in thin warmth. Smoke from burning incense bathed him and he pressed his tongue against the roof of his mouth in an attempt not to sneeze. He should be joining the acolyte who waved the incense stick in prayers. Instead his thoughts drifted to the upcoming ritual. To the spell his daughter would cast. To the remembrance of two feet instead of four, of flesh covering bones. To his mate.

Within the hour, Keara would cast the spell that would return him to human form, drain his magic, or kill him. Maybe all three. He hoped for the first option, keeping his magic intact, even if it meant never again covering himself in scales. Not having the ability to turn into a dragon was a price well paid. He'd spent enough time hiding behind scales and thick hide.

Time to reveal his true identity.

Fafnir shivered.

Within hours, hiding as a dragon would no longer be an option. What would Aryana say when she saw him? Bond with me?

He'd be lucky if she spoke to him at all. Not that he blamed her. If she'd been hiding under his snout for a month pretending to be someone else, her grand reveal would go over like a sack of stones. He'd forgive her. Eventually.

But would she ever forgive him?

To do so would mean giving up all she'd worked for, her dreams, her goal, the position of High Priestess. How could he ask that of her?

How could he not?

She might ask Ragnor to bond in her dream, but faced with him in real life she'd choose the priestesshood.

Fafnir sucked down a deep breath. Some things weren't to be no matter how predicted.

He still wanted out of his scales. He needed to admit to his father he lived. Even if it killed him.

Which it very well might do.

The thought of meeting Alviss as Ragnor sent another head-to-toe shiver cascading through his body.

"Is the water temperature too cold?" The white-robed acolyte assigned to assist him in the purification bath stood to the side of the pool, concern written in her green gaze.

Concern for his current discomfort or upcoming ritual?

What did it matter? He had enough problems in his own head without worrying about hers.

The temperature is perfect. Thank you for your concern.

She nodded. "I'm glad you find it so. The air is a bit chilly and that makes keeping the pools at a pleasant temperature a little difficult. If you are finished with your prayers, I can call one of the priestesses to take you to where the ritual will be held."

The ritual. The point of no return. Literally. If

everything went as Keara expected it to, then he'd never experience the thickness of a dragon's hide on a chilly morning again. He'd be forever locked in human form.

And he was complaining, why?

I am ready.

As ready as he'd ever be. The water would go cold and freeze before he thought of what to say to Aryana after he turned. What did you say to your mate when you'd been hiding behind a mask, refusing to admit who you were?

Surprise?

Since he doubted anyone else ever had his problem, he'd have to figure it out on his own.

Goddess help him.

Annaliese appeared beside the acolyte, her curly dark hair held off her face by a circlet of gold around her head. Gold embroidered dragons danced down the front of her white gown, a sign of her high rank in the priestesshood. A wrinkle twisted between her brows.

Maybe she didn't have as much confidence in Keara's abilities as she claimed.

She placed a hand on the acolyte's shoulder. "Thank you. You may go now."

The acolyte nodded to Annaliese before facing Fafnir. "I pray the Goddess surround you in her arms and grant you your request."

Which request? The no-more-dragon-form or the let-my-mate-still-want-me? Probably the former since he doubted the young acolyte had any idea of the latter. *Thank you for your prayers.*

A hint of a smile graced her lips before she disappeared with her sneeze-inducing incense. Fafnir sucked down a breath of fresh air. Ahhh.

"Are you ready, brother?"

As ready as I can be. No amount of time would prep him for what he feared to see in Aryana's eyes.

Annaliese took a step closer. "Do not fret about things. It will all turn out the way it should. No matter what happens."

As usual, she read his mind, stripping away the thin veneer he tried to use as a mask. *Well, that's one way of looking at things.*

Her chuckle wiped the wrinkle from her face. "It's always good to accept serenity. Provided you can pull it off. If I am truthful, I'm a bit worried."

Never would've guessed. He offered her a toothy grin.

"That obvious?"

It is to be expected. I'm more worried about Aryana and Father than I am about the ritual.

"As I said…"

It will all turn out the way it should. But would it be the way he wanted?

"No use dallying in the water. Come, now. It's time."

Time. No more hiding behind a mask of lies. Taking a deep breath, Fafnir walked up the slope leading out of the water until he stood dripping on the side of the pool. A quick shake to rid his scales of water droplets. No turning back. No more cowardice.

From this day on, he'd face his troubles head on instead of running from them. He'd talk to his mate and come to an agreement, whatever that may be. He'd admit to his father his failings.

All right, maybe not the last item, but he liked to

think avoiding Alviss made him more prudent than cowardly.

Whatever got him through the day.

What are you waiting for, Leesie? The pool to freeze over?

"You to stop shaking water all over the place." She flicked a droplet off her gown as she walked toward him.

It was one shake.

"That eliminated the need for watering for a week." Her hand rested against his shoulder, the warmth soaking into his skin. "Close your eyes. We're going to one of the secret rooms of the Temple."

Her transportation spell wrapped around him like a warm blanket, soft and comforting. Within seconds they reappeared in a cavernous chamber, the light from hundreds of candles brushing the darkness from the stone walls. Not a window to be seen, the ceiling sweeping upward into inky blackness. Dampness clung to the room, the dank scent of dirt and mildew. Not that he saw a speck of dirt or mildew. At least not where the light from the candles chased away shadows.

Underground. Deep underground in a chamber beneath the Temple.

Fafnir tried to remember exploring this room when a hatchling roaming around the Temple, running from his mother. Clearly, he'd never made it here. He'd have remembered that huge silver-runed circle etched into the stone floor.

No forgetting that thing.

Annaliese did not jest about the room being secret. He wondered how many of the priestesses knew of its existence and where it was located. Probably several of the former but only two of the latter.

Aryana stood on the other side of the circle, her back toward him, talking in whispers to Keara. Their words floated around the room like the buzz of insects, low and droning. Neither of them noticed his arrival.

"Step into the circle, face east, and don't move." Annaliese spoke in hushed tones, but her voice caused Aryana and Keara to stop their conversation and look at him. Both females offered a quick grin before returning to their conversation.

How do you know which way is east?

Annaliese raised a brow as if to remark on his dimwittedness. She glanced toward the wall on his left then back to him. He traced the path of her gaze. On the wall, lit by the flickering light of a torch, gleamed a painted sun.

Oh. Well. That solved that issue.

She patted his shoulder on her way to Aryana and Keara. Fafnir stood in the circle, tail wrapped around his legs, his flank to the females. His entire body fit inside the silver-lined circle with room to spare.

The females continued talking in whispers, little incoherent buzzes, as he stood wondering what the ritual would involve. The fear of a thing wasn't in the occurrence, but in the imagining. Constantly dwelling on the ritual and resulting aftermath drained him of energy. No use worrying. To paraphrase his sister, what would be, should be.

Candlelight flickered over the silver-etched runes, catching his attention. What did they mean? He focused on the rune closest to him. Maybe he should have paid closer attention to his lessons when a hatchling.

So many years ago. And these runes looked

nothing like what he'd learned.

Which didn't stop him from trying to read them.

"What are you doing?" Aryana stood next to him and Fafnir blinked. How did she get there so fast? Transported? Or was he so lost in thought he failed to see her approach? "You need to face east."

Well, what do you know? He'd turned several steps to the south. *Sorry.* Fafnir shuffled around until once again he faced east. *I was looking at the runes.*

"You can read them?"

Can you?

Pink tinged her cheekbones. "Are you ready?"

As ready as I'm going to be. But was she ready for who he was?

Probably not. Which meant things would soon get interesting.

"Hello, Fafnir." Keara walked around the circle until she stood beside Aryana. "I will light the candles and place them on the four directions, then start the spell. This is your last chance to back out." Her lips turned in a grin, but he read the lines of concentration framing her eyes.

No backing out. It's time for me to move forward. And leave the rest to fate.

Keara nodded, reaching out to touch his snout. *Everything will be fine.*

He wasn't sure if she said that for his benefit or hers. But he bumped his snout against her hand to offer encouragement.

She took a step back and walked out of his line of vision, returning with four candles. As she placed them around the cardinal points of the circle, she whispered words he couldn't hear before lighting their wicks.

Aryana and Annaliese took positions to the right and left of his head, outside of the circle on the periphery of his vision, leaving the area directly before him for Keara.

She stepped in front of him and he saw a glow of magic surrounding her head like an aura of pulsing blue-green light. The magic flowed down her body as she held a hand out toward him. When she spoke, thick and ancient words laced with a tangible power stroked across his scales, seeking inside him for a similar magic.

As soon as the spell touched his magic, he realized two things, setting loose a dance of pride and surprise twisting through his marrow. Keara possessed more powerful magic than he thought. And the spell only worked since she was his kin, his flesh, his daughter.

The spell called like to like. Kin to kin. Magic to magic. His magic formed hers. Hers transformed his.

A powerful spell. A dangerous spell. And one he was powerless to stop.

Strands of magic twisted around him, bathing him in a blue-green glow before slamming through his scales into his bones. Fafnir gasped. He couldn't help it. Pain like he'd never felt before radiated outward, consuming him in agony.

Keara paused when he gasped, eyes wide.

For Goddess' sake, girl, don't stop! He'd die if she failed to speak the rest of the spell, if she stopped before finishing.

Her voice cracked as she restarted the spell, growing steadier as her words flowed in a rush. The overwhelming agony disappeared, but the pulsating pain remained. Magic from deep inside him bubbled up through his scales, joining with Keara's magic, until the two formed one mass.

Keara held her hand out toward him, spoke a word, and yanked her hand back, pulling at their joined energies. Fafnir screamed as she pulled his magic from its moorings, freeing it from the confines of his body. Pain ricocheted across sensitized nerve endings. It might not be the most male-like thing to scream like a frightened hatchling, but the thought failed to stop the rush of air from his throat.

His human throat.

Fafnir dropped to the ground, to all fours, his scream echoing in his ears as it rose to the shadow-covered ceiling. His palms slapped against the stone floor, once, twice. He closed his lips. Ran his tongue over them. Lips. Human lips. Not the hard scales of a dragon.

His lungs inflated, sucking down air like a bellows, which meant no more screams erupted from his throat. But the air smelled different, not as damp or mildewy, blunted as if his nose was stuffy.

Or shortened.

Black hair brushed the backs of his hands. Long hair. Probably the same length as when he Changed all those years ago. He rubbed a strand between his fingers. Hair. Something he used to take for granted. No more.

He touched the back of his hand with a finger. Human flesh. Not dragon scale. Blue veins ran under his skin, rivers of blood to his heart. Black hair dusted his forearms, his thighs, the juncture between his legs.

Nice to know that part of him still existed.

Not so nice to know he knelt naked in front of his

daughter.

Fafnir focused on the stones between his palms, hair hanging around his face, blocking him from Aryana's view. He needed to look up, to see her face as she recognized him. To see as she rejected him.

Since he continued to look at the ground, he must be a bigger coward than he thought. Although that wasn't true.

When faced with the magical equivalent of a dissection, a coward would run in fear. Not volunteer for a change back into human form.

He was not a coward. Not anymore. He would face his mistakes.

Even if it meant rejection.

Fafnir raised his hands to his head, running them through his hair from temples to nape as he raised his head.

Keara stood in front of him, eyes wide, face pale. She swayed, one hand reached toward him. "Hello, Father," she whispered before crumpling to the ground.

He jumped to his feet. Bare feet against cool stone. But he only made it a step forward before Annaliese stopped him.

"Don't move out of the circle! I'm not sure if she ended the spell."

"What did she mean by father?" Aryana, his mate, his love, looked to him, then to Annaliese as she knelt by Keara.

"How—" his voice rasped like a thing unused and he cleared his throat. "How is she?" Definitely needed to practice on speaking.

But then what did he expect after twenty-four years of silence?

A moan answered his question.

"Keara?" Annaliese stroked his daughter's face.

"I'm fine. I'm fine." She pushed off the females' hands. "Just a little weak and very surprised." With help, she sat, resting her head on her knees for a moment.

When she raised her head and looked at him, Fafnir felt heat splash into his cheeks and covered his crotch with his hands. Not that he minded his naked-arse state, but that didn't mean he wanted his daughter to see him that way.

"Is he free to leave the circle?" Annaliese asked Keara.

"Oh, yes. Sorry." Her grin resonated within his heart. "As you can tell the spell worked, we just need to know if you can still work magic. Whatever you do, don't try to change into a dragon. I have no idea if you do, if you'd be able to change back into a human."

At the moment, changing into a dragon was the last thing on his mind.

Aryana's eyes narrowed as she stared at him. Fafnir noted the moment she realized who he was, the moment her eyes widened. "Ragnor?"

Ragnor died years ago, in his place Fafnir was reborn. "I am he who was once called Ragnor."

Her lips flattened, the happy surprise in her eyes morphing into anger. Like he thought. Not that he blamed her. "You've been back for a month and never said who you were? By all that's holy, what were you thinking?"

He shrugged, refusing to admit to his mate, sister, and daughter his foray into the land of guilt and shame. "It's complicated."

"Complicated? That's the understatement of the year." Aryana stood, her green gaze blazing. Good thing she couldn't kill with a look.

He hoped.

"You've followed me around for the last several days and didn't think about coming clean as to your identity?" Her voice rose in pitch. "How dare you? And here I thought there might be something between Fafnir and me."

His heart leapt at her words but he squashed the emotion. "There is something between you and me. We're mates."

"I can't have a mate." Her hands slammed against her hips. "I'm the bloody High Priestess!"

"I should have told you." *Instead of hiding behind lies.*

"Lots of good that does you now. Did you know?" She turned to Annaliese, pointing a finger at his sister.

"Once I saw him."

"And you didn't tell me either? I thought you were my friend." She turned back to Fafnir, stabbing her finger in his direction. "And if you'd stayed a dragon, I would've fallen in love with you."

Another squashing of his stupid leaping heart. "I'm still the same person."

"You lied to me! I can't talk right now. I need to think about this. Just, just leave me alone!" With a wave of her hand, she disappeared.

A sharp pain stabbed him in the chest, radiating outward until his limbs shook. His mate rejected him. Knowing the outcome of his transformation did not help the sting of her rejection.

"Well, that went better than I thought."

Fafnir stared at his sister. Had someone slipped her an insanity potion in her morning tea? If she thought their conversation went well, what was her idea of bad?

"Don't worry about it, Father." Keara smiled at him. "I said almost the same thing to Thoren and look how we turned out. Happy as a couple of singing birds."

Her words fell short of the desired effect. Not that he'd tell her, she spoke to comfort.

What would he do without his mate? How would he live? How would he ever discover the secret behind her ability to turn into a dragon?

A dragon. It had been less than a week since he prayed for a reason to live and the Goddess saw fit to drop Aryana out of the sky, setting him on the path of discovery. He had yet to find the answer, which meant hoped remained.

A spark fluttered in his heart, igniting his feeble hopes.

Aryana had another thing coming if she thought he'd roll over and give up on her. No male gave up on his mate. Even the cowardly ones. And since he'd thrown off all those cowardly traits like a moth-eaten blanket, he would convince Aryana they belonged together no matter how long it took.

Chapter Twelve

Aryana transported to a small garden outside the back Temple gate, her favorite hiding place to escape the stresses of the priestesshood. The garden, filled with dying summer flowers, still-green bushes, and tall shade trees, provided her privacy from the business of the Temple. Planted years ago, the garden provided a place for the High Priestess to find peace and relaxation.

Peace and relaxation. As if she could find those after the grand reveal she just saw.

Ragnor lived. Her mate, thought dead all these years, lived. And neglected to mention who he was for the last month. *A month.* What was that dragon thinking?

Oh, wait. He clearly wasn't. If he had a half a mind he would have told her who he was the first day he showed up at the Temple.

A month ago.

A growl hit her ears, and it took her a moment to realize it came from her throat. Steam wafted past her eyes, and Ari sucked down a breath.

Peace and relaxation. Relaxation and peace. Ari waved her hand to clear the steam circling her face.

Maybe she didn't need peace and relaxation. Maybe she needed a good dose of righteous anger coupled with a bit of oh-my-Goddess-what-am-I-supposed-to-do-now. Females with mates weren't allowed to be priestesses, let alone the High Priestess.

Why did Fafnir have to be Ragnor?

More to the point, what was she going to do about it? Ignore the fact like they had when young? Pretend the desire they felt for each other was nothing more than lust?

Neither option worked. She'd known Ragnor was her mate before he invaded her dreams. Why else would her dream self beg him to bond?

No more hiding.

But if she didn't hide, she'd have to give up her position, her dream, the goal she'd had since young.

How would she live without being the High Priestess?

Why couldn't Fafnir have been someone else?

Aryana remembered the underground chamber, Fafnir standing in the middle of the overlarge, silver runed circle, Keara casting a spell not spoken since ancient times. As soon as she saw the dragon shrink into human flesh, scales disappearing into skin, she breathed a sigh of relief. Keara lived. The spell worked. Then Fafnir—or should she call him Ragnor—raised his head, looked her in the eye, and her world tilted off center. Black spots dotted the periphery of her vision as she fought not to faint. As Keara seemed to already have that action covered, Ari managed through sheer force of will to remain upright and conscious.

If one could call shocked witless a state of consciousness.

No wonder she felt attracted to Fafnir. The bloody, lying dragon was her prophesied mate.

What was she to do now? She could almost hear

Alviss gloating over her predicament, hear the joy in his voice when he discovered his son still lived and she would have to abdicate her position. To his daughter Annaliese. Whom he thought should have been granted the position in the first place.

Maybe that's why her second-in-command failed to inform her of Fafnir—no Ragnor's—deception. Although thinking of Annaliese being sneaky and power-hungry was not possible. Her friend never appeared upset or spoke snide remarks upon Aryana's appointment to High Priestess. Not once. Even though Annaliese had wanted the position.

No, her friend probably acted on her brother's orders not to tell Aryana of his identity more so than a bid to steal her position as High Priestess.

Aryana sighed. Perhaps she would have done the same in her friend's position. Held her sibling's secret at all costs. Even if it meant pain to another upon the telling.

Moira's face flashed through her mind. The twinkle in her eyes when happy. The look upon her face when Jaythena was captured. The knowledge she'd kill the one who caused her sister pain without a second thought.

Keeping a painful secret meant nothing when put into that perspective.

So yes, she would have done the same in Annaliese's situation. If she would do it, how could she blame her friend for not informing her at once of Ragnor's appearance?

Their friendship had endured too many years not to forgive her.

Ragnor—or did he still want to be called Fafnir?—

was a different matter.

His betrayal stung. Why did he refuse to admit to his true identity? With sudden clarity, she remembered her dream, the feel of his body against hers as they moved together under a cloudless blue sky. Her shameless plea for him to bond his life-force with hers, a bond only performed by mates with a deep abiding love for each other.

How he refused her offer.

Aryana slapped her hand against a tree trunk, the bite of the rough bark shocking her with a jolt of awareness.

That dream had not been a dream from her own imaginings. She'd bet a chest of jewels he intruded upon her dreams, inserting himself into her unconsciousness.

A punishable action. Only priestesses were allowed to invade another's thoughts without permission.

Not that any of the priestesses admitted to doing so. Appearances dictated that they must seem to abide by the same rules as the rest of the Draconi.

She could punish him.

But she wouldn't.

No use in revealing to others she had begged him to bond. Even if it was in a dream. Those words also carried an action. An action she wasn't sure she wanted. Especially not now.

Or maybe ever.

Ari sighed. The years of lying to herself needed to end. Honesty in one's internal talk beat living a life of falsehood. Something she'd done for too long.

No one could accuse her of not doing everything in her power to achieve her goals. Except in this case, it wasn't a good thing. Allowing a childhood dream of being High Priestess to eclipse the fact she had a mate left a lot to be desired.

Not sure what that says about me.

Aryana pressed her index fingers against the bridge of her nose. Well, she didn't dive into this predicament on her own. She had help. From Ragnor. Like her, he refused to believe the old Seer, instead insisting the vagueness of the prophecy could apply to anyone.

Sure it could. And dragons could pass by a jewel without eyeing it.

For years her lying-to-herself ability convinced her becoming the High Priestess instead of taking Ragnor as a mate was a worthwhile trade. She possessed power in abundance. Took numerous males to her bed. Managed the welfare of the Draconi.

And did she mention the endless supply of magic available at the snap of her fingers?

But none of those things quenched the yearning inside. A yearning she tried to bury, to hide, to forget.

A yearning for a mate.

No wonder all other males no longer attracted her. No wonder she'd lost her desire for a night of bed-romping. At some level, deep inside, she missed her mate.

Her lying, hiding-behind-a-false-identity mate.

Aryana walked to the edge of the small reflection pool and sat, dipping her fingers into the ice-cold water. Winter approached behind the sunny day. Soon. And soon she would have to decide what to do with her life.

Refuse her mate and follow her dream. Or lose her dream and remain with her mate.

Things could be worse, right? She could be a

villager in Tyne with a burned home and destroyed family. Or her poor niece, Jaythena, who, although physically healed, carried deep emotional scars.

Not that the knowledge made her decision any easier or less stressful.

Aryana flicked the cold water off her fingers and wiped them on her gown. A sharp pain like an insect biting stabbed her upper arm, and she rubbed at the sore spot, knocking loose a small stick.

She held the stick up before her eyes. No, not a stick. A hollow tube whittled to a sharp point on one end. A dart.

What was this?

"I suppose I should thank you for making my job easier." The voice came from behind her, and she almost tripped on the hem of her gown jumping to her feet. The hollow dart fell out of her fingers, dropping to the ground.

Oh Goddess. Things could get worse. *Could?* Things just went from emotionally-distraught to life-in-danger.

Do not show fear, do not show fear, do not show fear. But the fear wrapped around her heart like a serpent, cold and writhing. *You are the High Priestess. Speak a word and he dies.*

Fasolt swayed before her. *See, he's weak, injured. Swaying.*

But which word should she speak? Weren't there words to stop him from approaching? To stop him from…what exactly? And why were the trees and bushes spinning as if she drank too much wine? Her legs trembled, the weight of her body too much for them to hold.

Oh. It's not Fasolt who's swaying, it's me. He poisoned me!

The slimy son-of-a-drunken dragon shot her with a poisoned dart. A rush of anger filled her veins. She was going to kill the low-down female-abusing bastard.

Right after she negated the poison's effects. How did she do that? A spell, yes, that's it. A spell. She knew one. Once. Before black spots dotted her vision and her world spun a dizzying dance.

The spell came to her in a rush of letters and syllables scattered through her mind, the disparate words fading as soon as they appeared. She tried to grab the words, to pull the syllables around her like a cloak protects against the cold. But her thoughts swirled away into darkness as she fell to the ground, a puppet with its strings cut.

****

Water dripped close by, a soft plink-plunk edging Aryana toward consciousness. Her tongue stuck to the roof of her mouth, thick and heavy and tasting of metal. Cold seeped through her velvet gown despite its thick warmth. Her arms ached, tightness cinched her wrists like a girdle on an overlarge female. Were her wrists tied together?

Moving half-numb fingers, she touched the rope binding her wrists. Well, wasn't this grand? Lying on her side on damp, hard stone trussed up like an offering. Could her day get any worse? First, she discovers her thought-dead mate lived, then she's poisoned by an insane male, and now she wakes to aching arms and going numb fingers.

Goddess help her.

All things considered, she'd rather deal with

Ragnor's deceit. Insane males like Fasolt failed to follow established behavioral patterns. Did he think for a moment she might be more powerful than him? Of course not.

Stupid fool.

Who managed to shoot her with a poisoned dart. It was past time she delivered him into the Council's loving arms. In order to do that, though, she needed to open her eyes, figure out where she lay.

Or maybe she needed to find out if anyone was nearby. Sneak attacks always worked better than frontal assaults. Keeping her eyes shut, she focused on the sounds surrounding her. Under the soft, steady splashes of water droplets against rock she heard the muffled sound of breathing. Pebbles crunched as someone shifted positions.

Her skin prickled. Was Fasolt watching her? Checking to see if she woke? Or did he expect her to sleep for longer?

Maybe she should break her bonds, surprise her captor, then render him unconscious. Maybe she should pretend to be unconscious and see if he said anything about the village attacks.

Oh, right. What were the chances of that happening?

Maybe she needed to take a peek inside the mind of the person nearby and see who was guarding her.

A quick touch of her mind to his and she tried not to alter her breathing. Definitely Fasolt. The slimy bastard. She saw his plans for her when she woke. But he didn't expect her to wake for some time.

So why was she awake if the drug should last longer? Aryana focused inward, seeking remnants of the poison coursing through her veins, and finding none remained. Nice to know the spell worked even when remembered in disjointed syllables.

What should she do? Breaking the rope on her wrists only involved a quick spell, but what would she do then? Not knowing where she was meant not knowing where to run. And while she could transport out of a cave, transporting through rock proved a tricky thing, even as a High Priestess. What if she got stuck in the rock by misjudging its thickness from the cave to the ground?

No, she'd have to make a run for it.

On foot.

After she showed Fasolt who was the more powerful, trussed him up like an offering and called the Council.

On the count of three. Open eyes. Take in surroundings. Break bonds. Smack Fasolt. Ready? Ari took a deep breath, but right as she started to open her eyes, heavy footsteps crackled and squelched against the damp floor, sending vibrations through the stone into her skin.

Who was that? Maybe, if she played unconscious victim, she'd discover the ones behind the village attacks. Fasolt helped them, why wouldn't they help him? Ari kept her eyes closed and her breathing deep.

The footsteps stopped nearby. "So you got her, I see." An unknown male voice wavered with age.

"Tranquilizing dart," Fasolt answered, closer than she thought from his breathing, and Aryana failed to stop the shiver cascading down her spine. "She came out right when I was about to go in. A true miracle in our favor."

"How much longer until she wakes?"

"Maybe an hour. Maybe less, maybe more."

"Have you given her the drug?"

"Not until she wakes. She must see who commands her."

"Are you sure you can control her? You already lost her once."

"Of course I can control her. That's what the drug is for."

Drug? What drug was he talking about? Then she remembered Jaythena, the blank expression on her face, the way she followed Fasolt's commands against her will. The same drug he'd given Keara before she arrived in Draconia.

And he thought he could control her with it?

Stupid male.

The only reason it took her awhile to counteract the poison in the dart had been because it caught her unaware. A little hard to pull a spell from a mind running full-tilt toward unconsciousness. But she managed.

And now that she knew his plans, she could counteract the drug with another spell.

It crossed her mind to kill the two males standing before her, but it was a little hard for the dead to talk, and talk they must. How else would their plans be thwarted? Not to mention she still had no idea where she was. Caves dotted Draconia like acorns on the ground, numerous and plentiful.

Most hid in cliffs a long distance from the Temple. Could Fasolt have taken her that far without being able to transport? What if he could transport? Maybe stripped powers really did return.

She could be anywhere.

Stripping a Draconi of his powers was not something she did on a daily basis. Or even a yearly one. As no one else had ever returned from their banishment, she had no idea how well her attempt at removing another's magic worked. Perhaps she always failed. Or powers grew back. Like all ancient writings, the explanation of the spell leaned more toward vague than clear.

If Fasolt possessed his magic, then subduing him might take more effort than she thought.

No problem. He'd troubled the wrong person for the last time.

"Once we show the Draconi we have their High Priestess, that she is powerless against us, then they will surrender. We will control them. We will prove that we are the stronger race." The other male's voice grew stronger, more fervent, as he spoke.

Fasolt huffed. "You are not stronger." The rustle of his clothes and the crunch of pebbles indicated he stood to his feet.

"We know what titanium does to a Draconi. Renders you powerless. Don't tell me you think you're stronger. You are nothing."

Flesh met flesh with a sickening thud. Ari risked a glance, peeking under a half-raised lid. Fasolt stood facing his opponent, a tall, older Watcher with short gray hair. Their sides were to her. Eyes narrowed, the Watcher rubbed his jaw. Neither male paid her any attention, too focused on the other to notice her open gaze.

Aryana shut her eyes. Who was he? An older Watcher, one who did not serve on the Council or she would have recognized him. Council Watchers and Enar were the only ones she knew by name. Many others she had seen, following their assigned Draconi, but as appropriate, she never met them. Who was this one?

"Proving you know how to hit does not make you stronger," the Watcher said.

"Maybe this will."

A quick intake of air greeted his words. Ari risked another peek. An energy ball sat in Fasolt's palm, weak and small. Sweat glistened on his forehead. From the strain of working magic or from tussling?

"Do not," Fasolt punctuated each word, "underestimate the Draconi."

Spoken true. Especially when applied to the Draconi High Priestess.

A brief, silent spell cut through the ropes binding her wrists together, a first step toward freedom. Remaining on her side, Aryana flexed her almost numb fingers. *Ouch, ouch, ouch.* Nerves tingled as blood rushed into her hands.

So much for moving fast. Dead hands apparently made for dead wits and slow speed.

"And you think that scares me?" the Watcher hissed. "I've seen hatchlings make larger energy balls."

Fasolt screamed and Aryana's lids popped wide as he threw his energy ball at the Watcher. Who jumped to the side with an agility surprising for his age. The ball slammed into the stone wall of the cave, exploding pieces of rock loose.

Aryana cast a quick spell of protection, a shield surrounding her prone body. Stones and pebbles pelted the shield and she heard the Watcher scream as the flying rock struck his body. Fasolt managed to cast a shield spell, but not a strong one. He dropped to the ground as rocks punched through his shield, striking him in the chest and face.

The ground shook, the earth's complaint against the energy ball. Maybe instead of draining Fasolt of magic, she had drained him of intelligence. Even a hatchling knew better than to pitch a ball of energy at a cave wall.

Stupid, stupid, stupid.

But it made her escape easier.

Ignoring her still tingling fingers, Aryana rose to her feet, keeping her shield in place. The ground no longer shook, no stones fell from the ceiling and she was definitely in a cave. Glow-lights dotted the perimeter of the large room, still shining despite the energy blast. Dust hung in the air like fog and she waved a hand in front of her face.

Apparently her shield spell needed tweaking to keep out dust.

The Watcher lay prone where the blast threw him, blood streaking his arms. Fasolt lay on his back a few feet in front of her. With a grunt, he began to shake the dust off his arms and legs. Luckily he hadn't noticed her standing.

Thank goodness for little things like exploding walls.

All she had to do was call the Council and they would come take Fasolt and his friend for questioning.

Thoren!

Silence greeted her mental cry.

She tried again. And one more time for good measure. Fasolt sat, his back to her, as he brushed dirt from his arms.

How could her nephew not hear her? *Thoren!*

What's wrong Aunt Ari? Ari breathed a sigh of relief at Thoren's voice in her head.

I have Fasolt.

What? Why didn't you wait for us?

Steam boiled in her throat, circled her face. *He kidnapped me.*

He what? Never mind. Where are you?

Good question. Unfortunately she had no idea. *I don't know. Can you transport here?*

Not without knowing where you are. I can only do that with Keara.

I thought a mate only transported if the other was in danger. While annoyed, as long as Fasolt forgot about energy balls, she was far from danger.

A mate can always find the other. If they want. But that doesn't help us with you.

Actually, it did. Not that she wanted to admit it. Or use that path. But what other choice did she have? She needed…Ragnor. Aryana swallowed a lump of steam.

By all that's holy, can this day get any worse? She needed to beg her deceitful mate for rescue.

How grand.

Aunt Ari?

I'm all right. For now. Go to the Temple. I'll try to send a message to Annaliese. She severed contact with Thoren before she lost the nerve to beg Ragnor for help.

What a mess.

And it got worse when Fasolt went to check on the fallen Watcher, whose arms and legs moved like he tested them for functionality.

Aryana closed her eyes. Drew in a deep breath.

Swallowed her pride and her anger.

"Your prize," the Watcher wheezed, pausing to cough. "Your prize is awake."

Aryana's lids flew open at his words, just in time to see Fasolt turn to face her. His eyes narrowed as his lip pulled into a snarl.

Her breath caught. Her hands shook. She was not scared of Fasolt. No, she was not. She was the High Priestess. She had more magical power than what he could dream. She. Was. Not. Scared.

She possessed the ability to cast a shield spell to protect her from any magic Fasolt might try to throw her way and a short-acting spell to hold both males in place. Unfortunately, the holding spell didn't work for long, which meant she needed to cast it several times before the Council came.

Provided they came at all.

It all hinged on Ragnor. If he would come. If he would help her. He had to come help her. Right? *Right.* And, according to Thoren, as her mate, he could find her no matter where she was. Including in a cave.

But after the way she shunned him, would he even bother?

Chapter Thirteen

Fafnir pulled up his trousers. Tied the laces. Stared at his reflection in the mirror hanging on the wall of Annaliese's room. He looked the same as he did the day he'd Changed in the titanium cell, long, curly hair to his shoulders and a beard to his chest. Not a look he wanted.

Although he had to admit, the hairstyle looked good. What were the odds Aryana would agree?

Picking up a pair of scissors Annaliese thoughtfully left sitting next to a razor, he cut the beard as close to his skin as possible. Then he used the razor to finish the job. His face looked different, older, years of captivity showing in the lines around his eyes.

Since when did Draconi his age have lines?

More importantly, would Ari find them attractive?

Fafnir ran a hand down the smooth skin of his cheeks. Her anger toward him did nothing to diminish his feelings toward her. How could he live without her? How could he even think on that possibility? A male was nothing without his mate.

And he would do everything in his power to convince her she belonged to him.

Right after he dressed. Thank the Goddess Keara thought to bring trousers and a shirt for after his change.

He grabbed the shirt, linen cool against the pads of

his fingers, and slipped it over his head. His shirt. His trousers. Clothes. Not scales. Clothes.

They had never felt so good against his skin.

He walked to the door, his clothing moving against his flesh, a soft tug and release he never realized he missed. Annaliese waited for him on the other side of the door. Waited in the hall for him to shave and dress. He appreciated her consideration of allowing him some adjustment time. Just as he appreciated her sending a protesting Keara to the healing room after the ritual.

His daughter needed to rest.

At least the day was not a complete failure. After all, he was in human form again. Even if it meant his mate disappearing in a snit of anger.

Not that he blamed her for the anger. Getting his head in the right place meant paying the price for his hide-and-lie strategy over the last month.

A twist of the dragon-shaped doorknob followed by a pull on the door and Annaliese stood before him, hands clasped in front of her waist. Her eyes widened as her gaze traveled across his face.

"You cleaned up well."

"Thank you for letting me dress in your room."

"It's the least I could do." She hugged him, her arms tight around his waist, his tight around hers, both using the hug to telegraph relief and joy. When she released him, one hand patted his cheek, her eyes shimmering as she blinked a rapid rhythm. Sniffing, she walked toward the soapy bowl of shaving water. "When do you plan on telling Father?"

Right after he passed his hand through dragon's fire.

No, no, no. He needed to tell his father he lived. No

more hiding his identity.

Even if thinking of the reveal brought a head-to-toe shiver.

He shut the door. Crossed his arms and leaned against it.

"Once I win Aryana." No other choice remained. He needed his mate. She needed him.

He hoped.

"She'll come around. But it might help if she knew why you kept your true self hidden."

Oh, yes. Just the thing he wanted to explain to his mate.

Fafnir made a noncommittal noise. "Do you know where she went?"

Annaliese turned to face him, one brow raised. "Perhaps she needs some time to think."

"I need to explain." And the sooner the better. He already made a muddle of things once.

A strange look passed over Annaliese's face, as if she heard a voice that surprised her. Her eyes widened right as a voice slammed into his mind.

Ragnor! I need your help.

Aryana. And she sounded panicked. Pain shot through his chest, his heart tapped an unsteady rhythm as he focused on her voice.

What's wrong?

Fasolt kidnapped me

He swore his heart skipped a beat. *What?*

He took me to a cave and I have no idea where I am. I can't transport out and I need your help.

Fafnir clenched his fists. When he said he wanted her to need him, this was not the situation he had in mind.

I'll be right there.

He stared into the wide-eyed gaze of his sister. "Aryana—"

"Is in trouble." Annaliese swallowed.

"How…"

"I saw her."

"So you know where she is?"

"Not exactly."

"Then I'll transport to her and let you know where we are so you can tell the Council."

She took a step toward him, placing a hand on his arm. "You might not have your powers. Outside of the obvious, we don't know the side effects of the spell."

"I don't care. She's my mate." And he was going to rescue her or die trying.

"You need to care. How can you rescue her with no magic? Don't be a dolt."

"What part of 'she's my mate' do you not understand?"

"The part where you put yourself in danger. At least be sensible. Try using your magic before you run off defenseless."

Fafnir took a breath and swallowed a lump of steam threatening an appearance. His sister feared losing him again. Of course she didn't want him running off without the ability to use his magic. But she seemed unable to understand he needed to go. He needed to prove to himself and Aryana his worthiness as a mate. And his lack of cowardice. Something he'd failed at this last month of hiding.

Taking a step away from his sister, he stared at the lines creasing his palm. A hand. A human hand. An appendage he never gave a thought to until stuck in dragon form. He ran a finger over his palm. Flesh. Not hard scales.

Get on with it, Fafnir. You can stare at your human body later. He closed his eyes. Thought of an energy ball floating in his palm. Opened his eyes. Pushed a little magic into his hand.

The energy ball popped into his palm, a swirling mass of magical fire burning brighter than he remembered. Nice to know he still possessed some magic.

"Good, good. Now transport from here to there." Annaliese pointed at the bed.

Curling his fingers, he extinguished the energy ball. A thought later and he stood by the bed. It appeared some of his magic remained.

But how much?

Enough to save his mate. "My magic is intact. I'm going."

"Thank you for humoring me." She walked toward him, stopping a few feet away. "Don't forget your boots."

Fafnir looked at his bare feet. Boots. How could he have forgotten about those? Easy. Dragons didn't wear boots. Going for expediency, he pictured the boots sitting by the bed on his feet and snapped his fingers. Warm leather encased his bare feet as he shifted from one foot to the other.

"Thanks."

She nodded, wrapping her arms around his waist. "I will contact the Council once I hear where you are. Be careful."

He returned her hug. "You too."

Fafnir took a step back from Annaliese. Closing his

eyes, he drew a mental picture of Aryana, her green eyes snapping ire instead of love.

What a sap.

He'd work on the shining love picture later. After he saved her.

Aryana's face firmly planted in his mind, Fafnir focused on her signal, that spark of light unique to her. There. A ways away. How did she get in a cave halfway to the Watcher village?

With a thought, he threw himself into a transport, his body breaking into pieces before hurtling across the ground toward his mate.

Fafnir reformed outside the entrance to the cave. Appearing inside of caves proved tricky. And dangerous. Unless he knew the depth between the ground and the cave chambers he could end up stuck in the dirt. Not an adventure he cared to experience.

Annaliese, I'm here.

Where's here?

He told her where the cave was located.

Be careful. I'll bring the Council to you.

How long would that take? Probably longer than he cared to wait. His mate needed saving. Now. Waiting around for the Council to make a grand entrance was not an option.

Light shone several feet into the cave, beyond that darkness snaked inky fingers into the inner depths. Fafnir strode into the cave, pebbles crunching under his boots. Forming a small light in his palm took no effort at all and cast a flickering blue glow across the stone walls.

Shadows swallowed him as he walked deeper into the cave, the only light coming from the small blue flame in his palm. He sensed Aryana to his left, behind a stone wall of indeterminate thickness. He cursed. How was he supposed get to her when he didn't know the wall's thickness?

Follow the path and hope it led to where she was?

What other choice did he have?

He shivered.

Her signal fell behind as he moved forward. The path split and he veered to the left, hoping to find a way to enter the chamber that held Aryana. His heart beat an erratic rhythm. What if she was hurt?

If only he'd killed Fasolt before that bloody dragon transported out of the fight. And he thought he acted cowardly? What kind of male transports away from a fight?

The dumb dragon should have escaped Draconia instead of returning to kidnap Aryana. All knew harming the High Priestess meant a death sentence. Not that Fasolt hadn't already renounced his life. Drugging Keara in Cautasia along with kidnapping and drugging Jaythena ensured a fast ride to the afterlife. Perhaps he knew death awaited him and he might as well continue his vengeance.

Or he was too dumb to realize he lay at the top of the Council's termination list.

And Fafnir was more than happy to help the Council dish out that punishment.

Light from the blue flame flickered shadows on the stone walls as he strode deeper into the damp depths of the cave. With each step he imagined his fist pummeling Fasolt's face. Bloody, slimy dragon. How dare he capture Aryana. His mate.

Would he ever find her? *How long was this path?*

Longer than a pebble's throw and his mate lay behind that massive wall of stone. He swore he'd been walking forever. Should he turn around and try another way?

The wall veered sharply to the left. All right, he'd look around the corner and if no entrance existed he'd turn around and try another direction. *Please Goddess, let there be some sign.* He took a deep breath and stepped around the corner.

Light poured into the path, cutting through the inky darkness, a beacon of relief. The energy pattern unique to Aryana spilled from a giant slash in the stone like a captive freed from bondage. Fafnir released his held breath.

Thank you, Goddess.

He extinguished the flame in his palm and pressed himself against the stone wall, peering around the corner. Glow-lights shone from regular intervals, bathing the cave in a soft glow. Dust floated in the air, originating from what looked like a recently disturbed pile of rocks. Some idiot had blasted a hole in the cave wall.

Judging from the scene before him, he had a good idea of the idiot's identity.

Aryana stood opposite the pile of rocks, facing who he assumed was an unmoving Fasolt. Scars lined the male's face as if raked by dragon claws. Black stubble and streaks of dried blood peppered his shaved baldhead, his cloak and clothing hung spattered with blood and tiny cuts. Anger radiated from the male like a fast moving mountain stream, dangerous and chill-inducing. Fasolt's fingers twitched a second before he stopped imitating a statue and began moving his arms.

"Stop freezing me, you stupid bitch, and start

fighting." His arms rose as if to throw an energy ball, but Aryana waved her hand and he froze, one arm drawn back for a pitch.

Fafnir snarled as he stepped into the room. "Aryana."

She turned, relief dancing across her face. "You came."

"Are you all right?" She looked unharmed, rumpled and dust-covered, but no blood. Thank Goddess. Fasolt still deserved to die. What kind of a Draconi harms females?

"Fine." Her jaw tensed as she turned back to Fasolt, whose arm twitched. Ari flicked her fingers and the Draconi stiffened. "I'm using a binding spell to keep them frozen. It works better on the Watcher than Fasolt."

"Watcher?" Fafnir walked closer to his mate, searching the room for another person.

"Behind Fasolt."

There. Prone upon the ground lay a Watcher, blood and dust covering him from head to toe.

"Who is he?"

"I don't know. Do you recognize him? He's older. Probably around before your captivity."

"Do you need me to help?"

"No." She waved a trembling hand. "I can hold him for a bit longer if you want to take a look at the Watcher."

"You sure?" Fatigue radiated from her body. What was wrong? Was she injured internally? Or did a simple spell cast over and again burn through magic like water in a desert? He took a step closer, but she waved him back. Pain stabbed his chest before he washed it away on a deep breath.

She'd accept him. Maybe not today, but soon. Patience, patience. For now he needed to concentrate on keeping her safe.

Although she seemed to be meeting that goal on her own.

"Go identify him for me." One finger pointed at the prone Watcher. "Before the Council shows up and hauls him away. I'm assuming you contacted them?"

He raised a brow. "Of course."

"Never thought I'd say it, but good."

He walked over to the Watcher as Aryana continued to bind Fasolt with another spell. How long could she keep spelling the male into immobility? The quicker he identified the Watcher, the quicker he could return to her side.

Not that she wanted him there, but that's where he needed to be.

Fafnir peered at the prone Watcher. Blood and dust covered him from head to toe and his breaths came in shallow gulps. Probably from all the cuts covering his body. Then the Watcher opened his eyes and stared at Fafnir. A couple of blinks later and recognition set in, a stomach punch to his psyche. Fafnir's eyes popped wide, his breath hitched deep in his chest as his mind churned, pulling memories from long ago into the present. Years had grayed the Watcher's hair and lined his face with age, but Fafnir would recognize that face anywhere.

His Watcher. The one who told the Cautasians about the effects of titanium upon a Draconi. The one who set him up for capture.

Fafnir growled, anger mixing with an unhealthy

dose of vengeance. "You. You told them how to capture me."

Latham narrowed his eyes, clearly making an effort to speak despite the binding spell.

"Release him!" Fafnir looked at Aryana.

Her brows furrowed. "Why?"

"I need to speak to him. Release him."

She paused, then shrugged before waving her hand.

Latham flexed his fingers as he sat. "Always butting in where you weren't wanted. Nothing has changed."

"You left me to die." Nice to know lips clenched shut didn't prohibit speech.

"Your death wasn't the plan. And it apparently wasn't a side benefit either."

"Why?"

"I don't know why you didn't die. You're a stubborn son of a bitch?"

Before his mind weighed in on the matter, Fafnir punched his former Watcher, knocking Latham flat on his back, before straddling his legs. As if possessed, he continued to pummel Latham, years of frustration erupting to the surface. At first Latham tried to defend himself against the blows, but after a few hits, lay immobile, Fafnir's cue to stop the beating.

But he couldn't. A beast buried deep inside him roared its freedom and he refused to rein in its furor. Latham jerked with each blow. Flesh hit against flesh. Again and again and again.

Until his fist froze in midair. He tried to pull it back and got all of nowhere.

"You can't kill him. We need him for questioning." Fafnir tried to turn toward Aryana's voice only to discover he lacked control over all movement except for breathing and blinking.

Rage exploded under immobility, boiling until it threatened to consume. How dare she hit him with a binding spell when he wanted to kill. Red clouded his vision and his skin hummed with pent up energy.

And then reason slammed into him, shutting down the drive to kill, popping some sense into his rage-saturated mind. Fafnir blinked until the red spots dotting his vision vanished. He took a deep breath. To kill another by beating was anathema. But with the rage clouding his vision he'd shoved that law into a dark recess of his mind.

Good thing Aryana cared enough about him to freeze his rage.

Even if the Watcher deserved it.

Did that mean she cared for him?

Great. He went from coward to sappy male in less time than it took a dragon to walk off with jewels.

At least the rage riding his veins dissipated, allowing him some measure of sanity. He glanced at the unconscious Watcher. Aryana was right. They needed answers about the Watcher rebellion. Along with the why of his capture.

He took a deep breath in. Blew it out slowly through his nose. Death would come to Latham, and most likely by his hand, but not until questions had been answered. Would he finally learn why Latham had told humans about titanium and offered him up for capture?

A yell snapped his attention to Aryana and Fasolt. It appeared the binding spell released Fasolt for a second, allowing him movement, but no harm to

Aryana. At least no harm by his hand.

A gray pallor hung over her face like a mask. His heart rate quickened, a frantic beating behind his ribs. Could the High Priestess become drained of magic? Or had Fasolt given her some drug? Either way, he needed to help.

How long did this binding spell last?

Aryana! Release me.

She glanced his way before focusing her attention on Fasolt. *Will you refrain from killing the Watcher?*

For now. *Yes. Let me help you.*

His fist sagged and Fafnir yanked it toward his chest. No use in her misunderstanding his dropping fist for a thwarted punch.

A glance to Latham showed he remained unconscious. Fafnir swallowed. One bastard down, one to go. Shaking his bleeding hand, he stood, turning to Aryana. He wanted to knock down Fasolt. To kill the one who harmed his mate.

But the Council would soon arrive to haul the male off for questioning. Not even his father could make a dead man speak. No, he needed to tend to his mate, not render Fasolt lifeless.

At least not now.

When he stood next to Aryana, he reached out a hand to touch her shoulder, to assure himself of her wellbeing.

"Don't."

His hand dropped mid-reach, pain spreading throughout his chest. No wonder when young he didn't want to be mated. A female possessed the power to stomp on a male's heart with just one word.

Sap, sap, sap.

Suck it up, Fafnir. Do you blame her? "Are you all right?"

"Of course. Child's play." She waggled her fingers and Fasolt froze, sweat beading on his brow.

The gray pallor of her face and the tremble in her hands betrayed her. She lied.

Not that he'd call her on it.

Appearances meant everything to the High Priestess.

Strain showed in lines at the corners of her mouth and eyes. But she looked better than Fasolt, whose scarred face was an overworked shade of red complete with sweat and a snarl.

"How did he get you here?"

"Drugged me. With a poisoned dart."

He growled as steam boiled out his ears. "Bastard."

Aryana's hand on his arm stopped him from taking a swing at Fasolt. Although no one could fault him for wanting to protect his mate. Even if she wanted nothing to do with him.

"The Council will deal with him."

Fafnir drew in a deep breath. Released it slowly. Fasolt deserved to die. And soon. But not now.

Fafnir! Where are you? Is Aryana all right? Annaliese's voice slammed into his mind.

She's all right. Take the path to the left. You'll see the light from the room. Fasolt and Latham are here.

Latham? She paused. *That's a name I never thought to hear again.*

You and me both.

We're on the path now. Be there in a minute.

"The Council…"

"Is coming. Yes, I heard."

"How?"

Breath hissed out her nose. Oh, right. Priestessly secrets.

"When we get out of here we need to talk."

Her glare made him want to take a step back. He stood straighter and returned her glare with one of his own.

She raised a brow. "Don't remind me."

"Aunt Ari! Are you hurt?" Thoren's voice boomed, shaking loose a few pebbles from the rubble of the fallen wall.

Aryana turned to face her nephew. "I'm fine."

As Thoren and the Council warriors walked into the room, Fafnir saw movement from the corner of his eye. He turned in time to see Fasolt pull his arm back like he prepared to throw an energy ball at Aryana.

Yells erupted, a cacophony filling the small room. Fafnir cast a binding spell. *Take that, you poor excuse for a Draconi.*

Smoke billowed around Fasolt, enveloping him in a cloud. When the haze cleared, the Draconi stood against the stone wall, bound with multiple strands of bright colored rope, his face a mask of pain and surprise. Fafnir looked behind him at six outstretched palms. It appeared the Council had augmented his binding spell by casting their own version.

"Is that the bastard who kidnapped my sister and drugged my mate?" Fingers clenched, Thoren snarled at Fasolt.

"One and the same," Fafnir replied.

"Who are you?" Enar stepped beside Thoren, clasping a hand on his friend's shoulder.

"Fafnir."

Thoren snapped his attention to Fafnir, joining Enar in raking him with a glare from head to toe. "You've changed."

"Nice form, my friend." Enar turned his glare to a grin.

"I…" *am not your friend.* Fafnir closed his lips to stop the rest of the sentence from escaping. No sense in saying words he no longer entirely believed. He settled for a shrug.

"We need to return this male for questioning." Balthor strode closer to his son. Fafnir caught his breath. Would the older male remember his almost brother-by-mating?

"And sentencing," Thoren added.

Fafnir breathed a sigh of relief as Balthor focused on Fasolt, not sparing him a glance.

"Don't forget about the Watcher." Aryana pointed to where Latham lay unconscious.

"Who is he?" Balthor turned in the direction she pointed.

"Latham," Fafnir snarled. "He's the one who told the humans about the effect of titanium on Draconi, which led to my capture."

Chapter Fourteen

Aryana blinked her eyes to wipe off the surprised look she knew covered her face. What was more shocking? That the downed Watcher used to guard Ragnor? Or that Ragnor continued to call himself Fafnir? Probably the Watcher. What were the chances?

"Tie him up." Balthor gestured toward Latham.

"He's injured." Annaliese appeared from behind Balthor, holding her skirt as she stepped over fallen rocks to the injured Watcher. Even from where she stood, Aryana knew that in order for the Council to question Latham, Annaliese needed to heal him. Unconscious males didn't talk. At least not without the help of a spell.

Something she kept to herself. No use in the Council discovering secrets of the priesstesshood.

What a waste of her friend's talents.

Leave him be, sat on her tongue, but she swallowed the words. The High Priestess should not be vengeful. Even if the male harmed her mate. Ari gritted her teeth. Did she actually use the word mate? It appeared so. Where was a convenient thought-removing spell when she needed one?

Mate or not, Ragnor—or should she say Fafnir?—did not deserve to be thrown into a titanium cell for over twenty years. Latham earned his punishment for that alone. But working with Fasolt sealed his fate.

With any luck, these two were the leaders of the Watcher rebellion and no more villages would be attacked.

"Let's get you out of here." Fafnir rested his hand against her arm, and she swayed into his touch.

Traitorous body.

But his touch evoked calm in her soul. Until she remembered his lies, his refusal to tell her his true identity. She jerked away. Sucked in a breath as the room spun.

Who would have thought constant use of an easy spell would drain her of energy? She felt like she could sleep for a week.

"Aryana, please. I know you are upset with me—"

She gritted her teeth and gave him her best glare. "Upset is the tip of the treasure."

"Fine. Thoroughly irked. I understand. But let me help you out of here. Let the Council bring in Fasolt and Latham."

Her jaw tensed. She hated asking for help. Admitting she needed assistance ranked lower than cleaning the latrines. But not nearly as low as showing the Council her weakness.

And the chances of that happening were less than Moira suddenly casting a spell.

The erratic dancing motion of the walls guaranteed her a bout of nausea. Spots sprinkled the edges of her vision. Taken together, it did not bode well for her remaining upright and conscious. How could constant use of the binding spell cause this reaction? Such an easy spell to cast, unlike others she knew.

Apparently, the High Priestess could drain her own magic. Someone should have told her that wonderful fact before now and saved her from swaying like a drunken dragon.

How embarrassing. The High Priestess, the receptacle of magic from the Goddess, couldn't even cast a simple spell without experiencing side effects.

"If you insist." It appeared she needed a bed.

Again.

This talent for injury needed to end. Sooner rather than later.

"Fafnir will escort me back to the Temple." Aryana gestured at the entrance to the room only to realize no one paid her any attention. Everyone focused on either Fasolt or the Watcher. Nice to know she held so much importance.

She shrugged. At least they couldn't accuse her of not informing them of her intentions.

Placing a hand against the small of her back, Fafnir urged her in front of him. She stepped to his side, slanting him a glance. Was it her imagination or did he duck his head when walking past Balthor?

Why did he not want others to know he was Ragnor? What did he fear? Clearly he feared something or he would have stated his true name first thing upon returning to Draconia.

What was it?

And how would she discover it?

Sure, she could hop into his mind, root around and uncover his fear. But she wanted him to admit his faulty reasoning on his own. Without her yanking the secret from his thoughts.

At least he came to her rescue. And was currently making an effort to escort her out of the cave.

They needed to talk. That was one thing Fafnir said

true.

Right after she took a long nap.

The cave opening gaped before them, a gateway to further darkness. Moonlight cast a pale glow over the ground as they stepped outside. A chill hung in the air announcing winter's coming.

No convenient rocks lined the cave's entrance for her to sit upon. But tiredness dictated she sit somewhere beside the pebbly floor of the cave. Good thing she knew how to remove dirt stains from her gown.

Ari stepped to the side of the entrance and sank to the ground. What was wrong with her? It couldn't be all the injuries she sustained over the last few days.

Of course not. She was the High Priestess, for Goddess' sake. Magic ran through her veins like blood.

"Are you all right?"

"Of course. I just feel the need to sit."

"Uh-huh." Fafnir squatted before her. "Try again."

"As if you're some paragon of truth."

He licked his lips, looked at the ground, a blush tingeing his cheeks. Bright green eyes met her gaze. "I deserved that. It's…difficult…for me. Being back."

"So you lied about who you were?" He made no sense.

"No. Yes. I lied."

"No?"

He sighed. Ran a hand over his face. "I—"

Footsteps crunched over pebbles as the Council and Annaliese walked out of the cave. Fasolt and Latham walked before them, hands tied behind their backs. Once everyone stood outside, two Council members grabbed the arms of each of the prisoners and disappeared, undoubtedly transporting them to the

Council Chamber for questioning. The other two Council members nodded to her before joining their brethren in a transport.

Annaliese knelt beside her. "What did you do?"

"A simple spell and yet it completely drained me."

"She kept repeating the binding spell over and over." Fafnir turned to Annaliese.

"Because it is a short acting spell." Aryana gritted her teeth. "I don't know a long lasting spell. The Council never saw fit to share that knowledge with me."

Annaliese touched her arm, closing her eyes. Ari felt warmth move through her limbs as her friend sent healing pulses to determine the extent of her injuries.

"You aren't badly drained. Rest would do you good. Are you able to transport to the Temple on your own or do you require assistance?"

Right when she opened her mouth to speak, Fafnir answered. "I'll take her."

"I—" But her words were cut off as he touched her arm, sending them both into a transport.

They landed in the healing room built to accommodate a dragon. The same room they had spent the night in. The same room where Ragnor visited her in her dreams.

He brought them here? Maybe he thought the room held special memories and she'd be more likely to forgive him.

Clearly he was insane.

"I can transport myself." She slammed her hands against her hips and tried not to sway.

"I'm your mate. It's my responsibility to see to your care."

"We're not mated. I relieve you of the responsibility."

The door popped open, Annaliese storming inside. "What are you doing in here?"

Both of them turned to her. Aryana gestured to Fafnir. Fafnir shrugged. "It's the same room we were in before."

"Which is the room for male dragons. Neither of you are in dragon form. A room better equipped for the High Priestess is down the hall."

Sounded good to her. The less time in this room the better. Any longer in here and she might consider forgiving Fafnir.

She shoved Fafnir's shoulder and got nowhere. How embarrassing was it to try to prove a point only to need help walking past the object of her ire. By said object.

She wanted to yank her arm free of his grasp. Yell at him for his stupidity. Berate him for lying to her.

Instead she allowed him to assist her to Annaliese.

The Healer placed an arm around her waist, escorting her across the hall and down a door to the room befitting the High Priestess. Or so Annaliese claimed. To Aryana it looked the same as the other healing rooms.

A bed. A nightstand. Water pump. Various healing items.

Shaking free of Annaliese's guiding arm and Fafnir's domineering presence, she placed one trembling leg in front of the other until she arrived at the bed. Lying down seemed like a good idea.

Tomorrow she would deal with Fafnir and his lies. Right after she marched on the Council and demanded

Fasolt's death. Something told her she'd have no problem with the convincing. Then maybe they'd tell her if Fasolt and Latham were behind the village attacks.

After that, listening to Fafnir explain his lies would seem easy.

Until she remembered a High Priestess couldn't have a mate.

Her position or her mate. Did she even have a choice?

Chapter Fifteen

Fafnir leaned against the wall, watching his sister tuck his mate under the covers, wishing his hands pulled the covers over Aryana. At least he had hands. All thanks to his daughter, who lay in another healing room.

Ack! Keara. What kind of male completely forgot about his own daughter?

He smacked his head against the wall, causing Annaliese to shoot him a raised brow. Life was so much easier as a coward. All he needed to do was hide and lie and avoid his family.

Now he needed to check on his daughter, tell his father he lived, and convince Aryana to renounce her coveted High Priestess position to become his mate.

And while he was at it, he could banish evil and create peace.

Right. When dragons stopped flying.

"Why don't you go check on Keara?" Annaliese pointed to the door. "She's at the end of the hall. I'm sure she'd be happy to see you."

A not-so-subtle hint to leave. He glanced to Aryana. She pushed up to her elbows, then raised a trembling hand to gesture at the door.

Pain, sharp and tearing, ripped through his gut. His mate rejected him.

Bloody sappy mated male. He knew her feelings.

Eventually they'd change—he would make sure of that—but she wanted nothing to do with him at the moment.

So why did his chest ache like his ribs were broken?

What a sap.

"Please." Her voice brooked no argument despite its weak, reedy sound. He fought the urge to rub his chest where he swore his heart spouted holes. "I...can't..." She waved a hand and fell back against the pillow. "Thank you."

Thank you? For rescuing her? For being her mate? For leaving?

As a mated male, he was nothing if not obedient to his female.

Sap, sap, sap.

Fafnir opened his mouth, thought better of the action, and shut it. A bit overly dramatic to inform her he would return.

A fact she undoubtedly knew and wished wouldn't happen.

He sighed, nodded to Annaliese, and stepped out the door. Cool air brushed against his skin and he shivered. Cold air, cold heart.

Enough with the morose thoughts, Fafnir. Get on with it.

When as a captive he prayed to have his life returned to him, he did not mean for it to be this complicated. And he thought he had it complicated? Because of him, Aryana must renounce the role of High Priestess.

Fafnir stopped, his hand halfway to the knob on Keara's door. No wonder Aryana refused him. Even as a child, she dreamed of becoming the High Priestess. Of possessing more magic than most Draconi. Once he told Alviss he lived and that Aryana belonged to him, her role as High Priestess would end.

Once that happened, would she resent him? Could he live with forcing the decision?

Life was much less complicated inside his titanium cell.

Not that he'd trade freedom for fewer complications.

Fafnir twisted the knob and poked his head inside. Keara lay on the bed, curled on her side, back to the door. At the squeak of the hinges, she rolled, her face lighting up as she recognized him.

"Father!" She pushed up against the pillows. "Come in! How are you?"

He closed the door and walked toward the bed. "Human again, thanks to you. Are you recovered?"

"Humph. Nothing to recover from. Since I've learned how to use my magic, things are easier." She patted the bed and he sat, propping a knee on the mattress. "It's amazing what magic can do when you know how to work it."

A swell of pride crested through his chest, strong in intensity. Did all parents feel this way about their children?

"I'm proud of you." A smile crooked her lips at his words. "And grateful. I never thought to see my hands again."

"I thought you'd stop by earlier. Not that I'm complaining."

"We had a…complication."

"What kind of a complication?"

Was telling her against some Council code? Good thing he wasn't on the Council. He thought she had a right to know.

"Aryana was kidnapped by Fasolt."

"Oh my Goddess! What happened?"

When he finished telling her, Keara sat wide-eyed and dropped mouth. "I don't even know where to start. Hopefully with their capture, the village attacks will stop. Will you ask for Latham's life?"

Fafnir opened his mouth. Shut it. Would he? And then another thought popped into his mind. What if Latham told the Council he was really Ragnor? Did his father already know he lived? Shouldn't he be the one to tell Alviss, instead of the old Draconi hearing about the matter from a captive?

"What's wrong?" Keara laid a warm hand over his palm.

"Just thought of something."

One brow asked her question.

He sighed. "I still haven't told Father I'm alive. He thinks I'm dead. But Latham doesn't know that. What if he tells Father I live? I need to tell him first."

"Why haven't you? You never did tell me."

He clenched his fingers together hard enough to pop the knuckles. She deserved to know. And he deserved freedom from the fear and shame choking his life.

"Embarrassment. What kind of Draconi gets captured by humans? What kind of a male leaves his daughter in a human village?"

"We've been through that before. You didn't know about me. You can't be held responsible."

"Knowledge doesn't negate fact. But I thank you

for your words."

"Grandfather needs to be told. Before he dies."

"And there's another reason."

"He's not going to char you for not telling him."

"No. It's Aryana."

"What about her?"

"A mated female cannot be a priestess, let alone the High Priestess. And all she's ever wanted is that role. What right do I have to take it from her? Once I tell Father, he'll insist she renounce the role."

"From what I gather, he's been insisting that despite your disappearance. Even thinking you dead didn't stop him from insisting she not hold the office since she had you as a mate. At least that's what I've gathered from listening to conversations."

"It's not nice to gossip. But what else did you hear?"

"Aryana thinks he wants Annaliese to hold the position of High Priestess, which is why he and she don't get along."

Fafnir growled. His father held issue with his mate?

"Now, now." Keara patted his hand. "Grandfather has never said one negative thing to me about Aryana."

A brisk rub on the bridge of his nose stopped the growling. Mated males clearly had protection issues. Did he really think his father would harm Aryana? And yet, he felt this almost overwhelming urge to defend her.

Sap, sap, sap.

"I should go tell Father I've returned. I've delayed this conversation long enough."

"He misses you, you know."

"Does he?" Fafnir straightened, trying to quell the little bud of joy unfurling in his heart.

"Of course. You were...are his son. He grieves your loss. He'll be overjoyed at your return."

"Until he realizes what a coward I've been."

"Eh. You weren't being cowardly. You were just, just...thinking things over before you made your presence known. That's called formulating a good strategy."

He couldn't stop the chuckle. Formulating a good strategy? "You've been around Thoren too long. It's not a good strategy. Who returns to the land of his birth and keeps his identity hidden? No one but a coward."

"Stop calling someone I love a coward."

Fafnir blinked, his morose thoughts grinding to a halt at her words. She loved him? Him?

"You are not a coward, Father. You've been kept in a cell for longer than I've been alive. Anyone would react to their freedom as you have. You're learning to deal with your new life and everything that's changed in it. He'll understand."

Doubtful. But as he hated to disappoint her, he formed what he hoped was a reassuring smile and nodded his head. "I'm sure you're right." Not that he believed his words. Alviss might forgive him for his lapse in revealing his identity, but would never let him forget it.

And the longer he put off the telling, the worse the lack of forgetting would be.

"I should go talk to him." But not if his father joined the Council in questioning the captives. No sense pulling his reveal with everyone around.

"Would you like me to call him? That way you

don't have to go in front of the Council."

Did Keara read his mind? No matter. He liked her suggestion. If Alviss decided to char him he'd at least be in the healing wing of the Temple.

Provided anything was left of him to heal.

Fafnir swallowed, his gaze darting to meet hers. "All right."

She nodded and closed her eyes.

No going back now. He swallowed. Drew in a deep breath. He was not afraid of his father. Was. Not. Afraid.

So why did his stomach feel like a writhing ball of worms?

Pop!

Fafnir kept his eyes on Keara, not needing to turn around to know his father appeared at the foot of the bed.

The ball of writhing worms seemed to solidify and grow, choking his breathing as sure as if they existed.

"What is wrong, Keara?" Alviss thumped his cane against the floor. "I've been called to a Council meeting." He paused, followed by a sharp intake of air. "Who is this male?"

No cue better than that one. Fafnir tried a swallow, got nowhere and licked his lips. Twisting around, he met Alviss's gaze.

"Hello, Father."

Alviss's eyes grew wide, color bled from his face, and he swayed, planting a hand on the mattress. "Ragnor?" His voice, pitched high and reedy, made him sound like a frightened hatchling.

Or a father reunited with a son thought long dead.

Fafnir drew in a breath past the lump in his throat,

blinking until Alviss's outline grew steady. "Hello, Father."

Alviss took two steps, his cane thumping against the floor like the pounding beats of an overexcited heart. One hand touched Fafnir's cheek, calloused fingers shaking in an invisible wind. Then he collapsed against Fafnir's shoulder.

"My son, my son." Alviss sobbed as he clutched Fafnir in an embrace tight enough to break ribs.

Not that he complained. Broken ribs were a small price to pay to hold his father after all these years.

When Alviss pulled away, he placed a hand against Fafnir's cheek, his touch like roughened parchment. "I never thought to see you again."

Now was the time to explain himself, to tell why he returned to Draconia and kept his mouth shut about who he was. Fafnir opened his mouth. Closed it. Opened again.

"Well, have out with it, son. That was you who fought Fasolt as a dragon, was it not?"

Fafnir's lids did a rapid open-close and one more time for good measure as if waiting for his lips to form words. No such luck.

"Did you think I would not recognize my own son? I was simply surprised. To say the least. Why did you not say anything?"

"I—"

"Wait." Alviss glared at Keara. "You know this is your father, do you not? And said nothing to me about it?"

"Um." Her gaze bounced between the two males as red tinged her cheeks.

"I asked her not to tell."

"But why?" Alviss's brows clashed together. "Why would you do that?"

Fafnir looked down at his hands, at the blue veins crawling beneath the surface. Crawling like the coward he was.

No, no, no. He was no longer a coward. He would admit to his failings come what may.

"I…" Emotions clogged his throat, feelings of hopelessness, of failure choking his windpipe. How was he supposed to tell his father?

"Well?" Alviss cocked his head to the side like a bird eyeing a worm.

Fafnir ran his hands through his hair. Stared at the ceiling. Drew in a breath. He could do this. He needed to do this.

When the words came they exploded out of his mouth, hot and blistering. "I failed my daughter! I left her alone. With humans. What kind of a male allows himself to be captured and treats a female like that? Not a real one. So what does that make me?"

"It's all right." Keara patted his shoulder, but he shook off her hand as he jumped to his feet.

"I'm a failure." Fafnir stalked away from the bed, jerking his hands through his hair as he shouted at the wall. No use in screaming at stones. He needed to face his father. See the rejection in his eyes.

Fists balled, he turned. "A failure." His voice dropped to a whisper. "Why would I want to admit that to my family?"

Keara made a small noise, like she was about to speak, but Alviss placed a hand on her leg and she closed her lips. Chest heaving, he stared at his father, waiting for the rejection, the pity. Banishment.

Anything but the raised eyebrows Alviss wore.

One second. Two. Alviss blinked his brows down. Took a deep breath. "Were you waiting until I died before telling my burning body you lived? Did you think of how I felt all these years, believing you dead, hoping you weren't? You let your fear conquer you, convince you it was right. I taught you better than that."

"You taught me better than that?" Fingernails bit into his palms as he glared at his father. "How would you have felt being captured by humans, told your child died at birth only to find out upon your escape she lived? That you failed her? That you were not the male you thought you were?"

Alviss thumped his cane against the floor. "I would have been happy she lived, you fool! Happy! I beat my captors. I would seek revenge."

"I already had my revenge. I cast a spell as they captured me. It was meant to kill, but instead rendered them all insane."

"That's my hatchling! Good for you. Now get over yourself. You could not help getting captured. Titanium would affect even me. And you have given me a blessing for a granddaughter." He patted Keara's leg. "Stop fearing repercussions."

"You don't blame me?" *Truly?*

"You are my son. You might have done some irresponsible things when younger, but you are still my son. Stop acting the fool, Ragnor, and get on with your life."

"It's not Ragnor." With his teeth gritted together the words came out like a growl. "It's Fafnir, Father. Ragnor died in that cell."

Alviss furrowed his brows, his head cocked to the

side. "Fafnir? Are you addled? Fafnir was the wolf's name."

"I liked that pet wolf." He crossed his arms, defensiveness bristling the hair on his arms. His father accepted his failings. Was happy to see him. So why did he want to punch the wall and scream?

"He was a good wolf. That doesn't mean you need to take his name. Ragnor."

Fafnir tensed his jaw until it popped. His father might accept him, but clearly failed to understand. Ragnor died. Fafnir emerged from that cell.

Alviss huffed. "I refuse to call you a wolf's name. You are my son. Ragnor didn't die." Using his cane as leverage, he pushed to his feet. "He just decided to act like a stubborn fool."

"I am not a fool." Although he might want to give that one another thought. Perhaps his father had a valid point. Actions that once seemed logical in retrospect appeared foolish.

Not that he'd admit to it.

"Stubborn dragon."

"Irascible old male."

"Humph." Alviss thump-shuffled over to Fafnir. "You will always be my son, but I must disagree with you. Now, I've been told the Council has captured Fasolt and your former Watcher, Latham."

"I know." He swallowed, clenching his fingers into a fist. "Latham is the one that told the humans about titanium and led to my capture."

Alviss's eyes hardened. "Did he, now? Well, you will want to attend the meeting with me. That way all will know my son lives."

Just what he wanted. *No, no, no.* His old way of

thinking had no place in his new life. He wanted to come clean about his identity. He needed to tell the Council who he was.

Before Latham clued them in.

He closed his eyes, drew in a deep breath. Shook off his bristly attitude. He could always find it again, if need be.

Tilting his head, he gave his father a nod.

"Then it's settled. You'll come with me." Alviss turned to Keara. "And you, granddaughter, will endeavor to heal quickly."

"Oh, I'm all right. I'm here more of a precaution than an illness."

"However you like to phrase it. Just feel better. Son, hold on." Alviss gripped Fafnir's forearm, throwing them into a transport.

Right into the middle of the Council Chambers.

Fafnir took a deep breath as Draconi and Watcher eyes turned on him. In less time than it took a dragon to snort fire, they would know his true name. And realize he lied to them about his identity.

His stomach churned, heat crept into his face as he looked around the room. Stone walls, a high ceiling, and polished marble floors lent a cold feel to the circular room. But not nearly as cold as he imagined the Council would look when they learned of his deception.

Who knew? Maybe they'd forgive him like his father had.

Stranger things had happened. As proved by Keara returning him to human form.

"I have joyful news." Alviss pulled him forward. "My son has returned. Ragnor has returned."

A weight heavier than a thousand gems settled on

his chest, restricting his breathing. Curious looks greeted his father's announcement.

"Fafnir is Ragnor?" Enar stepped forward, one hand gripping Thoren's forearm as if to hold him back.

Fafnir swallowed. He no longer acted craven. And part of his new bravery meant owning up to his mistakes. "I prefer to be called Fafnir."

"Nonsense. You are my son." Alviss banged his cane against the floor, punctuating his words with each thump.

"Why has it taken you this long to come forward?" one of the Draconi asked.

Wasn't that the question of the day? And one Fafnir had no intention of answering. He owed his family and Aryana the answer, not a group of inquisitive males.

But he needed to say something to erase the distrust and surprise hiding in their eyes.

"It was not the correct time. I needed to take care of some things first." Like eliminating his guilt and cowardice.

"Is that why you avoided appearing before the Council to tell about your experiences in Cautasia?" Balthor glared at him.

Fafnir swallowed. "Yes."

"Give the dragon some leeway." Enar gestured at Fafnir, his other hand clasping the forearm of an ear-steaming Thoren. "He's been locked in a titanium cell for almost twenty-five years. Who knows how that affected him? Do you really expect him to behave normally?"

Did Enar hand him an excuse or insult him? Fafnir shrugged, deciding to take the words as an excuse.

Perhaps Enar was a friend after all. Who would have thought he'd become friends with a Watcher?

Surprise, surprise.

Distrust morphed into understanding and pity as the Council members absorbed Enar's words. Pity. He hated pity. But it was better than distrust and disgust. At least no one called for his banishment.

Until Thoren broke free of Enar's grasp. "You bastard! I helped free you and you lied to us all about who you are!"

Two blinks later and Thoren stood before him, fist slamming into his jaw. Fafnir stumbled back. Obliterating his son-by-mating hopped to the front of his mind. Only to be squashed by reasoning.

He deserved that punch. He deserved a righteous hatred.

He also deserved to be forgiven.

As he rubbed his jaw, Thoren stood in front of him, fingers curling and releasing as a thin stream of steam trickled from his ears. Enar stepped beside him, trying to pull him back, but Thoren shook him off. Alviss pointed a finger at Thoren, a snarl pulling his lip.

One charcoal-the-Draconi session coming up.

"Leave him be, Father. I deserved that."

He gave Thoren a life debt when freed from his cell. The least he could have done was give the male his correct name instead of hiding behind a false one.

No wonder his son-by-mating punched him. He'd made him look the fool.

He deserved that punch. And many others.

Not that he'd let Thoren get another punch in. One proved the point.

The snarl turning Alviss's lip relaxed as he drew in

a deep breath. "Very well. Please state how you were captured, Ragnor."

Arguing about his name apparently proved to be a useless endeavor. Looked like he'd always be Ragnor to his father, no matter what name he went by.

Fafnir waggled his jaw before answering. Who knew his daughter's mate threw such a hard punch? "Latham told the ruling humans in Cautasia about titanium and its effects on Draconi."

Eyes widened and narrowed as he told about being captured, his time in the cell, Changing, his rescue by Thoren and Enar and how Keara returned him to human form.

When he finished answering questions, he glanced to his father, whose about-to-charcoal-a-Watcher expression gave him pause. For a fleeting moment he felt a stab of pity for Latham. But only for a moment. Latham deserved the punishment he would receive. Humans should never know the one thing that obliterated a Draconi's magic.

"Thank you, son." Amazing. Words really could come out of a jaw tensed tighter than a dragon's grasp on a gold piece. "Please return to the Temple and we will call you after we question the captives."

Fafnir nodded, but before he could transport, Alviss thump-shuffled over to him, clutching him in an embrace. Thoren might remain angered with him, the Council might feel pity and distrust, but knowing his father accepted him meant everything.

"Get on with you, now." Alviss released him, taking a step back. "We'll call when it's time for their punishment."

"Thank you." *For accepting me, for not banishing*

me, for wanting me to stay.

"You are my son. Now get on with you." Alviss flicked his fingers and Fafnir disappeared into a transport.

When he arrived in the Temple Courtyard, peace stabbed through his heart. For the first time since he escaped from his cell he felt a lack of worry. Good thing he never found a cliff tall enough to jump off. He never would have seen his family again. Never been accepted by his daughter. Never told his mate he loved her.

All right, so he hadn't experienced that last one. Hadn't totally realized it until standing in the midst of trees, shrubs and dying flowers. He loved Aryana.

And she deserved to know. Even if she refused to return his love.

A cold pain staked a hole in his chest. Without her love, he was nothing, an emptiness with no hope of being filled.

But would she choose him instead of her coveted position?

Chapter Sixteen

Birdsong woke Aryana, the happy chitter-chatter outside her window greeting the morning sun. She opened her eyes, took in another view of frolicking dragons painted on the ceiling, and stretched. Judging from the amount of light in the room, it was a little past dawn.

And she felt invigorated. Alive. Ready to start the new day.

"Good morning."

Ari started, clutching the covers to her bare chest as she sat up and turned toward the voice. Fafnir sat on the floor, back leaning against the wall. Fafnir. Her mate.

She just thought she was ready to start the day.

Could she give up the position of High Priestess for Fafnir? Did she want to? Would she be forced to?

How could she renounce the one thing she always wanted?

"Did you spend the night here?"

He ran a hand through his hair. "Not the whole night. More like the last couple of hours."

"Did Annaliese let you in?"

Red tinged his cheeks. "She doesn't know I'm here. She thinks I'm in a guest room."

Warmth bloomed across her skin, dropping lower until the sensitive skin of her core tingled. Knowing he watched her sleep ignited her desire. And how confused was that? If she allowed these feelings to dominate her reason, she would lose her position faster than she could strip.

Apparently her traitorous body wanted the strip, romp, and roll with Fafnir.

Her mind knew better.

"So why are you here?" Although she knew the answer.

He could no more leave her alone than she could stop her body from readying for his possession.

Where was a convenient stone to bang her head against when she needed one?

"Thought you needed watching."

And didn't that make her shiver with pleasure.

No, no, no. No shivering allowed. She needed to be in control of her emotions. To remain aloof. To not fall in love.

Why did she even bother? Resistance to one's mate was futile.

Being upset with his deception was an entirely different matter.

"Why did you lie to me?" She counted the seconds of silence with the heavy thumps of her heart while Fafnir stared at his lap like it held the solution to his problems.

Right when she feared he would not answer, he drew in a deep breath. Blowing it out, he met her gaze. "I was afraid."

"Afraid? Of what?"

"You."

"Me?"

He shrugged, gaze dropping to again stare at his

lap where his hands rested against his thick thighs. When he spoke, his voice rasped like stuck hinges. "I thought you might banish me."

"Banish you? Whatever for?"

Green eyes met her gaze, ribbons of pain coloring their depths. "Keara. I abandoned her with humans."

"Ah." No wonder he hid behind an assumed name. Guilt led to lying. "But there was no malice in the doing. You did not know. And you were a prisoner. Even if you did know, you could not have done anything about it." His accidental treatment of Keara gave her less grief than the knowledge he found love in another's arms.

Get over yourself, Ari. It wasn't like you even acknowledged his mate potential. Remember avoiding him?

His bed partners never bothered her before. What changed?

Her new-found belief in the old Seer's prediction?

"Everyone says that."

"Maybe it's time you start believing them. Does Keara know?"

"She knows."

"Am I the only one who didn't know you're Ragnor?"

Red tinged his cheeks as he glanced to the side and back. "I just told Father."

She cringed, a stab of sympathy shivering through her veins. Telling Alviss anything ranked at the bottom of her list. "How did that go?"

"Better than I thought. Until he transported us to the Council and told them about my return. It needed to be done..." His voice trailed into nothing.

"But it didn't mean you wanted to have to do it."

A smile turned the ends of his lips. "Exactly."

That little smile he wore gave him a hatchling-like appearance, a youngster's carefree expression after a day playing in the sun. It almost made her forgive him for lying to her.

Almost.

"I understand why you hid. Why you refused to admit who you were. But you lied to me. Me." Her hand performed double duty, slapping against her bare chest and helping to hold the sheet in place. "Aryana. Not the High Priestess, but me. The one you claim is your mate."

"Will you admit to it?" Hope shone from his eyes, drained from the pores of his skin, leaving him vulnerable to her words.

One wrong word from her lips and his desire would melt into repulsion. Despite her anger at his deception, she definitely did not want to destroy his love.

Apparently mated males weren't the only saps in Draconia.

"The old Seer might have been correct." More like was...not that she wanted to admit it to Fafnir.

"Come now, Ari, you know as well as I do we're mates. How do you think I appeared when you were in trouble? You drew me to you. You can't deny we are mates." He rose to his feet and walked to the side of her bed.

Ari clutched the sheet tighter, as if it offered her heart protection from his advance. What a futile gesture. Try as she might to fight it, he belonged to her, her mate, her love.

Did she really want to hide her body from his

gaze?

She dropped the sheet as he stepped to the side of the bed. Heat darkened the green of his eyes as his gaze dropped to her nipples. He swallowed before raising his head.

"You need to decide what you want."

"You." Did she really just say that?

"Now or forever?"

Why did he have to ruin the moment with logic? And correct logic at that?

Beneath the crumbling shield of her anger, the thin threads of their mating bond pulsed, growing stronger with each beat. The inevitable pull to mate with Fafnir, to join their bodies, grew stronger as he stood by her bed.

As did the knowledge the old Seer's prediction was true. Not speculation, as she desired when younger.

But how could she give up her position, her title? The power that filled her veins?

Ari looked into Fafnir's eyes, saw the hope glowing deep inside and knew he belonged to her. A tendril of pain shot through her chest, a double dose of knowledge and grief.

Maybe she didn't have to give up her position as the High Priestess. Maybe she could remain at the Temple.

And maybe dragons could walk by a chest of jewels.

Ari sighed. Was the power she craved worth losing her mate?

"I don't know." And she called him a liar? All her hesitation earned her was more time to prepare for no longer being the High Priestess.

Or any priestess.

Goddess. What would she do without serving in the Temple?

Mated females could not be priestesses. Even if they did possess enough magic to fill a jewel chest and transform into a dragon.

Not that she would admit to the dragon.

Some talents were best left unmentioned.

"That's what I thought. Until you decide, we best remain clothed."

Aryana pulled the sheet over her breasts, taking her time with it as lust darkened his gaze. "I'm sorry. Seeing you again is a surprise." Along with a disruption to her way of life.

"No, don't apologize." A hand raked through his hair. "I should be apologizing to you. For not telling you who I was."

"Have you told your father we're mates?"

He shook his head. "Not yet. We needed to talk about it before we let others know. For all they know, we feel the same way we did before my capture."

"I don't know if I can give this"—one hand gestured around the room—"up. It's all I ever wanted."

His jaw tensed. "So you don't want me?"

"No, no. I mean, I don't know. How can I have you and not this? How can I have this and not you? Do you have any idea how hard this is for me?"

"For you? Do you have any idea how hard being back in Draconia is for me? For most of the last month I didn't want to be here. And then you fell out of the sky into a berry bush, and I found a reason to live. Now you tell me you'd rather be a priestess than be my mate?"

"What do you expect? I thought Ragnor was dead!

I thought Fafnir was a dragon returned to home. I never suspected the two of you were the same person until you changed before my eyes. Then you pull out the we're-mates jewel and think I should wag my tail and follow you out the door? Do you have any idea how hard I worked for this position?" Her hand smacked against the mattress.

"You weren't supposed to have this position. You were supposed to mate me!"

"Oh? As if you didn't agree with me back then. I don't recall you flapping for joy over the Seer's prediction. I seem to remember you running off to Cautasia and forgetting all about me!"

"You didn't want me!"

"Don't act so high and flying. You didn't want me either. If I hadn't gone running off to Goleb, you never would have realized I was your mate."

"I always realized you were my mate."

"Then why did you rest your scales in every other female's cave?"

"For the same bloody reason you joined the priesshood and serviced males seeking the Goddess. Neither of us wanted someone else telling us what to do."

"I did not join the priesshood to service seeking males. I joined to receive extra magic."

"Is that how you change into a dragon?"

Aryana paused, mouth open. She snapped her mouth closed, her heart pounding a fast-tempo rhythm behind her ribs. Until he spoke, she forgot he saw her change shape. Not that she considered lying to him about it. *Liar, liar, tail on fire.* "I don't know. It started happening during the Harvest festival shortly after I became High Priestess. At first we thought it was something in the ritual, but Annaliese didn't change, even when she led the ritual. I always thought it was because of my inherent magic mixed with the circle's energy. Then it happened in Goleb, which was a surprise. I've never tried it outside of the circle."

"Why not?"

"I didn't want Alviss to know."

A smile turned his lips, crinkled the corners of his eyes. "I understand not wanting to tell him things."

"I'm sorry. He's your father. I shouldn't have said that."

"Really. I understand. He's a bit...difficult."

"That's a shortened way of saying it."

"What are we going to do"—his hand waved between them—"about us?"

"I don't know, Fafnir. I don't know."

He sighed, sat on the edge of the bed, ran a hand down his face. "A male is nothing without his mate."

"I'm sorry. I—"

"Am I interrupting?" Annaliese stood in the doorway, one hand on the knob, her face a mask of surprise.

"No, no." Heat splashed across Aryana's cheeks. "We were just talking."

Fafnir rose to his feet. "I wanted to ensure she was well."

Annaliese cocked a brow. "And how do you feel this morning, Aryana?" Stepping into the room, she closed the door behind her with a resounding click.

"Much better today. My energy has returned. Thank you." *Now can you do something about this mating predicament I'm in?*

Annaliese's eyes widened. Oh, no. Did she actually transmit that thought to her friend? Apparently so, judging from the glance the Healer gave them coupled with the slight turning of her lips.

"Glad to hear you feel better today. I've heard the Council has sentenced Fasolt and Latham to death. We are invited to attend the execution."

Relief slid through her limbs, a buoyancy freeing her from worry. "Does this mean the attacks will stop?"

"I don't know. All they told us was Fasolt was sentenced to death for his attacks on you and Keara and Latham for telling humans of titanium."

"When is the execution?" Fafnir asked.

"Three hours past sunrise on the Hill of Death."

Aryana shivered. Spirits of the executed haunted the Hill of Death since the hill itself prohibited the souls from crossing to the afterlife. Seldom did a Draconi perform an act requiring execution, so many years passed between her visits to that place. Good thing.

She hated going there.

Until today.

Fasolt deserved his execution. More so than anyone else she'd seen sentenced. And Latham. What Watcher in his right mind told humans about the bane of the Draconi? Watchers lived on the same land as the Draconi. Did they really want to give humans a reason to visit? Even the Watchers responsible for the village attacks weren't that stupid.

She hoped.

"Then I better go change." Fafnir took a step toward the door, only to come to a halt. "Wait. Do I have other clothes?"

"I'll bring you some. Go to your room and I'll be

there after I check Aryana."

"I'll wait."

"No, I need to speak with her. Alone." Annaliese opened the door, gestured between her brother and the doorway.

Aryana grinned. Leave it to her friend to force Fafnir to do something. A bristling Fafnir at that. Clearly someone did not like to take orders.

"We can go together to the Hill." Ari grabbed his hand, giving it a little squeeze. "I'll stop by your room after getting dressed. All right?"

He returned her hand squeeze, his fingers a warm heat against her skin. What would it be like to be held by him for real and not in a dream? As their gazes met, a thrill of pleasure shot from their clasped hands into her core, as warmth filled her veins. How long since she'd last wanted a male? Since desire tingled across sensitive nerves?

Years?

Yes, that was it. Years. Years since she desired a male's touch, since her body readied for his possession from only a gaze. Years.

And she actually thought the power of the High Priestess a better trade?

When he released her hand, the moment faded like fog over water, strengthening her wish to keep her magical powers. But a ribbon of want remained, threaded through her heart, a plea to take a chance on love, a chance on her mate.

Since when was a mating match so complicated?

The door snapped shut behind Fafnir, leaving bird song to fill the silence. Annaliese stood by the door, head tilted, regarding Aryana with a look that sent a shiver down her spine.

"What?"

Annaliese blinked. "You are mates, you know. I'm not sure what to do about it. You're the High Priestess. You can't take a mate."

Aryana shoved the covers off, swinging her legs over the side of the bed. "Don't remind me."

"You have to make a decision. It's evident you are mated."

"I am not mated. I merely have a mate. There's a difference."

"Only because you have not bedded him."

Aryana grabbed her gown off the bedside chair and held it up. Torn. Well, she needed to get bathed anyway. "I need to dress. We can have this discussion later. After the executions."

Annaliese nodded. "As you wish. But don't try to run this time."

As if that was an option. The High Priestess did not run from discord or danger. But then she was to no longer be the High Priestess, right? So maybe she could run all she wanted.

Which wouldn't solve one thing.

No, facing her problems headfirst was the only way to get them solved.

"I wouldn't dream of it."

Annaliese snorted. "I know you better than that."

"Then you know what a difficult choice this is for me."

"What choice? Not a choice. A decision. The choice is already made."

Her lip pulled into a snarl, and Aryana fought against the involuntary expression. No use in snarling at her second in command when she failed to like her words.

"I'm getting dressed. I'll see you at the Hill."

With a thought, she transported out of the healing room, away from the voice of truth, materializing in her own room.

Frolicking dragons danced across the ceiling, painted years ago, before her birth. A window overlooked the Courtyard. Open, it let in the scents of spring flowers, or the smells of a cool autumn breeze. Opposite the window, a door opened into a private bathing area, a courtesy shown the highest-ranking priestesses.

A large mahogany, four-poster bed stood in the center of the room, curtains concealing the mattress from prying eyes.

Not that any prying eyes would dare come into this room.

Her reward for amassing the most magical power. For testing better than Annaliese. For meeting her dream. Not everyone could say they had achieved a childhood dream.

And of those who did, how long did they keep it? Was a dream forever, or only until it became reality?

Aryana pitched the torn gown on a chair as she walked into the bathing room. Warm water heated from an underground hot spring lapped against the sides of a tiled pool. The relaxing energy running through this room always helped her work through problems.

But could it help her with the biggest problem of her life?

Chapter Seventeen

Fafnir ran his fingers across the smooth linen fabric of the folded shirt. His shirt. More specifically, his shirt from prior to his capture. Kept for him by his sister. Delivered to him moments ago in a bundle of clothing.

"I couldn't burn them as Father instructed," Annaliese had said, laying the clothing bundle on his bed before leaving him alone to dress.

Tears burned behind his lids. To be given a shirt to wear until he had his own made was one thing. To be given his own clothing meant he had not been forgotten. That his sister mourned his loss and waited for his return. Even though the titanium in his cell prohibited mind-speak outside of the dungeon, Annaliese knew he lived. Otherwise she'd have thrown out his clothes.

Her gesture touched the doubt smothering him, the doubt that whispered his family did not accept his return, sliced right through its snaking tendrils, allowing acceptance to take root. He was wanted. He was needed.

Just not by his mate.

Fafnir pressed fingers against the bridge of his nose. How was he to convince Aryana to want to mate him? If she didn't want him, then the choice would be forced upon her, a breeding ground for resentment. Which was no way to start a mating.

He shuddered. Resentment had no place in the mating bond. He needed to convince her choosing him meant greater happiness than remaining the High Priestess.

He'd have better luck jumping off a cliff.

Letting out a sigh, he left the stack of clothing lying on the bed and walked into the bathing room. After a quick bath, he chose the best linen shirt and leather trousers, amazed they still fit. As if nothing had changed.

As if he could slip on Ragnor's old life.

Could his two selves be reconciled? Did he even want them to be?

Fafnir pressed fingers against the bridge of his nose, squeezing his eyes closed. Returning to Draconia uncovered problems he never realized existed.

A tapping at the door startled him from his thoughts. He didn't need to open the door to know Aryana stood on the other side.

Two strides to the door, a twist of the knob, and Ari stood before him. Dressed in a green gown with gold trim, she wore a circlet of elongated gold dragons on her head, which held dual purpose of holding her straight hair off her face and showing the status of her position. The scent of cinnamon and cloves clung to her skin, his own personal aphrodisiac.

A jolt of attraction snapped through his system and he hardened. No chance of her not noticing his reaction. Leather pants tended to accentuate certain body parts.

She offered a knowing smile. "Ready?"

Stepping into the hall, he pulled the door shut behind him and reached for her hand. She stared at his outstretched palm as if it carried a soul-deep decision.

One blink. Two blinks. His breath froze in his lungs as he waited. Right when he feared his heart would burst, Aryana sighed, linking her fingers through his.

Her touch played with his senses, a gentle tingling racing through his veins, giving his limbs a false sense of buoyancy. She lifted her wide eyes to his as they stood motionless in the corridor, as her gaze devoured him, as he tried through his eyes to express his love.

Then she cleared her throat and the invisible ties stringing them together snapped. "We should go."

She spoke true, but he wanted to open his door, tumble her to the bed and prove his mating prowess.

Fafnir closed his eyes, drew a deep breath through his nose. Mated males were dangerous.

And idiots.

A tumble on his bed would lead to them mating and she needed to accept him of her own free will, in her own time.

Which hopefully would be sooner rather than later.

She tugged on his hand and he opened his eyes, following her out of the Temple. Once in the Courtyard, she transported them to the Hill of Death.

Draconi had already arrived, ringing the iron fence that surrounded the execution grounds, a breathing wall of magic. The stench of rot overlaid with dying vegetation permeated his senses and Fafnir slapped a hand over his nose. Did a spell exist to rid the air of foul odors?

A quick glance around showed most with a hand or cloth clasped over their noses. Maybe a spell didn't exist. Maybe someone needed to write one. How long did it take to become accustomed to a stench?

He refused to view the execution with a hand held

over his nose like a fragile hatchling. Dropping his hand, he sucked down an eye-watering breath. Then another. And another. And kept going until the stench faded like a background noise, present but not overwhelming.

Fafnir stared into the circular area surrounded by the tall iron fence. Dying grass waved in a wind that howled but never escaped the barrier of the fence. Fafnir shivered. Despite knowing about this place, he'd never come, never watched an execution.

Aryana squeezed his hand, pressing closer to him as if she also feared this place. And didn't that make a male proud, knowing his female depended on him to protect her?

Bloody Draconi sap.

I hate this place.

He nodded as her voice whispered through his mind. *This is my first time here, but I understand what you mean.*

It always gives me chills. The other side of the fence is worse. All those trapped souls.

Is that the wind?

Yes. That's why we aren't feeling it blow. The wind is comprised of all those who were executed. Their souls are trapped here for all time, never to pass into the afterlife, only to see the world pass them by. That area, her chin tilted toward the fenced-in area, *reeks of anger.* Another chill shook her and Fafnir wrapped an arm around her shoulders.

But they don't perform all executions here, right? I seem to recall some in my youth taking place outside of the Council Chambers.

That's right. Only the Draconi who commit

unforgivable crimes against Draconia are sentenced here. It's not often that it happens. I've only attended two or three. If the crime isn't as bad, then the perpetrator is only executed, not sentenced to remain trapped in this world.

How do they prevent a soul from journeying to the afterlife? How was that even possible?

I don't know. That's one power I don't care to have.

On that they agreed.

Who is the executioner?

Family members who have been wronged.

Then how do they trap the souls?

I don't know. Ask your father.

Did he really want to know that badly?

Some things are best unknown.

She tilted her face toward his, her lips turned in a grin not quite reaching her eyes.

He wanted to stare into her eyes until the crowds fell away, until the wind within the fence ceased to blow. He wanted to wake beside her each morning, to see happiness in her eyes when she looked at him, to know she loved him as he loved her.

Love. He had loved others, but none compared to the way Aryana affected him. A soul-craving love. Like ribbons threaded their souls together, a tightening bond, joining them together for eternity.

She had to feel the bonding. She had to want him. How was he to live without her?

A Draconi male was nothing without his female.

The poor, bloody sap.

Aryana broke their invisible communion by shifting her gaze to the wind-blown grass. A second later a series of pops heralded the arrival of the Council and the condemned.

Fafnir almost jumped out of his scales when a hand touched his elbow. Dropping his arm from Aryana's shoulders, he turned.

"Sorry." Annaliese stepped beside him. "I didn't mean to startle you."

"It's this place." He glanced over her shoulder. It looked like all the Temple priestesses stood in mass behind his sister. "Why is everyone here?"

"One of the priestesses has a complaint against Fasolt," Aryana said, drawing his attention back to her.

Of course. He should have remembered. "Will she help execute him?"

"No. Her father will stand in for her."

"Quiet!" Alviss's voice boomed across the hilltop, echoing in everyone's mind, sending a shudder through Fafnir at the amount of power in the command. The low murmur of voices silenced as all eyes turned to his father.

"This execution will now come to order. We are gathered here today to condemn to death the Draconi known as Fasolt and the Watcher known as Latham for their crimes against Draconia and the persons herein. We of the Council have questioned these two and discovered their link to the village attacks of Tyne and Goleb and for those attacks alone, they should be condemned to death. Along with those crimes, Latham has told humans of titanium's effects on Draconi, how the metal renders our magic useless."

Gasps rang out from the crowd, followed by a low hum of voices, the buzz of an enraged insect. Alviss waited until the crowd quieted before continuing.

"His telling led to the capture of my son Ragnor and his resulting twenty-four year imprisonment in a titanium cell."

Once again gasps rang, but no one seemed to recognize the Draconi formerly known as Ragnor standing in their midst. Alviss raised a hand, quieting the crowd.

"The Draconi Fasolt has been charged with physical injury to females." More gasps, another round of waiting for quiet. "He beat the priestess Ella, drugged my granddaughter Keara, kidnapped and drugged Balthor's daughter Jaythena, and kidnapped and drugged Aryana, our High Priestess." Anger like a palpable wave slammed through the clearing, strong enough to momentarily calm the wind, strong enough to drive Fasolt to his knees.

A shiver sank down Fafnir's spine.

"We are here today to balance these injustices. To right their wrongs. To execute them and refuse their souls entry into the afterlife."

Fasolt screamed, wrenching his arms as he pulled against his bonds, his voice a continual wail of no. But what did he expect? That he would escape punishment? Latham stood still, either not understanding Alviss's words, or not caring to see the afterlife.

As Fafnir watched Latham snarl at the crowd, a mixture of emotions roiled in his chest. Latham had been his Watcher, someone he had not liked, but trusted. To have that trust shattered, broken, snapped in two by betrayal, wounded him to the core. Stuck in his cell, he dreamed about Latham's death. Dreamed about killing the male. Quick and easy. Slow and drawn out. His dreams depended on the day and in some small way sustained him during his captivity.

But faced with the male's impending death, he was not sure he could watch.

"We ask if any family of the victims care to step forward to avenge their loved ones."

Balthor and Thoren stepped out of the circle of Council members, while a male stepped out of the crowd, pressing his hand against the iron bars of the fence.

"I will avenge my daughter, Ella," he said.

"Then come in." With a flick of his hand, Alviss transported the male into the circle.

Steam built in the back of Fafnir's throat as he stared at a screaming Fasolt. He might not be able to kill Latham, but he had no problem helping end Fasolt's life. None at all. The male had hurt his female. His mate. Not even in his cowardly state could such an insult go unanswered.

Fafnir stepped forward.

"What are you doing?" Aryana whispered, grasping his arm.

He placed a hand over her cold one. "Avenging you."

"You can't do that."

"I'm your mate," he hissed, the words warped with vengeance. "It's my duty to avenge you. What kind of male would I be if I didn't?"

Her mouth opened, closed, her face reflecting fear and uncertainty.

Then she squeezed his hand. Gave him a single nod, her face a pale contrast to her black hair. Fafnir stroked her cheek with his fingertips, a thrill of pride darting through him as she leaned into his touch.

Turning toward the fence, he stepped forward until he touched the cold metal of the iron bars.

"I wish to avenge Aryana."

Alviss's bushy white brows shot halfway up his forehead. "You do not wish to avenge yourself?"

"Perhaps. But I'm here to avenge the High Priestess."

"On what grounds?"

"She's..." He cleared his throat. Once he said the words, their path would be sealed. He glanced back to Aryana. She swallowed, took a deep breath and nodded. Permission granted.

Facing his father, he tried the words again. This time they rang throughout the hilltop, carrying over the howling wind.

"She's my mate."

****

Aryana swore the wind stopped blowing and everyone froze at Fafnir's announcement. Her breathing hitched, her stomach made a pit and shoved her body into the gaping maw while her heart tripped an uneven rhythm. No returning to life as she knew it. But what other choice did she have? Hide? Run? No, she must face her problems head first, even if doing so made her breakfast threaten a return appearance.

As if in slow motion, Alviss's bushy brows rose, eyes widening, the corners of his lips twitching. Like a cat with a mouse in his sight. She, of course, being the annoying mouse in the kitchen cupboard he finally caught.

Aryana straightened, returning his you're-caught look with a glare. She had faced scarier than Alviss. For instance that time...no, not then, how about...no, not that time either. Well, maybe nothing was scarier than Alviss, but she refused to be cowed.

A hum carried through the crowd, the low drawl of gossip spreading like a disease. Curiosity and surprise fell like a heavy mantle upon her shoulders as the crowd shuffled around to stare. At her. Short stabs of panic ran straight into her belly as she became the focus of their attention.

No need to fear. It wasn't their closeness or even attention she feared. No, not at all. For the moment she still wore the title of High Priestess, which meant these were her subjects. Her people. She had nothing to fear. Self-talk failed to stop a burning pit from forming in her stomach or her limbs from shaking.

She crossed her arms over her stomach as if to hold in the shivers. Annaliese stepped beside her, placing a hand on Ari's shoulder, a show of solidarity. Thank the Goddess for her friend.

Fafnir met her wide-eyed glare, stepped right between his father and her as if he possessed no fear.

It will be all right.

For you, maybe.

One black brow rose at her words. She wanted to scream at him, to shout he was wrong, she was not his mate. But lying was never her strength and lying to oneself took a certain ignorance she lacked.

No, it was best to face her problems head first. No denial.

I hope…

Alviss cleared his throat, slicing through Fafnir's words, focusing all eyes on him. "Ah, you have finally come to your senses. Glad to know, glad to know. Come in and exact your vengeance."

He crooked his finger and transported Fafnir through the iron bars.

And the crowd's attention again riveted on the accused instead of the about-to-be-removed High Priestess. No one but Annaliese and the priestesses kept their attention on her. Praise the Goddess.

Rubbing her hands up and down her arms, she watched as Alviss positioned Fafnir, Balthor, Thoren, and Ella's father opposite a stone column. Then two Council members dragged a protesting Fasolt to the column, chaining his wrists to the sides of the column so his arms hung to his sides, prohibiting movement.

The wind howled louder, a welcoming wail, full of anger and malice. Fasolt continued to plead for forgiveness, his scarred, baldhead bleeding from where he slammed it against the rough stone. For a brief moment, a stab of pity shot through Aryana, pity for the waste of life, for the sentence of death.

But justice must be served. And she must admit, Alviss was good at serving that justice cold, with no emotion.

The old Draconi waved a hand at Fasolt, his lips forming words unheard but nonetheless powerful. Then he spoke aloud to the males standing beside him. "Cast a killing spell and send this traitor into oblivion. For justice must be served and we are her servants." His hand sliced the air, a silent go-ahead for the death spells.

As one the males spoke their spells, colored streaks of light shooting from their fingertips to slam into Fasolt's chest. He screamed, high-pitched and ululating, a cry of an injured animal, the shards of sound dripping from the air to coat the onlookers with his pain.

And then the scream stopped, silence cutting like a dagger through the crowd. One minute Fasolt hung from his shackles, limp and lifeless, the next he vanished, the empty chains clacking against the stone column with an echoing finality.

Aryana shivered as the wind danced an angry jig across the tall grass. Did it make her a bad person to only feel relief instead of sorrow? And how was she to comfort his grieving parents when the Temple brought the first accusation against their son? Provided his parents grieved. The last time a Draconi was executed, his parents joined the crowd in condemning their son to death. Laws governing tranquility trumped blood.

She tried to remember Fasolt's parents when she banished him and drew a blank. Perhaps they were dead. Perhaps he was the last of his family and no comforting was necessary.

Perhaps after Fafnir's announcement she need not worry about comforting grieving parents and family.

Only priestesses offered comfort. And she hung on to that designation with a fraying knot.

One that continued to unravel by the second.

Crossed arms failed to stop a chill from spreading outward from her shaking stomach. What would she do if she wasn't a priestess?

"Chain the next accused." Alviss pointed at Latham, his voice booming over the howling wind. The same two Council members who chained Fasolt, grabbed Latham's arms, dragging him to the column and fastening his wrists with the manacles.

Unlike Fasolt, Latham did not utter a sound.

"Who of you seeks retribution against this Watcher?"

Several Draconi stepped to the fence and Alviss transported them into the circle. Ella's father, though, stepped back, seemingly through the iron bars until he stood among the crowd. Aryana recognized several of the villagers from Tyne and Goleb standing opposite Latham.

Where was Fafnir? He should be standing with the villagers. Instead, he stood against the fence as if trying to transport through it.

Alviss noticed the same thing, pointing it out like a dark spot on a white gown. "Ragnor, you also have complaint against this Watcher. Come stand with the other accusers."

Fafnir straightened. "There are enough accusers to cast spells. Another is not necessary. Let me pass."

Alviss tilted his head, clearly asking Fafnir a question using mind-speak and receiving an answer in return. He shrugged, leaned on his cane and thump-shuffled until he stood with the other accusers.

Facing the crowd, he spoke. "I will bring accusation against this Watcher for depriving me of my son, which caused my granddaughter to be raised by humans." He waved a hand and Fafnir transported through the fence.

Fafnir continued to stand where transported, as if transfixed by the scene before him, instead of coming to her. Why was she so bothered by his inaction?

"Cast a killing spell and send this traitor into oblivion." Alviss said. "For justice must be served and we are her servants." Once again he sliced his hand through the air and once again colored streaks of killing spells sped toward the accused, striking Latham in the chest.

The Watcher never screamed, never pled for mercy, and in an explosion of color he disappeared from life. Empty chains rattled against the stone column as the wind circled dirt into dancing columns of air.

Another shiver struck Aryana and she clasped her arms tighter around her torso.

Relief flooded her veins. She hoped with their deaths the village attacks would stop. Life would return to normal.

For everyone else. For her, life was about to take a turn in a different direction.

But would it be for the better? Or worse?

"Can we leave?" Annaliese whispered. "This place gives me the chills."

Aryana looked at Alviss, expecting the old male to make an announcement to strip her of her title, but he huddled with the other Council members talking about who knows what. The crowd began to disperse, clearly not wanting to stay in this place longer than necessary. Good idea. If Alviss wanted her, he knew where to find her.

"Let's go. We need to discuss—oh!" Aryana started as a hand clasped her shoulder.

"Sorry." Fafnir rubbed his thumb across her shoulder and another chill shot through her, this one having nothing to do with the location. "Didn't mean to startle you."

"That's all right. We were just leaving."

"Would you like to take the noon meal with me?"

Ari blinked, aware her fellow priestesses observed their interaction with more interest than a hungry dragon eyeing a herd of elk. "At the Temple?" *Where everyone can see us?*

"How about someplace more—" He glanced at the priestesses huddled behind her. "—private?"

Her heart tripped a thudding rhythm, her skin tingled a warning at the thought of being alone with Fafnir. Her mate.

No, no, no. She should not feel all warm and tingly about catching some private time with him. She should be upset, mad even, at his appearance causing such a disruption in her life. Yet the anger failed to appear, only a consuming sense of unease over her future. She couldn't very well be angry over him acting the way the Goddess in all Her wisdom designed him to act.

Resentment, though, was a whole different matter.

"Meet me in the Courtyard at noon and we'll go someplace private." Alone time coming up.

No, no, no. She should not look forward to spending time with Fafnir. She should want all that resentment to build, to overwhelm her senses, to drive a wedge between their budding relationship.

Instead she wanted to see what could happen between them, what life would be like with him as opposed to Temple service. Better or worse? How was her life to change?

"I'll be there." He reached for her hand, gave it a squeeze, his palm warm against her chilled skin. *Forever.* The word continued to echo in her mind after he disappeared.

Chapter Eighteen

"Love," Aryana overheard one of the priestesses whisper to another, "I would surrender my position here in a snap if I found out I had a mate."

Ah, but that priestess lacked the allure of power, of wielding a magic far greater than what she had inherited. The choice between serving the Goddess and taking a mate should be easy, given without thought, an instinctual decision leading to a lasting love.

But once she tasted a drop of the Goddess's power, she wanted more. To give up that magic was akin to knowing her favorite treat lay behind a door, but being denied entrance. Over the years she came to rely on that power, that extra magical boost given only to the High Priestess, rely on it like a cloak gave warmth during the winter. What would she do without that power? Not to mention renouncing her childhood dream.

You made that dream happen, a little voice inside her head pointed out. *You are the High Priestess. Now you have a chance to make the other dream, the one you squelched for all these years, happen.*

Bloody little voice.

But she couldn't deny she had squelched the desire of having a mate to chase after the dream of being High Priestess.

"We have much to discuss," Annaliese spoke to the cluster of priestesses, the corners of her lips twitching as if she knew Ari's inner thoughts, "before the noon hour. Come, let us go to the Temple meeting room."

The discussion with the priestesses. The relinquishing of her title, her power. Her identity.

Aryana forced a smile, hoping it hid the expression of panic freezing her features, and made her appear at ease without hinting at the nausea roiling her gut. Appearances meant everything.

"See you there." Throwing herself into a transport, she crossed the distance to the Temple and arrived in the meeting room before everyone else.

Located on the floor above the dining room, the meeting area spanned the entire length of the east wing. Glass windows overlooked the Courtyard and its main entrance. Mosaics of flying dragons danced across the chair-littered floor. Two chairs and a table stood at one end of the room facing the lines of chairs. She grasped the smooth wood of her chair and looked down the length of the room.

Here was where new High Priestesses were announced, charities planned, Temple matters decided. Here was where years ago she gained her title, her status, her power. And here would be where she lost it. The first High Priestess in memory to renounce the position.

A streak of anger danced through her, a lightning strike carving out a pit in her stomach. Her knuckles popped as the hard wood bit into her palms. How could she not feel upset over being forced to give up all this?

How could she not resent Fafnir just a little?

She sucked in a breath as a whisper of realization snuck past the ire. How could power seduce her into thinking it held more importance than her mate?

Ari slipped the gold circlet off her head, turning it in her hands, her symbol of power. Pops sounded in quick succession as the priestesses appeared. In an instant, murmurings filled the room, a hum of voices saturating the large space with excitement. The scent of fresh air swirled around them, carried in from their time on the Hill. Nice to know the rotten smell of death remained behind. No place for that stench in the Temple.

Annaliese placed a hand on Aryana's arm, her touch eliciting a sense of peace. Clearly a spell. Not that Ari was complaining. *Are you all right?*

Seriously? All right? It wasn't like she skinned her knee and needed a simple spell to heal. She failed to stop the exasperation from creeping into her tone. *What do you think?*

I think tough decisions are made with anguish and loss always hurts.

Well, there you have it.

You are making the correct decision.

I'm making the only choice given me. It's not a decision if there is no choice, now is it?

Ragnor is your mate. To experience that bond, that love—

To give up all I've worked for my entire life. It's hard.

A furrow appeared between Annaliese's brows. *Do you not care for him?*

Of course I care! I can't help but care. Along with want and desire, neither of which she'd mention to her mate's sister. Who wants to hear such things about their brother? *I want him for a mate now that he's returned, but this is all I've ever known or wanted to know.*

Annaliese patted Ari's arm as her brow smoothed. *In the end, you will want this decision.*

I hope you're right.

If she wasn't…Ari shook off a chill and glanced one last time at the circlet, at the dancing dragons experiencing a sense of glee she lacked. A burning ball of fire took up residence in her gut, anxiety twisting in its depths, a glove spiked with barbs. The gold dragons on the circlet symbolized power, magic, the highest rank of a priestess.

The ability to sacrifice one's own desires for the good of the Draconi.

The true test of one's gifts.

Swallowing, she raised her head, the movement stilling the hum of conversation as well as a shout. All eyes turned to her.

Nausea pressed against the back of her throat and she swallowed. The High Priestess shall not, ever, throw up in the meeting room. Even when what she needed to say made her stomach roil in protest.

Appearances were everything.

The coolness of gold cut into her fingers as she white-knuckled the circlet. No more delaying the inevitable. A wave of warmth washed over her as she spoke the words that sealed her fate. "You all heard Fafnir, I mean, Ragnor's announcement today. He spoke true. We are mates." Shocked mumblings greeted her words, and she raised a hand for silence. Words bubbled at the back of her throat, wanting escape before her nerve failed. "You have probably also heard rumors that we were predicted to be mates by the old Seer when we were young. This is also true. We, though, chose to believe her prophesy did not apply to us. I felt drawn to the priesthood and Ragnor felt drawn to other things. And then he disappeared, believed to be dead. That meant I no longer had a rumored or true mate and was free to accept the position of High Priestess. With his return, we realized the old Seer spoke true, we are mates. And as such, I can no longer hold the position of High Priestess. Or any priestess, for that matter. Therefore, I must—" Ari took a deep breath. She could say it. She must say it. No matter how badly it hurt. "I must renounce my position. I must step down and allow another to take my place."

Stunned silence reigned for a moment before the room exploded into chaos.

"But a High Priestess must hold the position until death. No one steps down!"

"Who can be in the running for a new High Priestess?"

"Can the rules change so you don't step down?"

"What will you do now?"

Wasn't that the question of the hour? And the one she had no answer for. None. What would she do when stripped of her title?

Annaliese raised both hands. "Quiet!" Like her father, one word from her lips dropped with the finality of a shroud, hushing the questions, settling the priestesses back into their chairs. "The rules are not ours to change. They were made for a reason and they will stand. A renouncement of the title of High Priestess has never been done, but there is no rule against it. And even if there was, the rule that mated females cannot be priestesses must stand for obvious reasons. No mated male could stand for his female to couple with other males. Anyone who thinks they are able can be tested for the position, but the winner will be judged by a panel of senior priestesses. You know this. As far as what Aryana will do and when this will occur, I do not know. Aryana?"

"I will step down when a new High Priestess has been found. I will help judge the contestants and seek the will of the Goddess on the matter. After that time, I do not know. What should I do?"

This time, her question elicited thoughtful consideration. At least she hoped it was thoughtful consideration and not shocked minds grasping for an answer.

Definitely shocked minds. The silence draped her skin in prickles and set a ball of writhing snakes twisting into her stomach.

"All right then, think about it." One of them was bound to come up with an answer she would like. Hopefully. "The tryouts will occur two days from now beginning at dawn. If you wish to be considered as a contender, please let Annaliese know by noon tomorrow. That is all. You are dismissed."

The females filed out, most offering her condolences or touches on her arm, small displays of support. Others stared, dropping their gazes when she noticed. When the room cleared, Annaliese pried Ari's stiff fingers from the circlet and set it on the table.

"Well, that went well, don't you think?" Annaliese's smile failed to reach her eyes.

Ari shrugged. "Rather like a stumbling dragon."

"At least the dragon didn't fall flat on his face."

"I'm not so sure about that."

"What do you plan on doing?"

"No idea. Do you plan on competing?"

"No."

Ari blinked. "No?"

"No. I am a Healer. Over the years, I've found I enjoy being second in command, not first. I no longer want the position. You're surprised."

To put it mildly. "I always assumed…"

"What? That I shared Father's ambitions? You should know me better than that." Annaliese crossed her arms.

"I'm sorry." Ari touched her friend's arm. "You are right, I should. It's just been…difficult since…" She waved her hand back and forth.

"I know." Annaliese picked up the circlet, twisting it in her hands, running her thumb across the elongated body of a dragon. Her voice dropped to a whisper. "Do you think you could still turn into a dragon without being High Priestess?"

"I have no idea." What an odd question to ask now. "Why should I try?"

"It's a special talent. Perhaps it's one you had all along and has nothing to do with your position, the energy of the circle or the excess magic in Goleb."

"It's the least of my worries. Alviss is going to gloat about this until he dies."

"Let him. It won't last. I won't be High Priestess."

Ari choked back a chuckle. "Oh, I can see him now when he finds out. A moment of glee followed by sorrow."

"More like frustration. Neither of his children doing what he planned. I love him dearly but sometimes he is just too much."

"Isn't that the truth?"

"Come now, you need to change before you meet

my brother."

What a polite way of saying Aryana should no longer wear her green gown with dancing gold dragons, the gown which showed all her status, her position. The gown she could no longer wear. Perhaps her friend meant she needed to dress in something more revealing. A gown designed to lure, not awe.

Although a little awe wasn't a bad thing when dealing with one's mate.

A thrill of anticipation shot through her veins, banishing the cold chill of anxiety. She wanted to see Fafnir. She wanted to mate with him. She just didn't want to give up her position.

Apparently male Draconi weren't the only saps around.

Chapter Nineteen

Fafnir sat on the sun-soaked marble bench in the Courtyard, warmth saturating the backs of his thighs, a picnic basket resting at his feet. The sunlight drifted through falling leaves and late-blooming flowers, planted to bring relaxation.

He fidgeted, shifting on the hard stone bench. Would she show? Would she want to eat the meal Keara prepared?

For that matter, did he want to eat the meal Keara cooked? After leaving the Hill, he found his daughter in the Temple healing wing, sorting herbs. Once he told her of his plans for eating the noon meal with Aryana, she volunteered to cook, transporting them both to the home she shared with Thoren. After watching her throw in enough spice to give a dragon heartburn, he understood why Thoren belched and set the drapes on fire.

Hopefully, Aryana wouldn't suggest going to a room with drapes.

Drumming his fingers against his thigh, he watched the ebb and flow of people walking through the Courtyard. One female with strange markings on her face strolled through the Courtyard, brushing her fingers across waist-high bushes. Her white gown marked her as one who worked in the Temple, be it assistant, acolyte, or priestess. But the tenseness of her stance and the way her gaze darted left and right as if she expected an attack, ruled out those choices. So who was she?

She caught his gaze, her eyes widened and she vanished down a tree-lined path, out of his sight. As if afraid of him. But what did a Draconi female have to fear from a male?

A burst of chatter drew his attention to the Temple entrance. Clusters of priestesses talked in low hums, their words indistinguishable at this distance, their gestures and body language indicating something big happened.

Wonder what that could be?

He pinched the bridge of his nose with his fingers. After his announcement today, he knew exactly what words the priestesses' whispers contained. The High Priestess had a mate.

Which meant she could no longer be a priestess.

How could Aryana not resent him for forcing her from her dream? What kind of a relationship could they have if she resented him?

Maybe he should leave her be. Not claim her as his.

His whole body reacted as if he received a blow. His heart pounded, his lungs froze, his stomach churned at the thought. She belonged to him. He belonged to her. Mates could not abandon the other, especially not for trivialities like a status in the priestesshood.

Walking away was not an option. Cowards walked. Real males stayed. He wanted her. All of her. The one female made just for him. His mate.

Pop! Fafnir started, turning to see Aryana standing by the bench, dressed in a low-cut green gown that accented her eyes and raven's-wing-black hair. He sucked down a breath. What a beauty. And she belonged to him.

His.

He rather liked the sound of that. But would she?

Fafnir stood, holding out a hand, which she grasped. "You look pretty. I like the gown."

Red tinged her cheeks. "Thank you." Her free hand smoothed over the front of her gown. "I haven't worn this one in some time."

"It looks good on you."

"What did you bring?"

"The noon meal." He picked up the basket, set it on the bench. "Keara made it for us."

"How nice of her." Ari glanced at the basket, her gaze pausing at his lips before focusing on his eyes. "I have just the perfect place to eat it."

"Where's that?"

"You'll see." Gifting him a grin, she touched his arm, transporting them a short distance to a walled-in garden. "This is my private garden. Was, I mean. For the High Priestess. Anyway, it's pretty."

"I'm sorry." It seemed like the right thing to say when faced with her resentment. Even if it meant lying.

She waved a hand as she walked toward a bench set on top of a stone patio. "What's done is done. And you're not really sorry."

Apparently she liked reading minds. "I'm sorry you have to give all this up. But you are right, I will not apologize for claiming you as mine."

"So what do we do now?"

He followed her to the patio, setting the basket on the bench. "Is there a table?"

"The bench is it. We can sit on the ground."

Fafnir opened the basket, pulling out plates and utensils, setting the containers of food on top of the bench. "I must warn you. She put in a lot of spice."

"Good. I like spice."

He made a non-committal noise and wondered if she'd feel the same after the meal.

After heaping their plates with the food, they leaned against the bench, plates in their laps. Fafnir held his breath and stuck a fork full of food into his mouth. The spice hit his tongue like a wash of warmth. Hot, but not as hot as he feared. Maybe he could get through the meal without burping fire.

"Mmm. This is good. I'll have to tell Keara."

"Glad you like it."

He shoveled another spice-laden bite into his mouth. What did he need to say to Aryana to convince her he was the better choice? To convince her not to resent him?

"I renounced my position. The contest for a new High Priestess starts day after tomorrow."

"Are you upset?" Dumb, dumb, dumb. Fafnir gave himself a mental smack. Of course she was upset. What kind of question was that?

One finely shaped black brow rose as if questioning his intelligence. "It was…not as difficult as I feared. I managed not to throw up."

"You were about to throw up?"

"It was a big announcement."

Ah, the understatement of the year. Or century.

"I'm glad you made it."

"As if I had a choice. It was either that or have Alviss force the issue. No offense."

"None taken. Do you even…" He swallowed, his words a thick paste on his tongue. "…want me?"

She choked on a cough and placed her plate on the ground. "What kind of question is that?" Her hand touched his leg, fingers stroking the muscle of his thigh. Fire spread outward, a tingle of desire centering between his legs, thickening his manhood. Her voice dropped to a husky whisper. "You know I want you."

She might still resent him, but he could work with what she offered. One hand grasped her wrist, placing it on his hard length, while with his other he put the plate on the ground. Aryana's eyes widened for a second before her lips turned up as if she found a treasure chest of gems.

"I want you too. Now and forever." Cupping her face, he stroked the smooth skin of her cheek with his thumb. She met his lips, her kiss sending a jolt of desire through his veins.

Dropping his hand from her face, he wrapped his arms around her waist, lifting her so she straddled his legs. She broke their kiss, her hands pushing against his shoulders until she met his gaze.

"Are you sure this is what you want?"

"Hey, that's my line." He grinned. "Do you think I'd be here if it wasn't?"

"I don't want to stop."

"I don't either."

"It's just…I want you, so don't take this the wrong way, but this isn't how I saw my life playing out."

"You never once thought of having a mate? Never? Not once?" Red tinged her cheeks as she lowered her gaze. Ah-ha. She had thought of him. "All right. If we're being honest—"

"Which we should always be with each other."

"All right, all right." A grin played along the corners of her lips. "I wanted to be High Priestess so much, I just squelched the idea of having a mate. And I hated adults telling me what I had to do when I was a child. If they said go left, I went right, if only to show them. Pretty stubborn and stupid, eh?"

"No comment. That would be like the gem calling the gold valuable. Do you resent me for calling you on it?"

"Maybe. A bit. Giving things up is hard to do."

"You enjoyed leading that much?"

Her gaze dropped to his chest as she untied the laces on his shirt. "If I'm being honest, not really. I enjoy the power that comes with the position. Of knowing I hold a drop of the Goddess's power. That I can tap into that power when I want. It's a rush."

"Power can be seductive."

"It is. But even that power can desert me. Like when Fasolt kidnapped me. I burned through the magic casting that easy spell continuously. Not sure why. I've never had that happen before."

"Well, you've never been kidnapped before either."

"There is that." Her fingers stroked down his chest until they came to his waist. She pulled his shirt up, running her fingers across the skin of his stomach and upward, brushing over his nipples.

Fafnir moaned. "I'm not stopping."

"Good." She grabbed his shirt, yanked it over his head.

He pulled her lips to his, drinking in her kiss, her desire. Telling her through his touch of his love. His hands stroked from her waist to her breasts, thumbs rubbing across her pebbled nipples through her gown. The gown needed to go. He needed to touch her skin, see her body.

He reached a hand to her back, fingers searching for the laces of her gown and finding none. How did she get the gown on? Magic?

Clearly dragons in the middle of bed-play with their mates failed to think straight. Of course she used magic to put on a dress that had no laces. Which was rather nice of her. Made for easier removal.

With a snap of his fingers, her gown vanished, appearing next to them on the ground. She pulled back, one brow cocked.

"It appears my gown vanished."

"Really? How do you suppose that happened?"

"Hmm. Maybe like this?" She snapped her fingers and his trousers joined her gown.

"Nice trick you have there."

She kissed his neck, her tongue licking as she whispered a breath across the wet trail. Fafnir shivered. "It is, isn't it?"

Her skin tasted salty as he licked his way from her neck, over the firm globe of her breast to pull her nipple into his mouth, teasing it with his tongue. His hand pinched her other nipple, rolling it between thumb and finger in time to the pulsing of his tongue until she rewarded him with a moan.

Then he switched sides.

She clasped his head against her breast, her hip moving against his, rubbing his length against her core. He lowered a hand to her sweet spot, playing with the small bud of her pleasure while her hand fisted around his length. If she didn't stop that, he'd explode before he made it inside her.

Peering up at her from lowered lids, he placed his hands under the globes of her arse and lifted. Taking his silent cue, she guided him to her wet entrance. A moan escaped her lips as he slid into the welcoming grasp of her warm core.

"You feel good." Her whisper against his neck sent a shiver coursing through his limbs.

"So do you."

Then she began to move, and he felt like his world tilted, shifted, until he lost all sensation of their separate bodies, only aware of the pleasure coursing through them. His mate. His love.

He pumped inside her, their hips moving together in an age-old rhythm. Sunlight sparked black diamonds in her hair as she rode him, head tilted back, her long hair brushing the tops of his thighs. His lips nipped her shoulder, at that sensitive place where the muscle joined her neck, licked higher where the large vein in her neck pulsed. The vein he'd bite to join their life-forces, to bond them together for eternity.

Would she let him?

"Do it," she hissed, her breath in short punches as her pleasure slammed through her. Her inner muscles gripped him as she cried out, spasming around him, carrying him over the edge like a waterfall of bliss. His body locked inside hers, joined them as mates. His incisors elongated, a sharp pain necessary to bond, one he welcomed. The spot on her neck he licked glistened a silent request for him to bite. He took it, teeth cutting through her skin, into the vein beneath, blood flooding his mouth.

A sharp pain struck the side of his neck as Ari joined him in the bonding of their life-forces. The sip of blood exploded on his tongue like a bright fire, the essence belonging to her alone. As soon as he swallowed, his teeth retracted, returning to normal size, never to lengthen again. He licked at the wounds on her neck, felt her tongue do the same to him, and watched as they vanished, shrinking into small scars, a visible reminder of her being mated.

His. Forever.

A thrill rushed through his heart, filled his veins with an ecstasy he never realized existed. Clasping both arms around her waist, he held her against his chest, the warmth of her skin a soothing balm.

His manhood relaxed, and he slipped free of her wet embrace.

"It's done then." Was that regret he heard in her voice?

"I love you." She needed to know their bonding meant more to him than instinct.

Her arms tightened around his neck, released. "I know. Where do we go from here?"

Not the words he wanted to hear. No reciprocation of his love. But she didn't tell him to leave her alone either. He could work with that. The Goddess saw fit to drop Aryana in his life—literally—which meant she would learn to love him.

He hoped.

"We need to find a place to live." His hand stroked the smooth skin of her back. "Then I need to see if I can get my position back in the cloth store."

"Oh. I didn't think of that. What will I do?"

"I don't know. What do you want to do?"

Wrong thing to say. Fafnir gave himself a mental smack. He knew full well what she wanted to do. And no longer could.

Aryana slid off his lap, reaching for her gown. Air hit his bare legs, a cool shock after her warmth. She tossed him his trousers and pulled her gown over her head, whispering a word to get it to fit her. Once dressed she shrugged.

"I haven't thought about it."

"At all?"

"This has all moved a bit fast for me. I don't know what I'm going to do. What work is available to a former High Priestess?"

Fafnir pulled on his trousers, leaving the laces undone, and reached for his shirt. "What is something you've wanted to do but never did?"

She paused, then shook her head. "I can no longer work in the various Temple positions as a priestess."

"Keara and Lily work at the Temple and neither are priestesses."

Her eyes narrowed, her gaze darting between him to some point behind him. "Something's wrong."

"There's nothing wrong with Keara or Lily working—"

"Not with them. Something's wrong in the Courtyard."

Fafnir stood, tying the laces of his trousers as he listened for anything not right. Birds tweeted happy tunes. Wind grazed yellow leaves, setting them rattling. A whiff of food and he glanced at the half-eaten meal. Nothing unusual.

"I don't hear anything."

"Of course you wouldn't. The priestesses are

talking to me."

"All of them?"

"Don't be ridiculous. One of them sees a Watcher approaching the gates."

"We need to go see. Make sure he's harmless." Although in his experience Watchers were far from harmless.

She held out her hand and he grasped her palm. That simple touch stirred his blood and he wanted her again. Did all Draconi males feel this way about their mates? How did they ever manage to leave them? He wanted nothing more than to pull her down beside him and keep her there.

He needed to concentrate on the incoming Watcher, not fantasize about the many ways he could take his mate. Plenty of time for that later.

"Ready?"

He nodded, and she transported them to the Courtyard in sight of the entrance gates. When he saw the Watcher, he blinked, confused. The male looked like an older twin of Enar and for a second Fafnir thought it was Enar. Except Enar never seemed to raise suspicion of the priestesses. After all, they saw him plenty when he came to visit Lily.

"Viktor," Aryana hissed.

"Any relation to Enar?"

"His father."

"And that's bad?"

"He's cruel. He claimed Ayla, Enar's mother, knowing she was a Draconi and abused her. We just released her a month ago. She's been living here at the Temple until she recovers."

"Enar has Draconi blood?" At her nod a memory

slammed into his mind. "Ayla wouldn't happen to have ceremonial scars on her face, would she?"

"Yes. Why?"

"I saw her in the gardens while waiting for you."

Steam snaked from Aryana's ears. "He's after her. Alviss banished him from the Council and freed Ayla from his control. He's supposed to leave her alone. Bloody idiot Watcher." She started for the male.

Fafnir grabbed her arm. "What are you doing?"

"I'm still the High Priestess. It's my responsibility to greet visitors."

"Even when they're cruel Watchers? What happens if he attacks you?"

"I'm still the High Priestess. Remember all that power I was talking about? I'll fry his cruel arse if he tries anything. Let me go."

Against his better judgment, he released her arm. "If he makes a move on you, I'll fry his arse for you."

She smiled. "I appreciate that. I'll be right back."

As soon as he saw Aryana, Viktor stomped toward her. "Where is she?"

"Where is who?"

"Ayla! My claim! You took her from me and I demand her back."

"You can't have her back. Be gone with you." Ari waved her fingers, gesturing toward the gate.

Viktor snarled and Fafnir took a step forward. "She belongs to me and I want her. Now."

"No. Leave."

Viktor didn't move, his snarl morphing into a crazy smile. He yanked a dagger out of a sheath, brandishing it before her face.

"Titanium, bitch. Your spells don't work on me.

Now give me that bitch I claimed and I'll let you go."
Before Fafnir could move, Viktor grabbed Aryana, dagger pricking the skin of her throat.

A snarl twisted his lip, steam poured out his ears as his body expanded. He felt the transformation sweep through him riding a wave of panic. If he changed, he could very well be stuck in dragon form. Changing was on the top of the do-not-attempt list. But what other choice did he have? His mate was in danger. His mate could die. What kind of male would he be if he didn't protect his mate?

Fafnir took a deep breath and roared, the change sweeping over him in a rush of lengthening bones and hardening scales until he stood as a dragon. An enraged, fighting-for-its-mate dragon.

Beware the male Draconi.

Something this Watcher was about to learn the hard way.

Chapter Twenty

Aryana gasped as the cold knife bit into her skin. This recurring experience of being a victim needed to end. In the last several days she'd been caught in a fight with rogue attackers, captured by an unstable Draconi, and now a deranged Watcher held her in his grasp. To make matters worse it appeared his dagger was made from titanium.

When she spoke her spell, he paid no attention. None. For all he noticed, she might as well have not spoken. What choices existed without using magic? The only things left to a trapped magic-less priestess were telepathy and turning into a dragon.

Maybe she could reach inside his mind, tunnel past his defenses, and shut down his higher functioning. Something she'd never tried to do before.

Why hadn't she paid more attention when Thoren tried to teach her self-defense? Oh, right. Why bother with hand-to-hand combat when she could speak a word and send an attacker tumbling?

Dumb, dumb, dumb. And now she must pay for all that pride.

She grabbed Viktor's forearm, trying to pull the knife away from her throat, but tugging on his arm seemed harder than pushing a boulder up a hill. He didn't budge. The air around Fafnir shimmered, drawing her attention to her mate, her fingers white-knuckling Viktor's arm.

He couldn't change. According to Keara, if Fafnir changed into a dragon, he might never return to human form. Not even with that complicated spell she worked. What would she do without him in her bed? Without sharing a home? With never hearing his voice again? Her gut cramped, froze right up along with her heart and lungs, as if someone dunked her in freezing water.

Her mate was about to sacrifice his form. For her.

In that instant, watching his bones elongate, watching as scales covered his skin, as he roared a ground-shaking warning, she realized she loved him. More than her life. More than keeping her secret.

And she never even told him how much she cared.

What a fool she'd been, giving greed for power precedent over loving her mate.

Her shout of "No!" died on her lips as Viktor's knife cut deeper into her skin. Pain marbled with fear shot across her nerves. Wetness leaked from the tip of his dagger, trickled down her throat, her chest. If she didn't do something, he would kill her.

And then Ayla darted out of the gardens, apparently attracted to the roar of an enraged male dragon, freezing as she saw Viktor.

The female drew in a trembling breath as color drained from her face. "Viktor?"

"Come over here, bitch. Don't just stand there like a fool."

Ayla's gaze darted from Viktor, to Fafnir to the cluster of priestesses standing useless by the gates. She took a step forward. Stopped. "Let her go, Viktor. It's not her you want."

"Of course it's not her I want, you stupid cow. It's

you. But it's your fault I have her. You left me. Now move your arse. Come here."

Ayla took a step toward him, her face the color of her white gown, her hands trembling like leaves in the wind. Fear morphed into anger as Aryana watched Ayla give a panicked glance to Fafnir and the cluster of priestesses hovering near the gates. As if an opened scroll, Aryana saw intent written in the ceremonial scars of her face, saw the moment Ayla believed the priestesses valued their own lives over hers. Clearly she didn't realize how titanium affected Draconi.

The press of the knife slackened as Viktor reached his other arm toward Ayla, releasing his grip on Aryana's waist. No better chance to escape than now.

She twisted, forcing the knife off her skin and stepped hard on Viktor's foot. He stumbled and the knife slashed through the muscle in her upper arm.

Pain slammed into her, streaking out from the gash in her arm, bringing with it a dose of murderous rage. How dare he hurt her? How dare he come here to terrorize and destroy? Ayla had just started to trust the priestesses after a month of living with them.

Fire shot outward along her veins, rippling her skin into scales, elongating her face into a snout as change twisted through her body. Bones snapped, lengthened, changed, until she stood on four legs, leathery wings beating eddies in the dirt, a snarl displaying her new vicious set of teeth. Teeth that she snapped together, sending Viktor hopping backward, his feet tangling under him until he sprawled on the ground, a look of this-can't-be-happening smeared on his face.

Ayla's eyes flared and stayed that way, her feet rooting her in place as her mouth fell open. Fafnir stopped chuffing, apparently deciding his impending fireball might char Aryana on its way to Viktor.

Smart thinking. Did scales protect against fireballs? What about leathery wings? Something told her even if the scales protected her, the wings would still char.

The low hum of shocked chatter echoed from behind and she turned her head. Oh, great. It seemed like the Council arrived right in time to see her change. Now what? What were the consequences of everyone knowing her little secret?

Surprise and dismay appeared to be the consequence winners. At least for the moment. The priestesses had been less stunned over the mate announcement. And the Council. As one that group of Watchers and Draconi stared at her as if they'd never seen a dragon. Judging by the look on Alviss's face, it was a wonder the old male hadn't died from a stopped heartbeat.

No more gloating for him. She roared, flapping her wings.

Are you hurt?

Aryana shifted so she faced a snarling Fafnir. *No. Cuts, nothing life threatening.*

Watch out!

She glanced down in time to see Viktor slash at her front leg with his dagger. Did the fool not give up? A stomp of her foot and he screamed, his arm trapped against the ground, while a sense of pleasure exploded through her at his terrified look.

Take that, bastard.

You've made an impression on the Council.

Aryana darted a glance at the still unmoving group of males. *Not for long. They'll snap out of it.* She paused, her eyes narrowing on Fafnir. Anger frayed the edges of her temper. *Why did you change? Keara said...*

I know what she said. Did you expect me to stand by while he attacked you? You're my mate. What kind of male would I be if I did nothing?

The kind who could share my bed, sat on the edge of her thoughts, but she refrained from mind-speaking the words. She hated to admit it, but he spoke true. Her respect for him would have plummeted if he hadn't tried a rescue. The anger coursing through her veins fizzled with that realization.

He loved her enough to risk his form.

What more could a female want?

"Release him!"

Aryana started, surprised to see Alviss standing beside her. Nice to know the old male recovered his shock. Not so nice to know he snuck up on her without her realizing he moved. She lifted her leg, freeing Viktor's trapped arm, while Alviss gestured at the downed Watcher.

"Oren, take him to the Chambers. We will deal with him later."

Oren squatted by Viktor, his blue eyes glittering rage. "He's injured."

"Do I look like I care? He escaped confinement, went after his ex-claim, hurt the High Priestess in the process, and all he got was a broken arm? I told you a month ago he should have been killed for his treatment of Ayla, but you insisted on keeping him alive. Get him out of my sight before I do something you'll regret."

Oren pulled Viktor's uninjured arm around his shoulders, lifting the whimpering Watcher to his feet and sticking the titanium dagger into his belt. After giving Aryana a glare that stabbed her straight to her marrow, he turned, leading Viktor toward the back gate, where they disappeared from view.

"Now," Alviss tapped her leg with his cane, "explain yourself."

Before she thought of a reply, Fafnir growled, snarling in the direction behind Alviss. Aryana craned her neck to see the mass of priestesses and Council members creeping closer, staring at her as if she was the main attraction in an oddity show.

Which she was. Since when did females change into dragons?

Aryana sighed. She should have let Fafnir handle Viktor instead of changing. But how was she to know a dose of righteous anger mixed with a bounty of fear led to a transformation? Well, she'd learned her lesson. No more scary situations for her.

"Well?" Alviss repeated the leg tap.

It started years ago. During the Harvest ritual. But I never changed outside of the ritual until I went to Goleb. Then it just happened when I was attacked. Like it did today. I don't know why. Or how for that matter.

"And you never thought to mention it to me?"

Why should she? Fafnir stepped forward. *It's Temple business.*

"I would think a female turning into a dragon would be more than Temple business."

Do you want people to know about Keara too? Aryana raised an eyeridge.

What about my daughter?

Lips pursed, Alviss narrowed his eyes. *He doesn't know?*

It's not my secret to tell.

What. About. Keara? Smoke drifted out Fafnir's nostrils.

She's a death raiser. Alviss spoke only to them as he leaned on his cane. *I consent, you've made your point.* Clearing his throat, he addressed everyone. "We will not speak of this...occurrence today. Is that understood?"

Aryana wondered if he sent a spell alongside his words since the crowd nodded in unison. All the better. She needed to speak with Fafnir. Alone.

Unfortunately, Alviss wanted more answers. "Why did you allow him to capture you in the first place? Why not cast a spell?"

Ayla inched closer, almost even with Fafnir, clearly intrigued by their conversation. Aryana projected her thoughts to the female, wanting her to understand why none of the priestesses came to her rescue.

He had a titanium dagger. Ayla, that renders our magic useless. That's why no one came.

Ayla stilled, her gaze darting to the crowd and back to Aryana. She nodded. Good. They had worked hard to build that female's trust and she didn't want to see it dashed to nothing.

Ayla appeared to be the only person happy with her statement. After Alviss repeated her words, the Council spoke in loud tones until he raised a hand.

"We will need to search the Watcher village again. This time for titanium weapons. Erase their memories if you must, but collect all the weapons. We cannot have that threat in Draconia. Go."

With one last glance her way, the Council members

vanished, presumably to carry out their leader's orders. Now if she could just get rid of Alviss and the priestesses, she could be alone with Fafnir. Assess the damage. Know if she would ever see his smiling face, run her fingers through his curly hair, feel his touch upon her skin.

"I need to speak with these two alone. You are dismissed." Alviss waved a hand at the priestesses and Aryana felt their ire in small prickles along the nape of her neck. Good thing looks couldn't kill.

Annaliese caught her eye and Aryana gave her friend a nod. She wanted to be alone with Fafnir too, but in her world alone meant minus Alviss.

"Father, she's hurt. He cut her arm and pricked her neck. I'm going to heal her, then you can talk."

"Oh. Of course, of course."

And, of course, he would not apologize for not noticing. Leaders of the Council apparently refused to admit mistakes.

When she finished healing the small cut in Aryana's neck and the gash in her arm, which was now her leg, Annaliese held out a hand to Ayla.

"Come along, Ayla. Let's get you inside." Ayla gave the two males darting glances before straightening her shoulders and quick stepping between them. As soon as she grabbed Annaliese's hand, the priestess transported them into the Temple. A quick glance showed the crowd of priestesses and acolytes pressed against the windows of the dining room and meeting room.

So much for Alviss's dismissal.

"When will you mate?"

As soon as you leave. Fafnir's eyes narrowed as he

stared at his father.

"The ceremony, son. Not the activities surrounding it."

Fafnir glanced her way, his wink hidden from Alviss. *We will have the ceremony as soon as the new High Priestess is selected. Isn't that right, Ari?*

Aryana swallowed, trying not to chuckle. No telling how that would sound in her current form. *Yes. In two days is the selection and then soon after that we'll hold the mating ceremony.*

Alviss beamed. "Good, good. Now my daughter can finally be where she should. I will see you at the ceremony. There are things I must attend to. Bloody titanium." A pop later and he disappeared.

He's going to be surprised when Annaliese isn't High Priestess. Ari flashed her incisors.

What do you mean?

She doesn't want the position.

Oh, ho. I want a front seat for that telling. Can you imagine the look on his face?

All too well. Her lip curled off her teeth as she thought of Alviss's dream being crushed. Served him right, meddling old male.

Who was now her father-by-mating.

And didn't that just take the wind out of her wings?

She sighed. Instead of gloating, she should be concerned about her mate. What kind of female was she not to ask after Fafnir? A bad one, that's what.

Not only did she not ask, but she still hadn't told him she loved him. Something she would remedy. As soon as she changed back.

Taking a deep breath, she found that spark of magic inside, the one holding her form, the one fueling her change. She brought the human form hiding inside to the surface, exchanging it for the dragon. Bones shortened, flesh eclipsed scales, her snout shrank into her face. Pain blossomed, dispersed, as her clothed human form appeared.

She walked to Fafnir, ran her hand down his snout, the small scales smooth under her fingers. "I love you."

He blinked. *You do?*

"Don't look so shocked."

I didn't believe you did. I thought you felt obligated to mate with me.

"I did. At first. I felt trapped. Forced to do something I didn't want. But the truth is, I wanted a mate. I wanted you. Ever since you landed in the Temple Courtyard a month ago I wanted you with a desire I never felt toward another. But I realized I loved you when you changed. When you risked something important to you for me."

Do you still resent me?

"No. Our fates were woven together before our lives began. Trouble comes when we don't follow the path set out for us by the Goddess."

Not all bad came out of it. I have a daughter because I failed to follow fate's path.

"And I had a position and title I loved. But power is seductive and convinces you to be something you aren't. Besides, I'm tired of all the attacks on me lately. I need a break from the action." She grinned, meaning to put him at ease, but instead he shuddered.

I'm tired of those attacks too. I don't like seeing my mate injured.

"Nor do I."

You need to think about what you want to do since

you can't be High Priestess.

"You were right earlier. Throughout Temple history, others served without being priestesses. Maybe I can work in the archives. Did you know how many scrolls are aging, crumbling to pieces? Think of all the spells lost. I can help copy them, preserve our history."

I never realized that. But you'd be good at preserving history. You can write yourself into some of those stories. The female who changed into a dragon.

"And then those stories could fade into fables."

Maybe that's how fables began.

"Perhaps." A quick pat on his flank and she stepped back. "Try to change."

What if I can't?

"It's only a form, Fafnir. I'll still love you." But it would be hard to wake each morning without him by her side. In her bed.

He closed his eyes, a fine tremor running across his scales as he drew in a deep breath. For a moment nothing happened, no change, no shimmering aura of magic. Breath locked in her lungs as she clutched her hands together.

Then she saw it, the shiver of magic pulsing outward, barely visible at first, growing strong with each pulse. Her breath released on a sigh as Fafnir shifted, as his bones shrank, scales disappearing into flesh, his clothes appearing a brief moment later as if he forgot how to change and have them appear. Dressed, he stood before her, straight and tall, his curly hair brushing his shoulders, his deep green eyes piercing her soul.

She reached a trembling hand toward him. Her mate. Her lover. Her friend.

Grasping her hand, he pulled her against his chest. "Forever?" One warm hand cupped her face, his mouth lowering toward hers, his warm breath caressing her skin.

"Forever." When his firm lips brushed against hers, she opened to his kiss, his love a steady flow through her heart. Why had she ever thought she didn't need a mate, could live alone, burying her innermost desire under a seduction of power? What a fool she'd been.

But no longer. She knew what she needed, a lifetime of experiencing the passion and love only her mate brought, desire only Fafnir gave.

Forever.

Chapter Twenty-One

Aryana stood at the front of the chapel, hidden behind a pillar. Sofie and Vendela, the twins who did everything together including being the first in history to share the position of High Priestess, stood before the altar, hands folded before their waists. Who would have thought twins would obtain the position of High Priestess simultaneously?

Definitely strange times. So many things happened over the last few days, it would take her a week to record them all in the archives. She turned into a dragon in front of the Council. A spell was found to turn a dragon back into human form. The Watchers, irate over Viktor's treatment, barricaded themselves into their village and threatened retaliation. What was next? A Halfling with non-typical coloring who proved to be powerless instead of powerful?

She glanced to Jamie, Thoren and Keara's adoptive Halfling son. The last time a Halfling possessed his brown hair and gray eyes instead of the typical red hair and green eyes she had been the most powerful Draconi ever born.

At least in the tales.

Jamie bounced in place until Thoren clasped a hand on his leg and Keara whispered into his ear. So far the youngster only showed a penchant for over-activity and getting into trouble. Typical boy behavior.

Her gaze caught on Enar and Lily as they walked to sit next to Thoren and Keara. She overheard Lily was in the early stages of pregnancy, not yet noticeable to others, but judging by the glow on her face others would catch on soon enough.

On the other side of the chapel, hidden behind a pillar similar to hers stood Fafnir, waiting for their mating ceremony to start. Her mate. Her lover. Her friend.

How could she have thought the position of High Priestess to be more important than him? Thinking of Fafnir now, she could not imagine not spending the rest of her life without seeing his twinkling eyes each morning.

To think, at one time she preferred power over love.

What an idiot.

Sofie and Vendela would make a good High Priestess. Or High Priestesses. Unlike Ari, they liked crowds, liked mingling with people, and did not seem swayed by the power boost the position provided.

Where was Fafnir? Aryana peered across the chapel, searching the shadows for her mate, finding nothing but shadows. She sighed and turned back to the attendees.

Alviss sat on the front row next to Annaliese, wrinkles and hair hiding his expression. Ari pressed her lips together in an effort not to chuckle as she remembered the look on his face when Annaliese told him she refused to test for the position of High Priestess. She almost felt sorry for the old male.

Almost.

Silence rolled over the crowd as Sofie and Vendela

raised their hands. As they lowered them, they each stretched a hand to Aryana and Fafnir. Ari stepped from the shadows at the same time as Fafnir.

His lips turned up as his appreciative gaze raked her from head to feet. Then he winked.

Heat splashed into her cheeks, pooled lower, and she returned his wink. A dark blue tunic stretched across his broad shoulders and matched his snug-fitting trousers. Tingles raced across her skin, straight to her core, as she remembered his touch, his embrace.

Why had she ever wanted to live without him?

What a fool she'd been. Good thing she had been given a second chance.

Fafnir held out a hand for her. His warm palm encased hers like an extension of herself, his fingers wrapping around her palm, her heart. She squeezed his hand.

I love you.

I love you, too.

Ready?

He nodded and they stepped forward, into their new life together.